Murder on Naked Beach

A Lucy Ripken Mystery

Murder on Naked Beach

A Lucy Ripken Mystery

J.J. Henderson

cds
BOOKS

New York

For information please address:

CDS Books
425 Madison Avenue
New York, NY 10017

ISBN: 1-59315-287-6
ISBN 13: 978-1-59315-287-1

Orders, inquiries, and correspondence should be addressed to:

CDS Books
425 Madison Avenue
New York, NY 10017
(212) 223-2969 FAX (212) 223-1504

Designed by Ruth Lee-Mui

Printed in the United States of America

10   9   8   7   6   5   4   3   2   1

*Dedicated to DD, true love, muse, and inspiration;
and to Jade, who rules my universe.*

Acknowledgments

Every writer has a history which needs acknowledging. This first Lucy Ripken tale—yes, there are more to come!—has been told by a writer who learned a love of stories from parents James and Jo Henderson, both writers. Through the years of bullshit, disillusion, enlightenment, and training, many friends kept the faith: especially all five of the Harris clan, Brooke, Jon, Jamie, Geoff, and their old man Walton; members of the less than famous Famous Writers Group in New York; and Group Six, also in New York. And also and above all Joey Freitas, agent, manager, best friend since forever, wise fool, and usually elegant and always eloquent character, who made it happen.

Murder on Naked Beach

A Lucy Ripken Mystery

1

Out of the Snow and into the Sun

Probably the worst thing about travel photography was the carry-on baggage. Lucy Ripken had this revelation every time she went on assignment, and today was no different. She staggered along under the weight of her overloaded camera bag, strap slung over her right shoulder; from her left shoulder hung her purse containing twenty rolls of transparency film, a potato chip novel to read on the plane and the beach, a notebook, her makeup bag, passport, four bottles of organic vitamins, three bottles of sunscreen numbered 8, 15, and 40, and the rest of her personal junk. She was upstairs in the east wing of the international terminal at seven-thirty in the morning, and she had just been informed by a friendly redhaired Irish woman—Air Jamaica shared counter space with Aer Lingus—that the Air Jamaica eight a.m. flight to Montego Bay would be leaving two hours late.

Lucy wanted food. She remembered a restaurant some-where along this desolate stretch of terminal, and that's where she was headed. She spotted it way down the endless arcade, adjusted her camera bag with a groan, and headed over. She trudged past a row of dark boarding lounges, one of which had posted her Air Jam flight number with, omi-nously, no departure time. Several stoic-looking Jamaicans slumped in the molded plastic seats, surrounded by sleepy children, overstuffed suitcases, and shopping bags. Beyond the lounge, a sundries shop, and then—praise be!—decorated with an assortment of plastic plants posed against a back-drop of plastic trellis, the restaurant.

Half a cup of coffee cleared her head, and her sense of anticipation arose in spite of the bleak surroundings. Air-ports were hateful, but they got you there, and this was a free-bie. Between Wills & Wilton, high-flying New York PR firm, and the Jamaica Tourist Agency, a couple of dozen Air Ja-maica tickets had been conjured up to provide complimen-tary passage for select members of the press down to Ocho Negros and the gala opening week ceremonies for the Grand Strand Hotel, a new high-end, all-inclusive resort. According to the Wills & Wilton PR girl, Susie Adams, the hotel's design was "simply fabulous," and so Lucy, sometime architectural as well as travel writer/photographer, had gotten on the list for the trip. She would have to work, interviewing architect and operator, and take at least a dozen architectural shots with her Hasselblad, but the rest of the week, aside from a few press events, would be hers, all expenses paid. What could be better than Jamaica mid-winter? Truth was, Lucy, nearly broke and with no work in sight, had been just short of desperate to flee the black ice of Broadway when this trip had landed in her lap.

"Hey, Luce," someone said, and she looked up.

"Mickey! What's happening?" Lucy grinned at her friend Mickey Wolf. This would surely be a good trip if Mickey was on it. "Grand Strand, eh?"

"Can you believe this bullshit? I called that bimbo Adams at nine last night, and she assured me the plane was on time today. But Air Jamaica is never on time. Fucking clowns."

"Hey, it's a freebie. I'm not complaining."

"Well, I am," said Mickey, pulling up a chair. She had a Heineken in one hand and a cigarette in the other. "My kid's girlfriend is pregnant, he doesn't know whether he wants to marry her or get her an abortion, and I leave town in the middle of—"

"You're going to be a grandmother?" Lucy said, unable to hide her shock. This woman was practically her contemporary, for God's sake. Lucy was still thinking about what it would mean to have a kid, and Mickey was about to be a grandmother? Shee-it!

"Damn, don't remind me," said Mickey. "Can you believe it? I mean, I was nineteen when Jesse was born, but . . ."

"No wonder you're drinking beer at eight a.m."

"Honey, I always drink beer at eight a.m. on these trips. I couldn't survive otherwise." She took a hit on the bottle.

"Right," said Lucy. It made sense. Mickey Wolf, thirty-eight, with whiter than white skin, lovely pale gray eyes, long stringy brown hair, and a spreading rear end, was the editor of *Best Travel Bets*, a weekly newsletter for the trade, and she did the junket shuffle probably half her time. She knew every hotel on every island in the Caribbean, the Mediterranean, and probably the Indian Ocean and the South China Sea as well. The glamour of tropical travel had long ago faded for her. "So how's life on Roosevelt Island?" Lucy asked.

"Same as it ever was," Mickey said. "Like the 'burbs, only right in town. Hey, I'm gonna get something to eat. You want anything else?"

"Nah, I'm fine, Mick. Thanks."

Lucy scanned the weather at top right on the *Times*, and felt grateful again. High today 27, tonight 14, tomorrow 23. And 86 degrees in Ocho Negros.

"So who are you shooting for?" Mickey asked on her return. She'd replaced the beer with a Häagen-Dazs ice cream bar and had a fresh cigarette in the other hand.

"Jesus, is that your breakfast?" Lucy said.

"No, the beer was breakfast, you silly girl. This is brunch," Mickey said, and bit into the ice cream.

"I don't know," said Lucy. "Susie Adams said there was definitely a design story in it, so I'm hoping for *Architectural Digest*, or at least one of the trades. I'm meeting with the architect for a solo tour, so I should be able to get a good interview. He said they used a lot of native building techniques and materials, so . . . ." She shrugged. "Somebody'll go for it."

"No doubt," said Mickey. "Maybe I'll be able to buy an image or two, Luce. Be sure and send me a set of samples."

"No problem. I'll download my test shots and e-mail them. You pick a couple and I'll send you transparency film." Lucy finished her coffee. "So who's on the boat this time around? You got any idea?"

Mickey dropped her half-eaten ice cream bar onto a napkin, then put her cigarette out right in the middle of it. "No, but I'm sure it'll be the usual suspects."

Three hours later, piña coladas hoisted, Mickey and Lucy took turns peering over the backs of their seats, slyly casing the traveling troops behind them. Scattered among the homeward-bound Jamaicans and the vacationing New Yorkers were two dozen members of the media—travel writers, editors, radio reporters, and video producers. Most of the journalists were half-crocked at eleven a.m., having indulged in Wills & Wilton complimentary beers and piña coladas in the airport from 9:15 on—anything to keep the restless editors happy—and on the plane since the seat belt light went off. Lucy, halfway through a piña colada, felt semi-wrecked herself. She had supposedly given up hard liquor, and never drank before five p.m. That was what she told herself, anyways, on the days when she had some perspective on the alcohol situation. Here it was not yet noon and instead of perspective she had a mixed drink in hand. But what the hell, this was a press trip, designed for excessive drinking. The camera bag and purse were securely stashed overhead and she didn't have any real responsibility until tomorrow morning.

"So tell me, Susie," Mickey said, leaning across the aisle toward Susie Adams, the Wills & Wilton PR girl. Mickey frequently danced on the drunken brink of obnoxious behavior, but she never went over the edge, no matter how much she put away. Lucy admired that quality in her. "Did Angus pay for his upgrade, or did you manage to talk Joey Ruskin into abasing himself before the Air Jam boys?"

"Oh, that's not for you to worry about, Mickey," said Susie, and smiled. "Angus is—"

"A double major pain in the butt," said Mickey. "But he only travels first class, of course."

"You know how it is, Mickey. We need him down there," said Susie. She smiled at Lucy. "How's it going, Lucy?"

"Oh, not bad. Now that we're on our way, everything's fine. How are you?"

"Well, we got off the ground just in time," she said. "Another fifteen minutes and I woulda had a writers' riot on my hands."

"No shit," said Mickey. "I was ready to burn down the terminal myself. Who likes to get up in the dark and rush out and sit at JFK for half a day? Nobody I know."

Lucy lowered her voice. "So tell me about Angus, Mick."

"Awful Angus. Angus Wilson. God, he's been Mr. All-Powerful in the travel mag biz since before they invented airplanes. My first job he was the boss, and he was a real nazi in the office, let me tell you. How he got so powerful I don't know, but I can't remember a time when the guy didn't practically control the fate of half the hotels in the Caribbean. And half the travel editors, for that matter. He's fucked up the careers of more than one person on this plane." She dropped her voice another level. "But confidentially, people are starting to not give a shit about him anymore. He's missed the boat the last couple years, people aren't taking him very seriously, and he hardly knows it. He gets all pissy about windsurfing and other watersports, likes to harken back to the good old days when a Caribbean trip meant you sat on your ass in a plantation chair under an umbrella on the beachfront verandah and drank gin till the sun went down, being waited on hand and foot by humble natives and complaining about the deteriorating level of service the whole time. He doesn't get the new travel scene, and it's just made him crankier than usual is all. You heard him back there at the terminal pitching a fit about sitting economy with the rest of us hacks? Well, that was just a warm-up, Luce. Wait'll he breaks out his color-coordinated resort wear and starts patrolling the hotel grounds and power-walking the beach. He is an awesome sight, let me tell you."

"So why's he still get the upgrade to first class?"

"Anything to shut him up is my guess. Right, Susie?"

"You might say that," Susie said, and grinned. Lucy had another look at her. Having talked to Susie Adams on the phone at least twelve times in the last month, angling for a seat on this trip, Lucy felt like she knew her. She looked about twenty-three years old, which would make her eight years Lucy's junior. Her age had actually surprised Lucy when they'd met at the airport. Lucy had assumed that she would be her contemporary but no, Susie was just a kid, and a cute one at that. But judging by her seven a.m. performance at the airport, Susie smoked way too much, and her voice had a premature crack in it. "Hey, did you guys get press kits?" she said, offering a pair of telephone book–sized, silver-embossed folders, stuffed with photos, press releases, and everything else anyone could ever need to know about the fabu new Grand Strand Hotel.

"Not for me, Susie," said Mickey. Lucy took one and flipped it open. In the right pocket, printed matter; in the left, a stack of black-and-white 8 x 10 photos. The first one showed a smug-looking, fiftyish, dark-haired man in a business suit. Lucy pulled it out and had a look.

"Who's this?" she asked Mickey.

Mickey glanced at the picture. "Jackson Hababi. He's the big guy at FunClubs. They're the owners. He runs half the hotels down there."

"Jackson Hababi? Sounds like a part-time Arab."

"Actually, he's Lebanese. Or rather, his grandfather was. There are a lot of them in Jamaica, and they seem to be better at business than anyone else. So they run the show. At least the tourist end of it. But bag the press kit, Luce. Don't you want to know who you're traveling with?"

"Yeah, right." She shut the press kit and put it on the floor, then smiled over at Susie. "I promise I'll read it later, Susie," she said.

"Whenever," Susie said. "There's plenty of time. But you might want to read the piece about the hotel design before you talk to the—"

"You can't seriously expect me to eat this rubbish," someone barked loudly in first class.

"Oh shit, there goes Angus again," said Mickey. "Right on time. Critiquing the eats in first class is one of his favorite pastimes."

"Um . . . excuse me, ladies," said Susie. "I've got to—"

"Yeah, yeah," said Mickey. "Tend to Mr. Wilson. Trust me, honey, it won't be the last time on this trip." She laughed. "But you already know that." Turning to Lucy, she went on, "Angus is such a prima donna, Lucy, you won't believe the shit he gets away with. Then again, he's not the only loser in this crew. Our fellow road-scribes are a bunch of half-wits in general. You see that bozo up there on the aisle, second row on the left?"

Mickey killed the next hour with her row-by-row, blow-by-blow take on the travel reporters. With the passage of the lunch cart down the aisle, the gossip tour ended. That was all right with Lucy—she'd have plenty of time to get familiar with the gang in a week of jollying it up at the hotel. Picking at her chicken a la airplane, she re-opened the press kit. Halfway through page one, she fell asleep.

An hour later her eyes popped open as they landed at Sangster International Airport, Montego Bay, on the north coast. After a short taxi, the flight attendants threw open the door and the sun-hungry troops quickly bunched up in the doorway, took in that first liberating lungful and eyeful of Caribbean air and light, then descended the rollaway stairs. The flags snapped in a warm salt wind: at least 18 knots, Lucy decided during the short stroll to the terminal. Windsurfing fever possessed her, like it always did when she walked off a plane into a hot tropical breeze.

She'd picked it up on Cape Cod six years back, taught by a summer romance, a year 'round North Cape carpenter who almost convinced her that his love was enough to keep her happy in Truro through the bleak, alcohol-fueled months of winter. Almost, but not quite. She'd left him after Labor Day, scurried back to Manhattan—but he'd taught her how to sail a board, and she had quickly grown to love it. She went every chance she got, at least a week or two every summer at the Cape or in the Hamptons and a week or two every winter down here in the tropics. One of the reasons she'd turned her professional photo focus toward travel was to get into the tropical wind as often as possible, and it had worked. Here she was, in Jamaica, and the wind was blowing.

She and Mickey, who was nursing a noon hangover, walked together up the stairs to the terminal and down the long echoey hallway to immigration. There they were greeted by six Jamaican girls swaying in a row, singing a syrup-flavored reggae welcoming song.

And then, before their very eyes, the ugly—or in this case just silly—American made a cameo appearance, in the person of twenty-three-year-old Allie Margolis. Fresh out of Bennington College, Allie was on her first press trip on her first job as an assistant travel editor at *Fiancé Magazine*, "that influential journal of pre-nuptial opinion," as Mickey had described it on the plane. A born-too-late-to-be-a-hippie Emily Dickinson type, all poetry and sensitivity, Allie proceeded now to demonstrate her multicultural awareness by joining the chorus line of Jamaican women, adding hers to the harmony of voices sweetly crooning "Stir it Up."

Ouch! Lucy found it hard to watch the girl, acne-riddled, white-skinned, and clueless under a big straw hat, her long black hair and long red skirt swaying as she missed the beat, humiliating herself before the few travelers brazenly sadistic enough to stop and watch. Fortunately it ended quickly, as the singing petered out and the Jamaican girls turned as one to gaze at the tourist woman and wait for her to go away. Allie got the message, skulked off, and life went on.

Stamped in and checked off, the writers milled around while Susie Adams expedited the baggage handling. Killing time, Mickey introduced Lucy to Harold Ipswich, a guy Lucy thought she had seen before. Five minutes of chat revealed that she had: he'd hung out at the same bar she did, back when she slept in a third-floor walk-up on Avenue A and Ninth Street and lived in Dan's Tavern on East Seventh. He claimed to be writing a novel and, like her, freelanced travel stuff. He was her age plus a decade, she guessed, and tall, with thick, go-every-which-way graying black hair and black-framed glasses. He had a droll way about him, seemingly amused by just about everything going on in this here tropical airport, and Lucy decided she liked him.

Eventually they got the luggage sorted out, and the writers dutifully followed the PR girl out of the terminal, pausing to pick up a couple of ice chests full of beer and soda for the road. On a quick rum-driven pit stop Lucy made the acquaintance of Louise Rousseau, a tall, super-chic dame in her late thirties, with spiky, Laurie Anderson–style hair dyed pure black. Lucy recognized her face, though she couldn't quite recall where they'd met. Had she been a model? Lucy left the question unasked for the moment as the two women together waded out into the heavy heat of the parking lot.

Nine other buses were lined up along with the pink-and-white-striped Grand Strand cruiser, and their engines were running. The air shimmered with heat and exhaust. Fast-talking dudes milled around selling Cokes, Red Stripes, and, with sly sidelong glances and suggestively raised eyebrows, also offered ganja, dope, marijuana—Jamaica's prime cash crop. Lucy turned them all down.

The hustlers didn't even try Louise, whose height, bearing, and high style were slightly intimidating even to these practiced scammers. According to Mickey, Angus Wilson long ago had hired and fired Louise in the six months following the six months in which he'd hired and fired Mickey herself.

They arrived at the bus just in time to witness Angus Wilson pitch yet another fit. "I am not going to ride in a bloody Greyhound for three hours," he snapped at Susie Adams. He and Susie glared at each other, head to head in the hot sun outside the bus.

"We can't give you a car and make all the others ride in a bus, Angus. Don't you see what problems that would cause?" said Susie patiently.

"I don't care about your so-called problems. You don't seem to understand. I do not . . . I am not going to ride on that bus, and that is that," fumed Angus.

"Fine," said Susie. "I'll get you a car and driver, but you'll have to pay for it, Angus. That's all we can do. I'm sorry."

"Oh, no," he said. "You can't seriously expect me to pay for a car. That is utterly ludicrous."

Lucy watched the sweat bead up on Angus's red forehead beneath the thin black slicked-back hair. "Get on the fucking bus, Angus," said Louise sharply. "We have a couple of hours on the road, and everybody's waiting."

Angus glowered at her, struck speechless. She glowered right back. He took out a handkerchief and wiped his brow. He looked at his watch, and then at the bus, and said, "You people are nothing without me. Don't you understand that?" Having scored his point, he climbed aboard and sat down huffily in the front row, left empty just for him.

"Nice work, Louise," Lucy said. "How did that shithead ever get away with firing you?"

"That was a long time ago," she said. "I let him push me around because I didn't know any better. Wouldn't happen today, you can bet on that." Lucy followed her onto the bus.

In front, Angus seethed behind the driver, with an empty seat on his right. Lucy left that seat for Susie, and took a closer look at the man as she headed toward the back. What sprang to mind as she took in his reddened, permanently irritated visage was Angus as the human incarnation of a hemmorhoid.

Lucy often took notes on long bus or train trips. On the way from Montego Bay to Ocho Negros, after a sporadic chat she wrote the following: "Slipping into prose here to slip out of talk with American-born Haitian white lady journalist called Sandy Rollins. She's almost glamorous but late 40s on the verge of terminal skin/sun OD, gonna be dried fruit another year or two. Moved from H. after Baby Doc chased out, now living in Sanibel. Yearns for the good old days of Papa Doc, when people like her 'lived extremely well,' as she put it. Sick bitch.

"Driving on the Brit side. The sea on the left, beaches, rocky low bluffs, blue-green aquamarine dream water, coral reef lines. High chop outside. Hope we get there in time for a sail today. Jerk chicken, fish, and pork stands, little grubby houses in exquisite beachfront locations—I hate thinking about real estate in places like this, but that's what life in Manhattan does to you. People here moving very slowly. What's the rush, mon?

"Passed through a town called Yarmouth. Dead donkey at the side of the road, all four legs extended, two handsome kids standing there in white shirts, ties, and shorts—school uniforms—poking the swollen body with a stick. Market day in town, we honked through, lots of beautiful fruit and cheap colorful stuff for sale. Faded pastel colonial architecture gone tropical. Driver's name is Big Wilbert, drives crazy, horn honking, passing on blind curves, laughing and talking all the while.

"Lots of new development since last time here. The ocean on one side, dark-green mist-wreathed hills rising beyond cane fields on the other. Coffee and ganja and Rastamen grow up there. Saw a Rasta walking along the side of the road, dreads to his waist matted and bleached to a golden blonde shade. Looked mellow, but you never know these days who's a real Rasta, and who's a gun-toting, dope-dealing, posse dude with dreadlocks—thanks to all the American drug money."

Soon they drove through Ocho Negros. As the driver proudly pointed out while dodging construction sites, cement trucks, dogs, pushcarts, and cars driving on the wrong side of the road, Ocho Negros had a McDonald's, a Burger King, and a Taco Bell. It was a little boomtown, Jamaica style. Dust swirled in the air, horns honked, and you could practically smell the odor of the hustle, of money conjured out of concrete and gasoline. Lucy didn't like it much, but what could she do? Jamaicans want their Big Macs just like everybody else. "Yo, driver," somebody bellowed. "We're outta beer back here."

Big Wilbert pulled over and looked in his rear view. "What's that?"

"I said we're outta beer, Wilbert." The guy stood up. He was a large, round man with a round head, crew-cut hair, and incongruously fashionable aviator-style glasses. His name was Dave Mullins and he worked the travel beat for the *Daily News*. Mickey liked him, she'd said, because he drank like a real old-fashioned, two-fisted reporter. In other words, like her. "How about another couple six-packs, Susie?" he said.

"The hotel is five minutes away, Dave," she said. "Can't you—"

"Why should I believe that?" he said with a grin. "You told us it was two and a half hours from the airport and its already been . . ." He looked at his watch. ". . . just shy of three."

"And we're five minutes away," Susie said. "C'mon, Wilbert, let's go."

"Hey, hey," Dave said, his tone heavier. "I want a beer. You think I like riding on a bus all day? We need some relief from this stress. Now Susie, why don't you direct Wilbert to drive by the nearest store and pick up a case of cold Stripers."

"Jesus, Mullins, do you have to waste everybody's time with your alcoholic bullshit?" Mickey snapped at him. She was sitting a couple rows back of Lucy, right across from Mullins. "The hotel is five minutes away!"

"Alcoholic bullshit?" he said, still grinning as he addressed the crowd. "This from a woman who drank an entire bottle of 151 rum in less than half an hour to win a bet?"

"Hey, shut up, you simpleton," Mickey said. "That was about a hundred years ago, and I'll thank you to stop with the story right now."

He paused, then sat down. "Ah, fuck it. Let's go. On to the hotel, Big Willie!" He caught Lucy's eye, three rows away. "You wanna know what she won?"

"Mullins, don't," Mickey said, and Lucy heard a plea in her voice. So did Dave. He winked at Lucy, but didn't say another word. Big Wilbert started up and they took off.

About a mile past town they hit the luxury hotel strip. The Grand Strand was the last one, and as was true with the four other hotels they passed en route, the grounds, the building, the beach, the whole landscaped and tastefully designed package was hidden behind a ten-foot-high, barbed wire–topped white plaster wall. The only ingress came via a weight-balanced lift gate manned by a pair of stone-faced, steely-eyed guards wearing dress uniforms, plumed hats, and pistols on their hips. One lifted the gate and waved the bus through. After cruising through an orchestrated tropical landscape dominated by a half dozen trees studded with bright red fruits, the bus pulled up under a porte cochere. Pink neon scrawled artfully on a white plaster wall spelled it out: The Grand Strand.

2

Wind, Dinner, and Death

As soon as she got off the bus, Lucy breathed a sigh of relief. One look and she knew she had a design story to tell. The architect, William Evans, had some moves.

Thirty yards of flagstone pathway led to the arched lobby entry. On the left of the path a white tile pool was enclosed by low white plaster walls. At its far end a waterfall splashed by a tiled verandah. The use of water and the clean, elemental planes reminded her of the work of the Mexican architect Luis Barragan. On the verandah, trellises planted with bright pink and orange hibiscus defined seating areas with low-slung Honduran planters' chairs encircling mosaic-topped tables.

The crowd of road-weary writers straggled to the verandah. A buffet table heaped with pastries awaited them, along with a silver tea service, champagne, and another cooler of Red Stripes. Smiling hosts and hostesses—young, black, handsome all—in white shirts and black bow ties welcomed them. A string quartet played Mozart.

The adjacent lobby had a natural stone floor echoing the pattern in the ceiling soaring overhead. Supported by marble columns, the octagonal roof rose to a peaked skylight above a brass chandelier. A series of arched portals opened off the lobby. On the right was the reception counter, with long-legged birds carved into its mahogany base. Lucy checked in and took a key.

She declined the tea and Mozart and headed for her room, strolling through the lobby lounge, with a life-size waterwheel on one side. Leaving the lounge, on her left she passed an enormous open dining area with buffet counters at one end and a stage at the other; on her right were three restaurants in a row, Italian, French, and Jamaican. She went on to the main bar, a horseshoe-shaped affair that separated the dining area from the pool and hot tubs, built into decks above the beach; beyond the deck was the beach itself and the two-story guest room buildings strung along the shoreline. She walked the path behind the guest rooms, putting off her first contact with the beach and the sea for one last tantalizing moment.

She entered her room, threw down her bags, and pulled open the drapes. A pair of glass doors opened onto a small patio surrounded by lawn. She went out. Beyond the lawn, clean, powdery white sand stretched twenty yards to the turquoise water of Blackwater Bay. She would have to find out where that name came from. This luminous liquid had not a hint of black in it.

Her bags arrived immediately, as she'd requested. Lucy quickly unpacked enough to find her one-piece blue suit, stripped and slipped into it, then ran out onto the porch. She stopped short, dashed back into the room, found her number 40 sunscreen, and quickly covered all exposed surfaces before heading out again.

She ran across the sand, splashed into the sea, and dove. Gliding along, she felt the water caressing her bones, washing away the winter chill of New York. She touched her hands on the sandy bottom, then surfaced and took a few strokes before standing up in the warm, waist-deep water to have another look at the terrain.

Lucy faced the eastern perimeter of the hotel grounds, on the west end of Blackwater Bay. To her left, the bay stretched eastward in a lazy curve for about a mile, lined with palm-edged white beach most of the way, then gently rising beyond a mangrove swamp to a rocky cliff at the end of the bay. A three-story, lime green nineteenth-century mansion occupied the prime spot overlooking the bay's east end.

Directly in front of her, the white security wall enclosed the hotel grounds. To the left, where the public beach began, a cluster of Jamaicans lurked, not daring to cross the line into Grand Strand territory. Possibly because of the security man sitting at the edge of the property in full dress uniform. A couple of the locals called out to Lucy. "Braid your hair? Boat ride? Glass-bottom? Ganja?" The last word was an undertone hiss. She smiled and waved, calling out, "Not today, thanks."

The hotel sprawled along the beach for several hundred yards, with a second guest room wing at the other end, where an open air restaurant under a multi-peaked roof rested on pilings over the water. Offshore of that west point a skinny little island stretched back into the bay. A stone tower about forty feet high rose up from the middle of the island, flanked by wind-bent palm trees and a pair of thatched-roof huts. The water was calm inside Blackwater Bay, but out past the point and the island the wind blew hard. A small dock jutted out of the island. Another extended out from the beach by the poolside terrace, and a couple of motorboats, including a sleek cigarette, bobbed alongside it. A catamaran and a large yacht lay anchored offshore.

Lucy went in and ran down the beach to where two perfectly built, handsome Jamaican men lounged by the sailing gear. Half a dozen brand-new sailboards, ranging from lumbering boat-sized trainers to short wave-jumping racers, were stacked in a rack. Nearby lay Sunfishes, plastic molded kayaks, and a little hut packed with snorkeling and diving gear. "Too late to go windsurfing?"

"You know how to sail?" one of them replied.

"Yeah, sure," she said. "Six years now."

The guy looked at his watch. "You stay here?"

"At the hotel? Yeah. Just got in. How's the wind?"

"You get out past de island and it blowin'. Take a wide tack if you go dat way, sister," he said, waving off to the east side of the little island. "There's some nasty corals out dere. Easier to slip tru deah," he added, pointing toward the narrow passage between the little island and the point.

"Yeah, but then I have to sail upwind the whole time, right?"

"Yeah, or we come get you in de boat." He grinned.

"No way," said Lucy. "So whattayou got?"

"You know how to water start?"

"Sometimes. There enough wind out there?"

"Past de island. Tell you what, sister, I rig you a floater with a 5.0 sail, then you water start if you can, uphaul de sail if you need to."

"Sounds good. But you got a 4.4 sail, maybe? I'm a little out of practice . . ."

"No problem. You wanta hip harness?"

"Definitely. By the way, I'm Lucy. Lucy Ripken. Just got here from New York."

"My name's Desmond," the guy said. "I'm de windsurf instructor and manager of the watersports department. And this is Leroy. Leroy," he addressed him, then slipped so far into patois Lucy lost track of it. While she adjusted the harness, then stepped into it and coupled the leg straps, Leroy pulled from the rack a medium-length sailboard—short enough to fly over waves yet long enough to float. After rigging it with the 4.4 square meter sail, he carried it down to the water's edge.

Lucy took a few deep breaths, then picked up the board and sail. She walked a few yards offshore and set the board down, pointed into the wind. Holding the mast with one hand, she stepped up quickly out of the knee-deep water onto the board and grabbed the boom with her free hand. She leaned the mast forward. The board turned downwind a few degrees, the sail caught wind, and she took off.

She pointed directly for the middle of the island, a hundred yards offshore, and relaxed into it. For all the gear and rigging, once you got the basics boardsailing was a simple sport. Stand on the board, put the wind in the sail, and let it take you. As she approached the island, she decided to come about with a jibe. Why not? The water was warm if she fell.

She moved back and brought the mast and sail across in front of her. The board swerved downwind. At just the right instant, hanging on to the mast with one hand, she flipped the sail; the board swung the rest of the way around, and she switched her feet.

She heard clapping and glanced toward the island, only twenty yards away. She had come about just in time to miss a bed of coral lurking beneath the surface. A trio of people— two men and a woman—stood at the foot of the tower applauding her smooth jibe. Lucy did a double take: they were all naked except for sunglasses and an L.A. Dodgers cap on the shorter of the two men. The flabby-looking woman in the middle had red hair, above and below. Could it be? Lucy grabbed another glance—yes, the redhead was Maria Verde, a travel writer from the plane.

Verde was not one of Mickey's favorite people. What was it she had said? Lucy had taken mental notes, and now they came back in a word-for-word flash: "An aging hippie type. Used to be Sophie Potts but changed her name to Maria Verde. So New Age, don't you think? Not a bad writer but all over the place, and never stops grinning and acting like she's your best friend. You being whoever she's talking to at the moment. I think she's a pothead." And apparently a nudist as well.

If so, the Grand Strand was the right place for Sophie "Maria Verde" Potts. The FunClubs chain had started in the swinging seventies, back in the pre-AIDS days when everybody thought they could fuck everybody else and it was just good if not quite clean fun. Between that hardcore crew and latecomers to the nudist movement from the same era, inevitably a small contingent showed up at these hotels ready, willing, and able to strip whenever they got the chance. Here at the Grand Strand the nudists had seemingly been given their very own island.

Lucy turned across the wind. Near the beach she cranked another jibe and headed north toward Cuba. Time to let fly.

Three hours later, in a state of exhaustion bordering on stupor, Lucy had a last glance in a mirror before leaving for the dreaded welcome-the-press dinner. She had a red patch on the left side of her forehead where she'd missed with her sunscreen. The makeup hadn't quite covered the ragged line between burn and slight number-40-sunscreened tan. And since she'd had two skin cancers removed in the past three years—left side of neck and right temple—sunburn was more than worrisome, it was threatening. Her arms, legs, and back ached from sailing. She stood back and had a last head-to-toe look—the white strapless sundress looked better than it had last night, now that she had a little color—then stuck her room key and a lipstick in a small bag and headed out.

Lucy considered the image she had just seen of herself in the mirror as she walked to dinner. She was not strikingly beautiful, but she had an interesting face—that of a tomboy aging gracefully. Cursed with cuteness, now she was maturing out of it into something more substantial. She did not love wrinkles, but her faint laugh lines actually enhanced the blue of her eyes. Her nose had gained a little weight with time, and its button effect had diminished. She looked older, but also rather more serious than she had, which didn't bother her too much. After all, there had been an entire decade between fifteen and twenty-five years old when she appeared fated to spend her whole life looking like a cheerleader. At thirty-one she still had a youthful body thanks to fairly obsessive exercise, but her face had taken on some gravity. A few years in Manhattan would put gravity in anybody's face. She was a serious person, and for a time it had been difficult getting people to take her seriously. Not long after moving to New York from Portland, Oregon, she had dyed her hair black and chopped it into angry spikes; she had worn sunglasses day and night; she had worn black clothes 365 days a year; she had learned to curse like a drunken poet; she had *been* a drunken poet, and lived with one, Jake Jones, their coke- and vodka-powered love raging among the East Village walk-ups until he took a part-time job on Wall Street, discovered a talent for management, and never looked back on the East Village or her.

She had not been in love since Jake Jones. Three years. With a lover, she imagined, like everyone without one did, that her life would be complete.

She let a quiet sigh escape. Jake Jones hadn't been the first, or the last, to tell her she missed out on things because she stood by taking notes or pictures too much of the time instead of being part of the action. But that was her job, taking notes and pictures.

The Jamaican sky glowed, thick with equatorial stars. The lilt of reggae carried on the wind, and she felt a surge of excitement. Harold Ipswich had been in the water, forty yards offshore, when she sailed in for the last time. He swam like a dolphin, he loved the water, and he had even asked her to teach him how to windsurf.

Les Poissons de L'Amour. The fishes of love? An odd name for a French restaurant, but perfectly Jamaican, and even more perfectly Grand Strand: groping for high style, they missed the mark and verged on self-parody. Lucy paused outside the door, had a look at the display menu, and grinned. The calligrapher who'd done the gracefully lettered menu had made just one mistake: across the top he had written *Poisons de L'Amour*. She gathered herself and prepared to enter. Mike Nack, another writer from the plane, abruptly appeared at her side in a synthetic safari suit with multiple pockets and short sleeves and many important-looking buttons and straps. He also wore a red bow tie clipped on his white shirt. One look and she knew that he had agonized over his wardrobe. "Hi. I'm Nack. Mike Nack. *New England Travel Digest.* Outta Boston. And you're Lucy Ripken." He stuck out a large white hand, trying not very hard to keep his eyes off her breasts, semi-exposed by the low-cut sundress. She looked at his hand and then at his slack white face, caterpillar mustache crawling, hairline receding, and regretted, as she often did, that she'd opted for sexy dressing.

"Nice to meet you, Mike," she said, and gave the clammy mitt a little shake. He held her hand a second too long, then let it go to open the restaurant's pale blue door and usher her in. She got a whiff of him as they walked in together. He smelled of mothballs, rum, and cheap cologne. He'd been sitting with Maria Verde on the plane. Mickey had described him as the kind of press trip guy who empties the guestroom mini-bar into his suitcase, daily if he can get away with it, and eats enough to feed an army, not because he's thirsty or hungry, but because it's free.

Inside, the primary colors were pink and pale blue, and the decor gave the impression of a salon in a turn-of-the-century French hotel. Or rather a bordello that specialized, perhaps, in underage courtesans. William Evans ran the architecture end of his business, but the interior design side was the domain of three lady decorators, and they had run amuck in this particular room. Ah well, thought Lucy. The Grand Strand clientele being what it is, most of them will indeed receive the intended impression—of upscale continental style, signified by pink plumpness and voluptuous draperies and pseudo-Empire furniture with elaborately scrolled legs and the usual royalist filigree. The only hint of the Caribbean came in the wooden chair backs, which had been carved into clamshells.

However, it didn't look so bad in the low light. The restaurant had been closed to the few dozen other guests of the hotel to accommodate the press group, and several large tables had been pushed together in the center of the room to form a single long banquet table. About a dozen people sat on each side, and two at each end. The light, from an array of faux gas lanterns and candelabras, was subtle and rich, and not so low that Lucy couldn't view the people she'd been traveling with all day, transformed by romantic light and semi-formal tropical evening wear into sophisticated visions of themselves.

In addition to most of the writer gang, she spotted Jackson Hababi at one end of the table and his son Jefferson Hababi at the other. The junior Hababi was deep in conversation with Joey Ruskin, who sat on his right. Ruskin, from the Jamaican Tourist Agency, was a gorgeous, golden-eyed black man, a charmer, Mickey had said, but a scheming mother-fucker as well. Such harsh words had caused Lucy to ask why, and Mickey had said, "When he was green and I was younger, I fucked him, and he fucked me over." Joey was the first to see Lucy, and as he smiled at her, his very teeth seemed to radiate light. Maria Verde, in a bright green low-cut silk dress, sat on Joey's other side. She glanced at Lucy, and gave her a complicitous smile, as if they were in this together. Thus far, they had not spoken a word to each other. Perhaps she felt that because Lucy had seen her flabby ass naked, they were now friends.

She spotted the seat that Mickey had saved for her. It was on Mickey's left. Harold Ipswich sat on Mickey's other side. Quickly heading over to beat Nack to the seat, she remembered Mickey's words of advice: "Grab the seat, and then grab Harold, because he's a great guy and you deserve it. I'll do what I can to get you guys going, but don't tread water, baby, take the plunge!"

"Hi, Mickey, what's up?" she said, taking her seat. Mickey shrugged, looking bored and cynical. "Harold, you look dapper," Lucy added. Indeed he did, in a muted green-and-gold-striped linen suit cut 1940s style.

"Thanks, Sailoretta." He grinned, and glanced around the table. "Welcome to the Marie Antoinette Room."

"Yes, it is rather frou-frou in here, isn't it?" said Lucy.

"I can't believe they'd stick a room like this in a contemporary Caribbean hotel," said Mickey. "It's totally . . ."

"Buatta," said Lucy.

"Buatta? What's Buatta?" said Harold.

"You don't know the Prince of Chintz?" asked Lucy, feigning shock. "Why, Mario Buatta for decades ruled the Upper East Side School of Interior Decorators."

"Not my part of town, Lucy," said Harold drily.

"Nor mine," said Lucy. "But I get around, and this joint"—she waved at the room—"would look quite correct on Park Avenue, in the forty-seven-room apartment of some arriviste stock merchant's wife intent upon declaring herself a queen even though she was a flight attendant last year."

"Lucy, you reverse snob, wise up and drink some wine," said Mickey, emptying a glass of red and waving at a tuxedo-clad waiter for a refill. He bustled over and poured for Mickey and then filled Lucy's glass as well. Lucy didn't even try to stop him. After all, she had to get through the evening. "You don't know from Park Avenue," Mickey continued. "And anyway, let's face it, this place missed the boat. They built it for yuppies and yuppies are extinct."

"Did you sail close enough to get a load of the island, Lucy?" asked Harold with a grin. "That was quite a . . ."

"You mean Naked Beach?" Lucy said. "Yeah, I checked it out. It's—"

"Naked Beach?" said Mickey.

"That's what the employees call it," said Lucy. "I asked Desmond, the windsurf guy. He's never been out there during daylight hours except to drop people off."

"You have to take your clothes off to go," said Harold. "I swam out, and they wouldn't even let me land unless I stripped off my suit as soon as I hit the beach. No clothes or cameras allowed."

"So naturally you peeled it right off?"

"No way. I'm not gonna barbecue my buns in the tropical sun, and not be able to sit for a week. I swam back to the beach." He lowered his voice, glancing down the table. "But I did see Maria Verde out there, in all her naked glory."

"I'll be sure and miss it," said Mickey. "These days, being seen in public in a bathing suit is crisis enough for me."

"Oh, come on, Mickey," said Lucy. "You're not so bad."

"Easy for you to say, Miss Muscle Butt," said Mickey with a grin. "Hey." She lowered her voice, eyes darting glances down the table. "Did you see Margolis? A braider got to her."

Lucy checked her out. Sure enough, the singing and dancing Allie Margolis, three seats down from her, had fallen victim to a braider. Lots of white girls got braided, their first time in the Caribbean. Ever since Bo Derek did it in *10*, it had been semi-popular, and every Caribbean beach had a legion of local women wandering around hustling tourist girls to get their hair cornrowed. What these tourist girls didn't realize is that nobody was looking at Bo Derek's hair when she bounded along that Mexican beach. "What a disaster," Lucy whispered to Mickey.

"She'll figure it out," said Mickey the Merciless.

Lucy glanced across the table. Louise Rousseau gazed at her with an odd, neutral expression on her face. Suddenly, Lucy placed her. She was the editor of *FastForward*, the ultra-hip, for the moment at least, downtown fashion mag. Lucy raised her wineglass and smiled at her. "Hey, I just figured out where I knew you from! Your magazine is really cool. I showed my book there last year but your photo editor seemed distracted, to say the least. So how'd you get on this trip, anyway? You don't do travel in your magazine."

"We're gonna do a resort wear shoot here in a couple of weeks. I'm scouting locations." She laughed. "It's a tough job, but someone's got to do it."

Ting ting ting tapped a spoon on crystal, and while the salad was served their attention diverted to the head of the table, where Jackson Hababi tapped and grinned. Facing Hababi at a 90-degree angle around the corner of the table, Mike Nack had managed to squirm close to the center of power.

Directly across from her, through a tangle of candles and orchids, on Louise Rousseau's right Lucy noted Sandy Rollins, and next to her, a grim-looking Angus Wilson, who glared at his salad. White people partying, thought Lucy, and had a look at a couple of the waiters. They were young, black, handsome, stuffed into tuxedos, trying their hardest to uphold Jackson's idea of continental elegance in the middle of this vulgar display. When she'd come in from sailing today Desmond had told her he made 50 dollars U.S. a week. It would take him over a year to earn enough to spend a week here. And the guests weren't supposed to tip.

"Good evening, ladies and gentlemen of the press," said Jackson Hababi with a grin, candlelight reflecting off his gold-rimmed spectacles and his solid gold FunClubs tie clip. "And welcome to FunClubs' newest, most posh resort: The Grand Strand. Let me say first how thrilled we are to have you here. I know you've all had a chance to look around a bit today, and I think you'll have to agree with me that the Strand is absolutely and without a doubt the finest all-inclusive resort in all of Jamaica if not the entire Caribbean Sea." At that point, Lucy's attention wandered, and she missed the rest of the speech. She came back into focus ten minutes later, as he closed. "Now"—he grinned—"I'll shut up and let you all get on with dinner. But first, I want to acknowledge a couple of people with introductions, and thanks." First, he introduced Joey Ruskin. Then PR girl Susie Adams. Then he acknowledged Michelle Stedman, a beautiful, honey-colored Jamaican woman who did in-house PR for the hotel. She was sitting next to Lucy, who'd been admiring her elegant bearing ever since she'd sat down. As soon as Michelle took her seat after standing for recognition, Lucy introduced herself. Before they had a chance to talk, Jackson Hababi closed: "Oh, I almost forgot," he said with a faint smirk. "Jeff. Jefferson Hababi, my son. Stand up, son," he said. Jefferson Hababi colored, half-stood, sat down again. "Jefferson is the employee manager here at the Grand Strand," said his father. "Don't ask me how he got the job," he added, and laughed. "Well, let's get on with dinner," he said, when no one echoed his malice-tinged giggle. Jefferson, facing him down the table, could scarcely contain the look of suppressed rage on his face as he raised his glass.

"To Jackson Hababi," he said. "My stepfather, who made the Grand Strand dream come true."

Running through a couple of conversational tacks over the mediocre vichysoisse, Lucy discovered that Michelle Stedman came from the school of PR that held that honesty was the best approach to all publicity. And so, the two women bonded. "So tell me, Lucy," said Michelle softly in her elegant anglo-patois, "Is that Michael Nack person," she glanced down the table, "is that what you Americans call a yuppie?"

Lucy laughed. "He wishes," she said. "But I'm afraid he's too . . . nerdy . . . if you know what I mean."

"Nerdy? No, I do not, but I can imagine by the sound what this word signifies." She grinned. "And what about Mickey, is she a yuppie?"

"No, Mickey's too . . . real. Press people don't usually qualify for yuppie status, Michelle. We're too poor. Now, if Jefferson Hababi lived in New York, he'd probably be a yuppie."

"Because he's . . ."

"Young and well-off."

"But I thought all yuppies were sophisticated."

"Only in what they buy, hon. Not in what they think. They're masters of consuming and little else."

"Sounds distressing."

"It is . . . or was. They ran New York for a few years, but now things have changed. The yuppies got old."

"Yes, too bad for us, eh?"

"Yeah. This place would have done better a few years ago. Power vacations. Hah."

Michelle laughed. "Oh, my God, you saw the brochure. What an embarrassment. Well, so it goes. Or went, at least, with that particular advertising agency. Jefferson Hababi's choice. A school chum of his set up to look like a professional but lacking, shall we say, finesse. Anyway, ten years ago a couple of Rastas and their American hippie friends lived in huts here," she said. "Now, French restaurants, hotel rooms, and . . . yuppies on power vacations."

"Hey, Lucy," said Harold from the other direction. "What time's my windsurfing lesson tomorrow?"

"Whenever you want, Harold. Just be ready to get tired. The first couple days are brutal. By the way, Michelle." She dropped her voice. "Whose idea was Naked Beach, anyway?"

"Naked Beach? Oh, you mean Tower Cay?" She grinned, and admonished Lucy with a wagging finger. "You've been talking with the staff too much, Lucy. But there's a big demand for nude beaches here. Americans arrive in the sunshine and seemingly feel compelled to strip. The cay is perfectly situated, eh? A nudist ghetto. Boat access only, except at low tide, when you can almost walk all the way out there."

"You ever go there?"

"Me? No. Never." She laughed, reddening. "We Jamaicans are modest people."

"The British legacy, eh?"

"Something like that. What about you, Lucy? Will you be patronizing Naked Beach?"

"No way. I, too, am a modest person."

The next course was a white fish mixed with some weird egg-like stuff in a sauce so salty it was nearly inedible. "What's this eggy junk?" she said softly to Michelle. "It doesn't taste like anything."

"Ackee, honey," said Michelle. "It's our national dish. It's . . . subtle."

"And it can kill you," said Mickey from down the table.

"That's right," said Michelle. "You saw those trees with the red fruits out in the garden? Those are ackee trees. This"—she poked at the goop on her plate—"is the edible part, and you can only get it from inside those red fruits after they have opened and released the poison gas inside. If you eat them before that, you die."

"Really? Jesus," said Lucy. "What happens?"

"The stuff eats away the lining of your insides," said Michelle. "Like ptomaine poisoning, only much worse, and very painful." Lucy picked a piece of it up on her fork, looked at it speculatively, and then put it in her mouth.

"It still doesn't taste like anything to me. Kind of tofuish," she said. "But I like the idea of the national dish being poisonous," she added. "It has a certain charm."

"This is absolutely inedible," barked Angus loudly enough for all to hear. "Please remove it." A waiter, his face a mask, did so. Angus turned to Sandy Rollins. "And they claim the chef is cordon bleu," he sniffed. "Miss Stedman," he went on, with a glance across the table, "would you mind being a good girl and seeing if they might broil me a piece of plain fish, please."

Michelle stood. "Certainly, Mr. Wilson," she said pleasantly, and smiled, as if there was nothing in the world she would rather do than take condescending shit from Angus

Wilson. She pushed her chair out. "I'm sure we can accommodate you." Angus sat back, crossed his arms, and looked satisfied as Michelle moved away from the table, called over a waiter, and conferred with him briefly, glancing just once at Angus. The waiter headed for the kitchen, and Michelle reclaimed her seat. "Coming right up, Mr. Wilson," she said.

"You going to serve him some raw ackee fruit?" Lucy said quietly.

"Don't tempt me, honey." Michelle laughed.

By the end of the fish and ackee course, exhaustion and wine had taken their toll. Lucy made her brief good-byes, fingers lingering on Harold's for an extra second, and left for her room before the roast beef arrived.

Strolling out of the restaurant and back toward her room, she watched the theater lights being tested on the stage. A band was setting up, and the lead singer wore a James Brown pompadour and a gold lamé jumpsuit. Apparently, at the Grand Strand they took their reggae Las Vegas style. Wandering past the bar, she noted two fortysomething women in transparent blouses perched on bar stools. Displaying their gauzily draped unbound breasts, they clutched cigarettes and drinks and chatted noisily with the handsome young bartender. Lucy wasn't sure if she admired their free-spirited nerve or found them pitiful.

Above it all, a three-quarter moon cast a ribbon of shimmering white light on the sea. Lucy, asleep on her feet, didn't even see it.

In the room, she turned off the air conditioner and opened the window, then took off her dress, brushed her teeth, and lay down on the top sheet. The bedspread had been folded down, and the chambermaid had left a gold-wrapped chocolate coin embossed with a grinning pirate's head and a tiny pink and white orchid on her pillow. She threw them aside and fell asleep.

She woke up aching and praying it was six a.m. She checked the bedside clock: 1:37. "Damn," she muttered aloud, and glanced over at the window. The moon had sunk low: silvery horizontal beams shot between the curtains.

Lucy knew she wouldn't get back to sleep for hours. She decided not to bother trying. She got up and went over and drew the curtains open. The gibbous moon had dropped close to the smooth, still sea. She closed the curtain, turned on a desk lamp, and fished around in her suitcase until she found shorts and a T-shirt. She slipped them on and headed for the door. Just short of it, on an impulse she stopped and went back. She pulled her camera bag out of the closet and dug out her digital camera. She checked to make sure it had a fresh battery and a fresh memory chip, tested the flash, then slung it around her neck and headed out.

She went down to the water. The tide had dropped, and she had to walk a dozen yards farther to reach the edge of the sea. The energetic surge told her the tide was on the way in again. She got her feet wet, and then strolled west along the hard low-tide sand. Snatches of music, the throb of a reggae bass line underpinning shreds of faint laughter, drifted past. On her right, the black silhouettes of the tower and the catamaran and the yacht were etched against the moonbright sky. Ahead of her, dim pole lights cast a sodium glare on the dock. One of the motorboats was beached by the low tide, and the pilings that supported the dock were exposed. To the left she could see a couple of people still hanging out at the bar, unwilling to let the evening go. Now the bar music, Marley and the Wailers doing "No Woman No Cry," hit her full on. Two heads leaned close together in the hot tub next to the pool. Watching them, awash in late-night dreaminess, Lucy's heart ached for romance.

She ascended to the pool deck. She stopped to snap a few Hopper-goes-Caribbean shots of the isolated cone of light from a sodium lamp, the beached motorboat captured in it, white edge of tidewater rising into the frame. She flipped to review and had a quick look: the images were green and dark, but the rich, lonely mood was there, and would probably still be there when she downloaded and printed. Then she continued along on the promenade to the west. She could hear, beneath the music, the sweet, high, birdlike sound of Caribbean whistling frogs. Ahead, the restaurant pier loomed, a multi-layered silhouette. She headed out onto it. She strolled through the open air dining rooms in search of unusual angles. She would shoot it by day, of course, but sometimes darkness revealed interesting elements. The pagoda-like Colonial Regency roof was supported by an exposed understructure, a maze of angular wooden struts, support beams, and poles, and even in the faint moonlight Lucy picked out a couple of architectural details she could shoot in the early morning, when the sun would reach up under the roofline.

Then she spotted a wonderful night picture. She made her way through the tables and chairs to the end of the restaurant, pulled up a chair facing out, and sat down to have a better look. She could hear Marley clearly drifting across the water now, singing "Songs of Freedom." Joined to its own reflection, the moon appeared full, a disc of white fire afloat in the water. She set the camera up on a wooden railing and peered through the lens, quickly framing her composition before the moon disappeared. Suddenly a piercing shriek came from out in the bay. From somewhere in the vicinity of Naked Island.

Lucy looked up, froze for an instant . . . and then leaped into action. She snatched up her camera and charged back toward the shore, knocking tables and chairs aside. She ran down to the beach, on the way passing a kayak lying on the sand. A woman's hysterical voice came from the island, repeating, "Omigod omigod omigod." Lucy ran out to knee-depth, then stopped—the onrushing tide had filled in the channel—and hustled back up the beach. She grabbed the kayak and a paddle and dragged it into the water. She jumped in and began paddling.

The island dock was forty yards away. She got there fast. Just before she reached it, the bottom of the kayak scraped across the top of a coral reef with a shuddering jerk, almost turning over. She righted herself, took another stroke, and hit the dock. She grabbed a ladder and climbed. A few seconds later she set foot on Naked Beach, and stopped short.

She felt a surge of fear, crouching low as she quickly took stock. Between the palms she could just make out a wooden sunbathing platform raised up a foot above the sharp coral rocks surrounding it. Before her rose the round black stone tower. Light glowed from an arched opening in its base. She stepped softly to the tower entrance. On both sides, black coral rock glittered in starlight. The moon had disappeared. She crept up to the entrance and looked in.

Stone interior walls gleamed in the dull light. There was a pile of sun mats on one side, a self-serve bar with a beer tap and a stack of plastic cups on the other. The light came from a dim red lamp attached to the wall. A stone stair wound up from the back of the circular interior. She followed it with her eyes. There was another level above. She heard crying close by, stepped back, and quickly circled the outside of the tower.

On the other side she found another sunbathing platform, visible in the dim glow from a pair of lights hung from wooden posts that flanked a wooden bench on the far side of the platform. On the bench, Allie Margolis—Lucy recognized the long, beaded braids instantly—huddled, hugging herself and softly sobbing. She was naked, and blood flowed from a large, bright red scrape on her left leg, just below the knee. Between the two women, steam rose from a hot tub built into the sundeck. Lucy could see the back of a man's head resting on the edge of the tub, his arms spread out and slung over the edge. A pile of neatly folded clothing sat just to the right of his head. Allie suddenly looked up, spotted Lucy, let out a sharp cry, and burst into tears again. "I didn't do anything," she wailed. "I was swimming, and cut myself on the coral so I had to come onto the island."

"It's all right, Allie," Lucy said, putting aside the questions that arose as she surveyed the odd scene. "It's just a coral scrape. There's a hotel doctor. I've got a kayak. I can paddle you in."

"In there," cried Allie, as Lucy crossed the deck to get a better look at the mystery man lounging in the tub, so rudely watching yet ignoring this injured, naked, hysterical girl. "I tried to help him, but . . . it's Angus Wilson, and he's dead!"

"Oh shit," Lucy cried, when she saw his distorted, bug-eyed face. "What . . . Angus . . . Angus, wake up!" She knew it was ludicrous, the man's eyes bulged open, unseeing, past caring, he was a dead and ugly duck, but she went on anyway. "Angus . . ." She moved closer to him.

"He's dead," wailed Allie. "I cut my leg, and came in, and he was facedown in the tub. I—"

"Did you see anyone else?" She looked around, suddenly fearful again.

"There was no one. He was drowned, already . . . facedown dead in the water when I got here. It was just a minute ago. I . . . I pushed him up and got his arms out to hold him up. I thought he might be passed out or . . ." She burst into tears. "But I . . . he was gone. He must have had a heart attack and . . . I don't . . ."

Lucy could see red welts on his neck. His head tilted back

at an awkward angle. "Did you touch anything? I mean be-sides—"

"No," she wailed. "I didn't know what to . . . Oh, God, why did I—"

"Jesus Christ, calm down, Allie. Shit, cover yourself with this, for God's sake!" she hissed, grabbing a towel off a pile next to the tub, and tossing it to Allie. "We've got to get off this island and talk to the management. And the cops. Now hush up," she said sharply, whispering. "There might be someone else around."

"What . . . what makes you say that?" Allie asked in a scared voice.

"I don't know," said Lucy. "But I'd rather not stick around to find out. Let's go. We've got to get to the police." While Allie wrapped herself in the towel, Lucy, moving quickly, turned on the flash and quickly took six pictures of the plat-form and the surrounding area—and of Angus as well, blithely seated in the steaming hot tub, naked, dead.

Then she took Allie by the hand and led her down the path and onto the dock. When they reached the end, Lucy looked around, then cursed. "Oh hell, the kayak's gone. Well, the tide's higher now. We'd better swim for it. Come on."

"But what about the coral . . . and the body?" Allie cried.

"Forget about the body for now, Margolis," Lucy snapped. "We'll have to finesse it over the coral. We've got to get out of here. Come on. I'll go first," she said, and stepped onto the ladder and down. She lowered herself gingerly into the warm water—ever since *Jaws* she had a bad habit of seeing herself from the shark's point of view when swimming at night, when sharks feed—and turned around to watch Allie, who paused atop the ladder and unwrapped the towel she had draped around her body. She had a great figure, Lucy couldn't help but notice. Nothing like being twenty-four years old. "You'd better bring the towel. Wrap it around your neck. No, the other way, so it flows behind you. Now follow me . . . and slow. The coral's just ahead." Holding her camera aloft with one hand she did a one-armed backstroke softly, not splashing, kicking rapidly but softly to keep herself close to the surface. As she moved away from the dock, she reached carefully under the black water, feeling for coral. The water and the task of swimming seemed to calm Allie, who followed her, stroking strongly. Lucy hit a sharp rock with her hand. "Ow! Okay, here's the reef. Now stay close, and keep yourself on the surface if you can." She paddled tentatively, checking for coral, and passed over the reef without a scrape. Once she'd reached deeper water, she stopped and waited for Allie to pass the coral. Overhead, a million stars twinkled in the warm black sky, and Lucy thought, He was murdered. And whoever killed him was there when I was, and then took the kayak. Or had it simply drifted away? She hadn't tied it up, the tide was moving, anything could have happened.

"Ow, damn," Allie hissed. "I've done it again. My arm. It's bleeding."

"It's okay, Allie." Shark thoughts again. Blood in the water. Shit! Stay calm. "Come on, we've got to get to the beach." Lucy waited for Allie to catch up to her, then began kicking strongly. Allie kept pace with her. They reached the shallows and hurried up onto the beach. Lucy helped Allie wrap herself in the towel and then they ran down the promenade, headed for the bar, screaming like characters out of a bad movie: "Heeeelp, help! Murder!! There's been a murder!" Maybe, maybe not, Lucy thought, even as she yelled—but either way, there was definitely a dead guy out there.

By the time they reached the bar Allie's hysteria had infected Lucy as well, and the two of them speed-babbled at the bartender and the one man sitting at the bar—of all people, it was the unctuous one, Mike Nack, his head sunk in a glass of rum and coke. He smirked at the nearly naked, hysterical Allie, until a look from Lucy cut his look off at the knees. The bartender called the office, and within minutes Jefferson Hababi arrived on the scene. They talked at the bar, the barkeep poured brandies, and Jefferson dashed to the hot tub area to fetch towels and robes off the stack of freshly laundered ones kept close at hand.

Then Jefferson called the local police from the bar telephone. He was doing his best to stay on top of the situation, but it was Lucy who told him to fetch the robes and call the cops. She could hardly take the kid seriously, but Allie warmed to him, particularly after she'd downed a few gulps of brandy.

Shortly thereafter Acting Corporal Chauncey Billingsworth, neatly uniformed in his Green River Substation cop garb, arrived with a tense-looking Jackson Hababi leading the way.

The senior Hababi dashed up to Lucy. "Oh, Miss Ripken, so sorry, so very sorry about—"

"She's the one that's hurting," Lucy said with a nod at Allie. "She's the one that found the dead guy. He's out on the island. Maybe you want to go out there, Corporal Billingsworth, is it, and see what you can find."

"Yes, that is a good idea," said the young cop.

Then he glanced at Hababi, who shook his head just once. "Better we tend to the ladies first, don't you think, Corporal?"

"Yes, the ladies." The cop nodded. He tried to appear serious, but he looked like a boy playing soldier, like he didn't know what the fuck he was doing and Hababi would have to tell him.

Hababi shifted his attention to Allie. "Ah, Miss . . . Margolis, is it? My goodness, what a terrible thing to have happen to you at our hotel. We are so sorry. My dear, what shall we . . . perhaps we can extend your stay a day or two . . . yours as well, Miss Ripken, since this day has ended so very badly, so very, very badly. Let's move to a table, please, so that Corporal Billingsworth here can take your statements, please." He helped Allie up. Lucy declined similar help from Jefferson. They moved to a dining table. Hababi sat close by while the nattily uniformed constable, not more than twenty-five years old and so deferential to the hotelier you would have sworn he worked for him, interviewed them. Jefferson Hababi perched at the next table, behind his father, and like his father he listened carefully to both their statements. They told it as they'd seen it, no more, no less . . . well, a little less, since Lucy did leave out the fact that she'd shot a few pictures.

After the interviews Billingsworth asked to be taken out to the island. "Yeah, let's go," said Lucy, who'd recovered from her shock and now felt alert and into the scene, in spite of her exhaustion. "I'll show you where the corpse is." She wanted another look around out there. View the dead guy and all. It wasn't every day, after all, that you saw a corpse on location.

"That won't be necessary, Miss Ripken," Jackson said, smiling smarmily. "You beauties need your beauty sleep. Please, I insist. Jefferson, why don't you escort the ladies back to their rooms? We'll take care of the matter from here on out. Again, ladies," he said, ushering them to their feet, "we're very, very sorry about this matter, but don't worry, please don't worry. Corporal Billingsworth and I will handle it."

Against her better instincts Lucy gave in—to her weariness more than anything else. She bid goodnight to them all, and even managed a "sleep well" to Mike Nack, who'd lurked at the bar the entire time, picking up on the whole drama being played out. Well, nothing wrong with that, death was usually the most interesting thing around, especially when least expected.

Jefferson Hababi left her at the door of her room and started up the stairs with Allie. "Allie, wait," Lucy said as they reached the stair landing. They stopped and looked back. "Are you going to be all right?" she asked the younger woman.

"She'll be fine," Jefferson said before Allie had a chance to answer. "She'll be just fine." Lucy was too exhausted to push the point. What was the point, anyway? Allie looked tired and scared, but safe on the arm of Jefferson Hababi. Lucy closed her door, locked herself in, checked her patio door lock, and pulled the curtains. A quick shower to rinse off the salt, and then to bed. At 3:17 a.m. she set her alarm, and quickly fell asleep.

3

Design Chatter, Political Matters, Barroom Blather

The beeping alarm saved her. Seven-thirty a.m. She slapped it off and sat up, immediately possessed by a rerun of . . . The Night Before! Featuring a chorus line of corpses high-kicking across the moonlit stages of fabulous Naked Beach.

How could she not be possessed by that lurid scenario? Still aching from yesterday's manic sail, she dragged herself into the bathroom to put on a face and get organized. Her official morning would commence at eight a.m., when she was due to meet the architect, William Evans, in the lobby lounge for the grand architectural tour of the Grand Strand. It always seemed to work out that way: on a day she needed to be on full alert, she was running on empty.

She dressed in light cotton pants, flip-flops, and a pale blue cotton T-shirt. She brushed her hair for about ten seconds and left the bathroom. Into her purse she put a lipstick, a notebook, and two pens. Turning on the digital camera, she reviewed last night's images—a couple of moonlit mood shots followed by half a dozen views of a dead man and his surroundings—then turned it off and stuck it in her bag.

She marched out of the room, William Evans and the grand tour of the Grand Strand awaiting her. Words and pictures. Work.

But first, a cup of coffee. This involved a plunge into La Terrazzo Grande. Beneath the ruggedly beamed ceiling, the huge, skylit space, by night a dance hall and schmooze and booze zone, was by day a cafeteria. Lucy paused by the bar and had a look. The place was shot through with morning sunbeams, lovely in the cool early air. Several groggy-looking guests milled about in front of the long food service counter, with its diamond-tiled front, and a dozen servers dressed in white stood behind, ready to dish, while white-shirted waiters roamed from table to table with coffee and orange juice pitchers. Lucy, in search of coffee, eyed the goods as she wandered past.

The cornucopia began with an array of silver trays heaped with slices of cantaloupe, honeydew melon, watermelon, papaya, mangoes, pineapples, and oranges, as well as halved grapefruits and huge bowls of figs, grapes, blueberries, and strawberries. Next to that stood a multi-stacked rack of cereal boxes and pitchers of milk and cream. Then the heavy geography started, with a mountain of sweet rolls and danishes flanked by smaller hills of croissants and doughnuts. Next came the serviced area with its white-clad cooks standing coolly behind the counter. Vats of hot cereal flanked pans

of scrambled eggs and trays laden with waffles, pancakes, ackee, and eggs with salt codfish. French toast, steak, bacon,
sausages, and ham were lined up atop steam tables.

She shoved a slice of papaya in her mouth and legged it
for the lobby, a fragrant cup of Blue Mountain coffee steaming in her hand. Tomorrow, maybe, she'd indulge.

In the lobby lounge she spotted her new pal Michelle
Stedman in a flowered blouse and jeans, with a short, handsome, pale-skinned black man. They stood by the waterwheel
on one side of the lobby. The man wore an immaculately
pressed seersucker jacket with short pants, white suede shoes,
pale yellow socks, and a jaunty straw hat.

"Michelle," said Lucy, approaching them, her voice raised
over the rhythmic splash of the waterwheel. "How are you?
God, what a night, eh?"

"Lucy, good morning," Michelle said. "This is William
Evans, the architect."

"Hello, Lucy," said Evans, offering a hand, which Lucy
shook. It was warm and dry. Evans had slightly Asian eyes.
"I'm happy to meet you. Loved your piece on Columbus in
Jamaica in *T & L*. A fascinating and little-known—up there in
North America, anyway—tale. This should be of interest to
you," he went on, not missing a beat. His voice blended the
training of English public school with an island lilt. "I was
just explaining to Michelle the . . . symbolic importance of
the waterwheel in the history of Jamaica. I insisted that they
install this here so that the guests could, at least for a moment, reflect on that history."

"I see," said Lucy. "The legacy of imperialism, slavery in the cane fields and sugar mills. It's an admirable idea, and a wonderful architectural object. I love the sound of falling water, but I'm not sure the kind of people who come here will have the faintest idea—or interest, for that matter—in this kind of—"

"It's the responsibility of hotel management to inform them," said Evans sharply. "That's why I placed it here."

"Right, William," said Michelle quickly. "And they will, if I have anything to say about it."

"Speaking of the management, did they tell you what happened last night?" asked Lucy.

"I'm sorry I didn't make the dinner," said Evans. "I had another engagement."

"You don't have to lie to Lucy, William." Michelle grinned. "William is not a great admirer of Jackson Hababi," she added.

"Not many architects are, of their clients," said Lucy. "Particularly by the end of a project. But I wasn't talking about dinner. Michelle, you heard what happened out on Naked—I mean, Tower Cay, didn't you?"

"What's that, Lucy?" said Michelle.

"Angus Wilson died in the hot tub out there last night," Lucy said. "I can't believe they didn't—"

"What?" Michelle cried, her face turning white. "Angus Wilson dead?"

"That's right," said Lucy.

"That idiot Jefferson didn't say anything when I came in this morning," Michelle said. She seized control of herself. "You'll have to pardon me," she said, distraught, furious. "I've got to look into this. What happened? Was he . . . I'm sorry . . . I'm sure you two can figure out what you need to talk about without me butting in anyway." She stuffed her notebook into her bag.

"We'll be fine," said Evans.

"See you later, Michelle," said Lucy, as she and Evans watched her hurry off. "Strange, not telling their own PR people about something like this."

"Frankly, I'm not surprised," said Evans. "Who wants a dead man spoiling the party on opening day?"

"Good point," said Lucy. "Besides, Angus Wilson was not exactly among the dearly beloved."

"Never met the man myself," said Evans. "But how did you happen to hear about this unfortunate incident?"

"Actually, I was wandering about admiring your work in the moonlight, and I heard a shout. Another guest had just found him." Lucy shrugged, pulled out a pen, flipped a notebook open, and made ready. Later for Angus Wilson. There was work to do. "Well. As they say in New York, people die and clubs open. Let's do the grand tour. It's a great-looking place, by the way. I'm amazed at how many facilities you've gotten under one roof without losing control. And the restaurant on the water is exquisite."

"Thank you. Getting this place organized was an exercise

in . . . architectonic logistics, shall we say," said Evans, an expansive, somewhat pedantic tone emerging in his voice. "And, of course, the usual head-butting on budgets.

"Shall we begin with the lobby," he went on, wandering that way. "I had to train the local workers on how to cut this stone—it's native, of course—so you'll have to forgive the rough edges. I had the chandelier done by some friends in Florence. I used to live there, you see . . ."

Two hours later, Lucy had the basics of her story, her photographic plan sketched out in thirty-six digital images, and more: she had a deeper understanding of Jamaican politics, race, and architectural history, and how all three had played roles in the creation of the Grand Strand hotel. Now she and William Evans sat at the edge of the poolside verandah, and Lucy asked a waiter for another hit of the Blue Mountains. To conclude the interview, she gently, obliquely, nudged her way into the personal side of things, where the real stories lay hidden.

"Why anybody would want to spend time in the video lounge when they have this"—she gestured at the sea and sky, and the pagoda-like rooflines of the Colonial Regency-style Chinese restaurant suspended over the water—"is beyond me."

"You don't have to euphemize, Lucy," said Evans. "It's not a video lounge, it's an orgy room. And there is still some demand for a room like that. But things have changed. When I designed the Sybarites all-inclusive next door, let me think . . .

nearly twenty years ago, it was my first hotel. The quote un-quote video lounge—they called it the 'Relaxation Chamber' in those days—was almost a thousand square feet of redlit adult romper room. All that space goes to restaurants now. People have come 'round to admitting they'd really rather be eating than . . . well, you can imagine what went on in there." He grinned. "But organizing a room for an orgy is a pretty simple task, really. It basically designs itself. Talk about form following function! All you need is mood and mattresses."

Lucy laughed. "The good old days of free love, eh?"

"The good old days when I got along with Jackson Hababi."

"You mean this current . . . rift . . . is new?"

"Well, we always had our disagreements. I'd like to blame it on the budget problems, but they're almost predictable at this point, like part of the deal, you know? But Hababi's never taken overruns so seriously before. Maybe he's in over his head this time, I don't know. Perhaps Dexter's threatening to raise the room tax again, and put the squeeze on him. I can't say for sure."

"Dexter?"

"Hanley. The prime minister. He's a friend of mine. Like me, he's mixed race—he's Afro-English, I'm Afro-Chinese. And as I said before, we mutts form one contingent, and the Lebanese form another, and the power seesaws back and forth. The differences between us are, well, let's put it this way: none of their ancestors were slaves. Right now, although the tourist industry is doing well, and Hababi and his crowd still have all the money, we're holding the reins, and Jackson doesn't like it."

"So the last thing Jackson Hababi would want today, with Hanley on the premises, is anything that might appear to weaken his position, such as an open investigation of an unexplained death."

"Actually, I heard from the hotel doctor that Angus Wilson had a heart attack, Lucy. But no matter. Hababi and Hanley don't even speak except on ceremonial occasions. I always thought I could bridge this racialist gap, but with money and power at stake, I'm beginning to wonder." He looked at his watch. "Well, I've got to run."

"William, just one last question: what was the budget overrun on this project?"

He grinned at her from beneath his straw hat. "Oh, forty percent or so." He laughed. "But we opened only two weeks late. Now that is incredible for Jamaica. Good morning, Desmond," he said, as the sailboard instructor appeared tableside.

"How you doin', William Evans," Desmond said. "You going to finally learn to sail?"

"No time, my friend. No time. Got to keep building hotels."

"Right, and pretty soon there won't be no beach at all for us local boys, mon." He grinned. "Way it go, I guess. Now this Lucy here, she's a fine sailor," Desmond said, and looked out at the horizon. "It maybe going to blow later, Lucy. What time you want to sail today?"

"I don't know, Desmond. Grand opening today, you know. I have to stand around and watch."

"So," William Evans said, rising. "You're comfortable with your photographic plans?"

"Absolutely," said Lucy. "The eleven definite shots we discussed, plus those other ones if I have time. It's gonna be a stunning story, William."

"Great. I'm sure my office will want a set of transparencies. Here's my card. We'll stay in touch. I suppose I'll see you this afternoon, anyways. Dexter would be terribly disappointed if I didn't put in an appearance." They shook hands and he left.

Lucy went back to her room and lay down to attempt a nap beneath the lazy turning of the ceiling fan. She closed her eyes and saw Angus, awful, naked Angus floating toward her in the hot tub, dead and staring. Had she seen those welts on his neck? What did they mean? Had there been a murder? And if so, how was it that everything seemed so calm, so . . . normal this morning? Before last night, the only corpse she'd ever seen was her grandmother's, in a coffin in church. She'd been ten and only had a look at Gramma because her father had insisted.

Last night was different. With this murder, or whatever the death had been, something in the air had changed. And yet, as she'd walked back to her room just now, there was not even the hint of it. Instead, in bright, hot sunshine the employees were busy putting up balloons and bunting, flags and folding chairs, in preparation for the gala grand opening event. The only suspicious-looking characters she'd seen were a couple of secret police types, skulking about scouting security for the PM, Dexter Hanley. She wondered if Hanley would get wind of the death of Angus Wilson. She wondered what that cop had found out on Naked Beach. Tower Cay. Whatever. Allie Margolis. Where was she this morning? Well, Allie Margolis hadn't had to interview an architect for two hours, so she'd probably slept in. Lucky girl. Lucy hadn't slept in in about six years.

Sleep wasn't possible. She got up and changed into her swimsuit, ran out the door, dodged past a prone body—registering only afterward that it was Susie Adams, in an itsy little string bikini, fully greased and baking in the sun—and dove into the shallow waters of Blackwater Bay. Eyes open, she skimmed the bottom, watching little silver fish catch flickers of light and dart away. Earlier, William Evans had explained to her how Blackwater Bay got its name. In the nineteenth century, Caribbean whalers had brought their catch into the calm waters of the bay to butcher. The water ran so heavy with the blood of slaughtered whales that it turned black.

She surfaced, gasping for air in the dazzling light. Her early morning nightmare had placed her father, passed out in his standard drunken beatitude—the only redeeming quality of his alcoholism was its non-violent nature—in a hot tub, dead.

Lucy swam fifty yards out and headed east, parallel to the beach, swimming at a steady pace. Four hundred strokes later—the equivalent of forty laps in the pool at the club back in the city—she turned around and did four hundred more.

One advantage to traveling heavy on photo equipment was that it forced you to travel light on clothes. After a shower, Lucy spent all of thirty seconds deciding she'd wear the strapless red summer dress from Bongo Girl rather than one of the two Digital Dogma dresses she'd gotten in exchange for shooting their next summer catalogue a couple of weeks back. She slipped the hot red item on braless over bikini underwear, put on her face, and ran a brush through her hair, currently almost shoulder length, all the while psyching her weary self up for the gala grand opening of the Grand Strand.

Lucy stuck her mini tape recorder, a notebook, a lipstick, and a couple of pens in her bag, locked up her room, and wandered over. She pulled up to the horseshoe-shaped bar and had a look. La Terrazzo Grande, a half-dozen steps below her, swarmed with tuxedo-clad waiters pouring champagne, hotel guests, management personnel, and dignitaries from all over the island and the Caribbean. At the edge of the dance floor, Susie Adams in a semi-formal summer dress conferred with Jefferson Hababi, who wore a purple tux and his awkward grin. Sandy Rollins, in black pants and a pink top, with an orchid in her hair, huddled with Mike Nack and Maria Verde, bursting at the seams of a yellow dress, near the small podium that had been set up before the stage. Onstage, a band of white-jacketed, black-tied musicians, including strings and horns, played Muzak Marley. A dozen long tables had been set up with white linen and orchids, and in the middle of the floor, a huge ice sculpture of a swan, wings half-spread as if verging on flight, dominated the central table. The rapidly melting swan was surrounded by carefully arranged orchids and lilies, and myriad platters heaped with desserts, fruits, breads, cheeses, and other eats. More massive quantities of food. Gluttony equated with luxury.

"I'm gonna need major liposuction back in the city," said Mickey, sidling up next to her. "Look at this hogfest."

"Mickey, how're you doing? Nice dress," she said, admiring the lavender kimono-style wraparound. "Hey, Dave," she added, as Mullins hefted into view.

"Hiya, Lucy," he said, and turned to the bartender. "Yo, barkeep, set me up with a Wild Turkey and a Striper." He grinned at Lucy. "God, I love these open bars."

"I'm okay . . . but how are you?" Mickey said. "I heard about last—"

"You did?" Lucy said quickly. "From who?"

"Didn't I tell you? My room is right next to Margolis's. All kinds of commotion in the middle of the night. I'm a journalist last I heard, so I checked it out."

"You should have seen him, Mickey. He was—"

"As ugly in death as he was in life, I bet. God, poor Angus. He wasn't such a bad guy that he deserved this. Christ. What the hell was he doing out there in the middle of the night?"

"More to the point"—Mullins smirked—"what was that little petunia Allie Margolis doing with him?"

"She wasn't with him," Lucy said. "She found him."

"Yeah, right," sneered Mullins.

"What, you think they planned a rendezvous, Dave?" she said. "Allie Margolis and Angus Wilson? Please. I would call that about the least likely love match on the island of Jamaica. No, Mick, I don't know what the hell he was up to out there, but I can tell you one thing, you seem to be the only person who gives a shit."

"What do you mean?"

"Well, look at this." Lucy waved at the festivities. "Does this look like a murder took place last night?"

"Murder? Allie said the doctor told her he had a heart attack."

"Doctor! What doctor? What time did you talk to her?"

"I don't know," said Mickey. "It must have been . . . well, by the time I went back to bed it was four-thirty . . . so, I guess around four-fifteen." Almost an hour after Lucy had set her own alarm. Allie Margolis and Jefferson Hababi had walked away from her door around three a.m.

"And she said she talked to a doctor?"

"The hotel doctor. Some quack named Babcock. She was pretty woozy at that point. I think he must have given her a Valium or something."

"Well, he didn't give me a thing, and I went to sleep before three-thirty."

"So what's the big deal?"

"I don't know. I thought I saw these marks on his neck, like maybe someone had . . ."

"What, you think he was bumped off?"

"I don't know. But it's all too . . . tidy . . . today. I saw Michelle Stedman this morning, and they hadn't even told her."

"Luce," said Mickey. "Have a beer. Hey, Walter," she said to the bartender. "Couple Red Stripe drafts here, my man. Now listen, Luce: there may be a dozen people on the grounds of this dump that believe they wouldn't have minded seeing Angus dead—and I count myself among them—but hey, none of us could or would have actually done him in. The guy's a . . . was . . . a bloody institution! C'mon! Besides, there's several million dollars at stake here, you see?" she said, looking over the crowd. "Look, there's little Jeffy Hababi chatting up Allie now." Mickey waved, and Lucy glanced that way. She caught Allie's eye. Allie looked away. The bartender set them up. "Have some brew, doll, it'll do you good." Lucy sipped. The cold beer did taste great. She took a larger gulp, and spotted Harold, in another dapper 1940s-cut suit, wandering over from the guest room wing. "So anyway," Mickey went on, "You don't really expect that Jackson Hababi, with all he's got into this place, and with his arch-enemy Dexter Hanley coming here to actually participate in a grand opening ceremony—this is the first time Hanley's ever done this for a new hotel on the island, and it is supposed to signal, at last, his support for the tourism industry and his acceptance of Yankee imperialist dollars—with all that at stake here today, you can't really expect them to bag the opening because some not particularly well-liked hack journalist dies in a hot tub, of a heart attack, at that, can you?"

Louise Rousseau and Joey Ruskin strolled into view. They weren't touching, but the body language was there to be read: they had fucked last night. Louise, in black pants and a silver sleeveless top, was positively glowing; meanwhile Joey extended the distance between himself and Louise as they approached. "You're right, Mick," said Lucy. "I just want to . . . hell, I don't know." She threw down the rest of the beer. "Harold, what's up?"

"Not me, I'll tell you that," he said. "Wars are fought and won, famines come and go, there are hurricanes, tornadoes, revolutions, and volcanic eruptions . . . and we are here to exercise our brilliant journalistic talents on the opening of an all-inclusive luxury hotel."

"Get serious, Ipswich," said Dave Mullins. "Nobody held a gun to your head to get you down here."

"Really," said Mickey. "Spare me the identity crisis, Harold."

"Hey, sounds like the action's about to start," Harold said, wincing at a microphone squeal. Lucy nodded at Louise Rousseau waltzing by, sporting a pleased post-coital grin, looking like the New York kitty that ate the Jamaican canary except that Joey at her side acted like he didn't know her, and she wasn't aware of it. Joey, slick in a yellow seersucker suit, tossed a not-very-subtle "fuck me" kind of glance Lucy's way as he passed.

The band blared a somewhat martial tune, and everybody paused as the power surge of the approaching PM rippled over the sea of well-dressed citizens. These were the people that ran this island. They had power and prestige, and it showed in the way they dressed, talked, and moved. Now those who were seated rose to their feet; and as the stately music played, Prime Minister Dexter Hanley and his entourage appeared at the edge of the lobby lounge, paused, and looked down over the crowd. As several waiters began clapping, firing up a round of spontaneous applause, Hanley led the way down the long, wide staircase to the main floor.

"Love your suit, Harold," Lucy whispered. "Who's your tailor?" She watched Hanley as she spoke, and was impressed. A Creole, he was exquisitely handsome, with a big square jaw, salt and pepper hair, thin mustache, and golden skin. He appeared to be in his late fifties. Dressed in an off-white linen suit, he was tall and slender and utterly charismatic. Lucy wasn't around politically powerful people all that often, and was usually unimpressed when she was. But Hanley had an aura that glowed all the way across La Terrazzo Grande.

"Daffy Dan, who else?" said Harold. "Shall we find a table?"

Michelle Stedman appeared at the podium, dressed in an off-the-shoulder white top and matching three-quarter-length skirt with gold threading that gleamed subtly in the sunlight. She looked elegant as hell, Lucy thought. The girl had some style. "Good morning, ladies and gentlemen," she said, "and welcome to the Grand Strand's Grand Gala. My name is Michelle Stedman, and I'm the manager of public relations for FunClubs. Welcome, welcome to FunClubs' latest and greatest: The Grand Strand. And isn't it another lovely day in Jamaica? We've got a magnificent lunch planned for you, but first, as you know, the Right Honorable Dexter Hanley is here to say a few words, along with Mr. Jackson Hababi, president of FunClubs . . . and then we'll do lunch and the official opening ceremony. So if you'll all take a seat, we'll get on with the festivities."

Lucy followed Harold and Mickey down onto floor level in search of empty seats. En route, she passed Allie Margolis, seated between Mike Nack and Maria Verde at Jefferson Hababi's table. "Allie," she whispered over her shoulder, "how are you feeling today?"

"Good morning." Maria Verde jumped in quickly, grinning at her like a deranged doll. "How are you, Lucy?"

"I'm fine, Maria, if a little exhausted. I'm sure Allie told you about—"

"Yes," said Maria, her thick, dark-red eyebrows knitting together tragically, but the grin remaining below. Her face had this odd quality of appearing to be doing several things at once. "How sad for Angus. But let us not—"

"Allie, did you manage to get some sleep?" Lucy interrupted Maria. Allie had stuffed her snake braids under a scarf, and wore dark glasses. She had, thus far, simply refused to acknowledge that Lucy was talking to her.

Now she glanced up, and from behind her shades, dully, she said, "I'm fine, Lucy." Valium? She sounded like they'd given her a shot of Nembutal last night; and maybe another one for breakfast.

"Thanks for . . . helping out last night, Miss . . . Ripley," said Jefferson Hababi. Lucy gave him a look.

"That's Ripken," Lucy said. She looked again at Allie Margolis, but Allie had gone back to staring at her plate. What was up here? Lucy followed Harold to a table, sat down, and got out her notebook.

Jackson Hababi concluded his five uninspired minutes by introducing the Right Honorable Dexter Manfred Hanley, Prime Minister. Lucy fished out her tape recorder and notebook.

A moment later, she wrote: "Eloquence, coming from a politician after so many years of hearing American bullshit and blather, is almost shocking, so unexpected is it. Shocking, and then refreshing, like a splashing fall into very cold water. But eloquent is the only way to describe the words and style of Dexter Hanley, Jam's PM." She recorded the whole speech, and later transcribed the high points:

"You'll have to forgive me if I take a few moments to get started. I was dragooned into a lunch with a former American vice president yesterday in Venezuela, and I have to work my linguistic way back from this strange dialect . . . um, shall we call it Quaylespeak . . . to English." The crowd laughed, except for a few of the American reporters. "First off I want to say hello to all my poorly paid, overworked friends, the ones who are waiting on you, ladies and gentlemen. I want to remind you to look at them, and see them, and don't forget who they are, for they are my people." At this the waiters, cooks, and busboys stopped, put down their trays wherever they could, and began applauding. Soon the served were embarrassed into joining the servers in applauding as well. After basking in it for a moment, Hanley continued. "Now I know I have a reputation for resisting this kind of . . . extravagance," he said, waving at the surrounding hotel, "as representative of the worst aspects of colonialism in its late capitalistic form . . . and the reputation is well deserved, I might add," he muttered aside, drawing a nervous laugh. "But I have no desire, and have never had any desire, to allow the Americans to make of Jamaica another Cuba, isolated, abandoned like a ghost ship at sea. I have spoken with my friend Fidel many times about this, and he will be forever embittered at how in the old days the Americans made his revolution so dependent on the fat, pale, humorless missionaries of the Soviet Union. On the other hand, this is not Puerto Rico, this is not the fifty-first state of the USA even if we are"—he glanced at Jackson Hababi—"in some respects, somewhat overdependent on the largesse of certain American bankers. Nevertheless, I want to say that I welcome . . . I welcome Mr. Jackson Hababi's efforts at developing hotels for the American tourists. If it be Grand Strands we need to bring in the dollars, then let a Grand Strand bloom on every beach . . . or every third beach, anyway, since we want to keep the best beaches open for the people of Jamaica, for it is they, ultimately, who should benefit from these properties. Which reminds us, Jackson, how would you and your fellow hoteliers feel about another point on the room tax?" Hanley grinned as Hababi blanched, then recovered with a nervous laugh. "I've been thinking, with the rates a place like this charges, and the wages you pay your workers, there must be some space in that vast margin for a little more money for the government—for, say, perhaps, a new people's health clinic here in Ocho Negros, and some new air-conditioned buses for the public transit system that delivers these hardworking people to your hotel each and every day, and . . . well, as we all know here, ladies and gentlemen, the list is endless, for ours is a poor country. A most beautiful country, but very, very poor."

He went on for another ten minutes in the same combative, populist vein, drawing more enthusiasm from the waiters and busboys than from the bourgeouis troops seated at the tables. After the speech, which ended with an invitation to a press conference after lunch and the grand opening moment, Hanley sat at Jackson Hababi's table, but they were at opposite ends.

There was no wind that afternoon. Lucy lay on a lounge chair beneath an umbrella, looking out at the flat horizon where blue met blue. In the middle of her range of vision sat the stone tower and graceful palms of Naked Beach. Her body felt torpid from champagne and Red Stripe, but her head was humming.

"I can't believe anyone would want to lie in the sun out there," she said to Harold, lolling in a lounge chair by her side. He was reading Derek Walcott, poet laureate of the Caribbean. What a guy, reading poems on the beach! He looked up. "It's hot enough to stop a clock."

"God, no kidding," he said, squinting out at the island. "Look at that heat shimmer. Carcinoma Cay." He put the book down, and grinned. "But we really should be able to banish the sinners to the island, don't you think? Stick 'em out there and make 'em strip in the hot sun. Start with that Rollins woman, to be exiled for her foolishness at the press conference."

"Really. Accusing Hanley of being anti-American. What a dimdome."

"Hey, you know, the guy had an independent thought. How dare he! Hey, we could send that Nack clown out there, too. What a worm!"

Lucy laughed. "No shit. I'm surprised he didn't simply crawl up there and lick Hababi's feet like a dog might."

"He is a dog, isn't he? Christ, thanking Hababi on behalf of all of us for a fucking press trip. Like the place won't get six tons of free PR out of the deal. A brown-nosed lap cur if ever I saw one." Harold sighed, gazing out to sea, and grew pensive. "But then again, we're all dogs on this gig, aren't we? Christ, for a minute there I thought Hanley was going to break that bottle of champagne over Hababi's head instead of on that idiotic 'official welcoming' post, you know? I mean, there's a real story here, in the political doings on this island—but all we get to report on is the quality of the sand on the beach."

"It is great sand though, isn't it?" Lucy laughed. "That was weird, wasn't it, christening the damned hotel like a sailing ship. But Harold, there is another story here, too, for God's sake. You saw what happened when I asked Hababi about the death of Angus Wilson. He just brushed my question aside."

"Lucy, he answered the question," Harold interrupted, a little impatient. "He simply said that Wilson died of a heart attack."

Lucy sat up. "And I'm telling you it isn't . . . it can't be that simple, Harold! I saw the guy dead, and Allie Margolis is acting really weird today."

"Jesus, she's just a kid, she found a dead guy last night, it's not surprising she's acting weird."

"Fine, Harold, say what you want. But I'm going to look a little further into this Wilson thing. I know it isn't politics, but it's life and death, and it means a lot more than critiquing the clam chairs in green sauce in the poison fish love cafe, or whatever they call the place. I think something happened out there. I'm gonna find out what." She touched his shoulder gently. "I could use your help."

She didn't get his help that evening, for Harold, the beer-sodden swine, slept through the call for all reporters to gather at the porte cochere for the ride into town to Jack's Joint, where they were to be escorted by the indefatigable

Susie Adams through the legendary island moment of Sunset at Jack's.

Sunset at Jack's, Susie informed them en route, was where and when everybody in town gathered for cocktails, gossip, and dealmaking. "Like Rick's in Casablanca," she said, facing them from the front of the bus. "Everything happens there." Lucy had seen it before, in Puerto Vallarta, in Provincetown, in Key West, all hip resort towns have their sunset spots. Every ganja dealer in town would be there, along with the hangers-on, hookers, gunrunners, drug runners, lowlifes, rumor mongers, and sleazoids of every elegant and not-so-elegant description who tended to congregate at such places. Jack's westerly siting on a little point sticking out of the coast did make it one of the best locations to watch the sun go down on the entire island. The sunsets were so consistently stunning, in fact, that almost every night, at the moment of sunset, every conversation would cease, every dealer would pause, every pick-up artist would hesitate, and all, all would applaud the miracle of the setting sun.

Lucy shared a seat on the bus with Louise Rousseau. After Lucy had admired Louise's outfit—a white silk shirt, black pedal pushers, and black sandals—and Louise had likewise expressed her approval of Lucy's black tank top, long, tight black bike shorts, and black platform sandals with enough criss-crossing ankle straps to subliminally evoke, as Louise put it, "the dominatrix dynamic," they got down to business. "So I gather you and Joey hit it off," Lucy said, her tone noncommittal.

Louise grinned a Cheshire grin. "Yes . . . he's quite a guy, I must say. Haven't slept so well in ages, it seems. You forget sometimes what a good bump in the night can do." Her tone changed abruptly. "But God, I heard what happened to you. I meant to ask earlier, but there was just so much going on. When Joey told me I couldn't believe it!"

"When did he tell you?"

"When I got up this morning he had room service breakfast for the two of us waiting. I guess the waiter must have told him." She giggled. "I . . . we must have . . . slept through all the excitement."

"Yeah, it was pretty intense," said Lucy. "By the way, where is Allie? She's not on the bus. I can't believe she didn't want to experience Jack's."

"Joey said he was going to arrange for her to see a local shrink this evening. That's why he's not on the bus now."

"It was a pretty awful sight, I must say. Well, here's the Joint," Lucy added, as the bus rolled into an overgrown dirt parking area. Two old VW buses, painted 1960s style, were marooned on one side, enveloped in huge vines of green and yellow pothos leaves. The parking lot was thick with red and orange hibiscus. A pair of ackee trees overhung the entrance-way, their lovely poison-red fruits dangling; and a pair of ancient Dewey Weber surfboards were crossed like spears over the facade of the palm thatch–roofed arcade leading to the double swinging doors that opened into Jack's Joint. From inside drifted the ubiquitous reggae. The journalists in their crisp New York resort wear climbed off the bus and clustered in a group, waiting for instructions. Lucy and Louise drifted away and headed in on their own.

Inside, everything was driftwood and green leaves and soft lights, fishnets and shafts of sun peeking through the vines, reggae smoking up the air. You passed down a long hallway framed with old surfboards, paddles, boat signs, tropical plant life, and a couple of parrots and parakeets squawking in wooden cages; you stopped at a palm thatch booth where, from two red-eyed smiling Rastamen, you bought the tokens with which all transactions were accomplished at Jack's. Money was not allowed, and the plastic tokens were white poker chips with a marijuana leaf stamped onto each one. Lucy bought ten bucks' worth and finished the stroll to the bar alone. The bar formed a long, freeform curve, and the view from the cliffs beyond the bar was north and west, full of sea and sky and clouds and ships drifting past. The bar was jammed with Ocho Negros' beautiful people, and to Lucy's trend-jaded New York eyes, the place felt time-warped in a good way. The late sixties inspired the scene. The first guy she focused on in the lively crowd looked like John Lennon in his long center-parted hair incarnation, only this guy was wearing a Balinese-style wraparound "skirt" in a green jungle print, and a white tank top. He sat at the bar between two gorgeous black women in mini-skirts, high heels, and low-cut tank tops, and another guy was videotaping the three of them from across the bar. The way the Lennon-clone sniffed and grinned, Lucy suspected he was a cokehead. And the girls looked like Tenth Avenue hookers on holiday. Lucy slid past them and up to the bar, took a seat, and ordered a Red Stripe from the bartender, a flower child with long blond hair and a happy, vacant look in her eyes. Probably showed up here crewing on a yacht out of Boston, ran into a ganja cloud, and got shipwrecked. Lucy now had a chance to scope out the video man more carefully, and he was an odd one: a white boy with dreadlocks—now that took some work, when you had straight, honky blond hair—wearing, of all things, a white suit, circa John Travolta in *Saturday Night Fever*. He pointed the camera at her, said, "Hey love, give us a smile." She turned away just in time to find Louise.

"God, this place is quite a scene," Lucy said. "I'd forgotten."

"You've been here before?" Louise asked.

"Years ago. But I was pretty deranged at the time," Lucy said. "Some serious overindulgence in local product."

Lucy emptied her Red Stripe, ordered two more, threw five ganja chips on the bartop, and chased Louise across the patio, dodging through a swarm of tourists and around two white guys in tie-dye, long-haired, bearded, who had assumed the lotus position in the middle of the bar area on a table top, facing the sunset, so as to share their moment of spiritual transcendence with the crowd.

Up ahead, three sunburned American boys picked their way up a trail over the rocks between the dining area and the cliff. One of them suddenly jumped, flew thirty feet, belly flopped in the water below, and emerged to a round of applause. He swam out of the way, and another leaped, from a higher spot, and pulled off a smooth dive.

Lucy and Louise found a spot by the railing and watched a dozen dives, each more drunkenly brilliant than the last.

And when in a cloud-crowned blaze of ephemeral brilliance the sun landed in the embrace of the sea, the stoned and boozed-up troops applauded on cue. Then Susie Adams found her and said there was an early bus back and a late bus, and which did she want to take? Exhausted, Lucy took the early one. When she got to her room she set her clock for five a.m. and fell asleep before nine p.m.

4

Picture This

Up at four, Lucy beat the alarm by an hour. Not bad: nearly seven hours of sleep. She rose quickly and opened the sliding doors to step onto the patio. Cool air soothed her, sweet with the scent of night-blooming jasmine. The magic hour.

She went inside, dressed in shorts and sandals and a T-shirt, and packed her gear. Into the camera bag went the Hasselblad, with wide angle and close-up lenses, along with the digital camera to shoot test images, and her light meter. Then she organized the transparency film, putting eight rolls of daylight and eight rolls of tungsten for the Hasselblad into separate compartments of the bag. She stuck a notebook and pens in another compartment for keeping track of shots, threw in spare batteries, and was ready to go.

Extracting the digital camera from the bag, she sat at the desk for a moment to review the images she'd shot the day before. For the most part her instincts had been right, but she could see ways to improve several of the shots. She also had another look at the series of dark, green-tinged pictures she'd shot the night before—a beached motorboat, a sinking silver moon, the death scene of Angus Wilson. After a moment, she turned off the camera and put it back in the bag, shaking off the grisly scenario. She got up and grabbed her tripod, slung it over one shoulder and the camera bag over the other, and headed out into the early morning darkness.

She passed the bar area, for once still, and went first to Les Poissons de L'Amour, where she found the door unlocked per arrangements made the evening before. This room could be shot with artificial light only, and therefore could be done before dawn. She went in, put down her gear, and started playing with the lights. After she'd set them at a level bright enough to create some contrast between the highlighted tabletops and the darker surroundings, she positioned the camera, got out her light meter, and did some readings around the room. Then she attached the digital camera to the tripod, set it to automatically adjust to the existing light levels, and took a couple of pictures.

After looking them over, she adjusted the tripod. Then she got out a book of matches, lit all the candles in the candelabras, did another light reading, adjusted a few flowers in the direction of the camera, and shot several more digital images. She had a look. Just about right. She loaded film into the Hasselblad, surveyed the room once more, then took the picture three times, on three different settings, to bracket the exposure. Shooting digitally was efficient but made you lazy about light readings. The bracketing would pretty much guarantee a useable transparency.

She repeated the process from another point in the room, shot half a dozen details with the digital camera set for wide angles or close-ups, made some notes on the shots, then packed up and left.

As she had planned, the sun was on the verge of rising when she got outside. By the time she'd figured out the precise composition of the most important overall Terrazo Grande shot, positioned her tripod, and set up, the morning rays bathed the terrace in rich golden light. The food service counter was clean and clear, gleaming brass trimmed with copper; each perfectly placed table wore white linen, crystal, silver, a bird of paradise in a bud vase; the wood floor shone. She shot her test shots, had a look, moved the camera six inches, and took her pictures.

The sun had risen high enough now to shoot the entrance and the lobby. Before heading up there, Lucy took a deep breath and looked out to sea—to Naked Beach and its stone tower. William Evans had told her the tower was a pint-sized version of the Tower of London. Lucy had viewed the Tower of London six years ago on a trip, yet she hadn't made the visual connection until he told her. The tower on Tower Cay, in early morning sunlight, showed two black arched holes, glassless windows like enormous empty cartoon eyes. To complete the face, the arched doorway formed a distorted Munchian cartoon mouth, open, shrieking, yet still and silent.

She would have to shoot from there sometime today. The definitive territorial site shot could be taken from the island and nowhere else.

Lucy hauled her gear over to the hotel's main entrance and did two shots of the entry passage and the pool. Next came the lobby. She was humming along. It was after eight now, and hotel guests were straggling through, en route to town, breakfast, the poolside bar, the beach. Now she wished for an assistant to play traffic cop and keep people out of the lobby.

With permission from the demure young black woman behind it, Lucy set up in front of the reception desk—she could shoot the desk itself afterward, with the digital camera set on close-up to get the richness of the wood detailing—and pointed the Hasselblad across the octagonal lobby. The double wide arched doorway into the lobby lounge, flanked by a pair of elegant Biedermeier knock-off sofas, formed the center of the image. This would be the definitive interior shot, and run as a full-page vertical, if there was to be one. Lucy got behind the camera and made ready. Grabbing shots between passing guests and hotel workers, she soon had the lobby work done.

She shot a dozen details, dodging the bodies passing through, closed with a couple of portraits of the receptionist smiling at her desk, and had just packed up and readied herself to move to the adjoining lounge to photograph the waterwheel more directly when into the lobby marched Jefferson Hababi, wearing an ill-fitting iridescent green suit and hefting a suitcase in each hand, followed by Allie Margolis, dressed to travel in her big hat and a white cotton dress, and Maria Verde in a pair of bright yellow harem pants and a purple bikini top. Maria had draped a huge turquoise and silver necklace around her neck, matching oversize earrings dangled from her ears, and a dozen jangly bracelets rattled on each arm. She looked like a hippie hooker. Jefferson did a double take upon seeing Lucy, then quickly recovered with a big, fake grin. "Lucy, how's it going?" he said, trying for cool but sounding like Daffy Duck gone Caribbean.

"Fine, but . . ." She looked past him to Allie and Maria. "Allie, are you—"

"She's heading out today," Maria said, a half-grin, half-frown creating unintended havoc on her face. "The other night, finding Angus . . ."

"Allie, I'm sorry," said Lucy, quickly approaching and standing right in front of her. Allie had her shades on again, and her head down. "I'm sorry we haven't had a chance to talk about the other—"

Jefferson butted in: "Pardon me, Miss Ripley, but the last thing she needs right now is to talk about what happened."

"How would you know that, Jefferson? I was there."

He backed off. "I don't . . . I don't know, Lucy. I'm only telling you what Dr. Ernst told her last night." His voice had a whiny edge to it.

"Dr. Ernst? I don't give a damn about Dr. Ernst. Allie, what's with you? Are you really leaving? It's not like you did anything wrong, honey, but ever since we separated the other night I—"

"Lighten up, Lucy," said Maria Verde. "Can't you see that she's not in any shape to discuss this?"

"Bug off, Maria," Lucy snapped. "I'm not harassing her, I'm trying to help."

"I'm sorry, Lucy, I . . . just want to go home," said Allie, her voice dull. "I just want to get away from here."

"You see?" said Maria. "There's no need to yell at me, Lucy Ripken. Allie has had an upsetting experience. This is where it happened, and as nice as this hotel is, she wants to get home. I personally don't blame her."

"Me either," said Jefferson. "I think Miss Margolis has seen enough of Jamaica this time around. Right, Al—Miss Margolis?"

"Okay, Jefferson," Allie said.

"So where's your tambourine?" Lucy said to Maria.

"What are you talking about?" Maria said with a gap-toothed grin, but her eyes betrayed distrust. "What do you mean?"

"Those clothes you're wearing, you oughta be banging a tambourine. You know, playing a revival of *Hair*. That's all I meant," said Lucy, and turned her attention back to Allie. "Well, what the fuck. So you're out of here, Allie. So you're gonna walk away from what we saw out there. So you figure that's the way to handle it." She picked up her tripod. "Well, Allie," she said, looking not at Allie but at Jefferson Hababi and Maria Verde as she said it, "I figure otherwise. So have a good trip."

She waited for a response, watching Allie's sunglasses. The pause stretched for a few long, uncomfortable seconds. Finally Jefferson Hababi broke it. "Nothing happened out there, Miss Ripley. Except that Mr. Angus Wilson died of a heart attack. I don't understand why you keep making such a big deal out of it." He sounded not at all like the forceful young man he imagined himself to be, but like a petulant eight-year-old. "And now our driver's waiting. We should be going."

"I . . . I'm sorry, Lucy," Allie said. "It's just that . . . I don't know what happened out there anymore," she wailed, and burst into tears.

"Now look what you've done to her!" Maria snapped, and took Allie by the arm. "Let's go, honey." She half-dragged Allie past Lucy.

Lucy stayed in the way. "Allie, take care of yourself," she said, trying to get a look through the sunglasses. "I'll be here till the end of the week, if you want to talk." She thought she sensed a flicker, a little quiver of a cry for help darting out from somewhere behind the sunglasses as she stepped aside.

Lucy watched the three of them cross the lobby and head up the flagstone path to the porte cochere, where a cab was waiting. They stuck the suitcases in the trunk, climbed in, and took off.

Lucy could have kicked herself for not taking the time to track the girl down earlier. Now it was too late. Too late, too bad. Back to work.

She got a nice shot of the waterwheel in sunlight; the moving water would make for a poetic blur in the sharp, crystalline image. She shot a bunch of details of rattan furniture groupings and some pieces of wall art. Then she did the other restaurants, finishing off the indoors shoot by noon. She wandered around the grounds for an hour with the digital camera, and eventually this led her to the foot of a huge tree growing out of a stretch of lawn behind the west wing of guest rooms, at the opposite end of the hotel from her own room. She was setting up to shoot it when a young Rastaman with shoulder-length dreads and the usual scruffy never-cut beard appeared, sat down on an exposed root beneath the tree, and began playing a little wooden flute. He wore a tattered multi-colored shirt, bright red pants, no hat, no shoes. Mr. Tambourine Man. Hippies didn't die, they just moved to Jamaica and turned a mellow shade of brown. "Yo," said Lucy in his direction. "How are you today?" He looked over, spotted her behind the tripod, continued to play his flute, a pretty little melody with a vaguely African undercurrent. Lucy stepped out and walked the fifty feet over to where he sat beneath the tree. The root system was exposed aboveground, an intricate web of interlaced branches that roughly mirrored the network of branches above. "What do they call this tree?" Lucy asked. "It's intense."

He stopped playing his flute and grinned at her. His eyes, like so many of the Rastas she'd met, were red from ganja, yellow from jaundice, but also merry and mellow—this too from ganja. "They call this the Hangin' Lady Tree, sister," he said. "Been here over one hundred years. They want to cut it down but Dexter Hanley make dem build the hotel around it, see? Seems that in the way back when, two lady pirates, they were hung here, from these branches."

"Lady pirates! No shit."

"No problem. String 'em up in dresses and bonnets, you see?" He grinned.

"But why? I mean, who were they?"

"Mrs. Bluebeard, one of dem. And her friend." He stuck his flute in his pocket, pulled a little drum out of a woven shoulderbag, and banged out a little rhythm. Then he began to sing, chanting non-word syllables in a high falsetto, smiling at her gleefully as he did so. Lucy lifted the camera and started snapping away. His smile broadened, and he showed a set of perfect white teeth.

After a moment, he paused in his chant and dropped his drumbeat to a low volume. "You want to meet the pirates of today, go to Jack's Joint," he said, singsong. "Jack's in de afternoon is where it is, when you want to see Ocho Negros."

"Yes, I was there last night," said Lucy. "Quite a scene."

"Last night is good, yes, but de night is a party for tourists, you see. Today, the ganja pirates gather for business, you understand me, no problem?"

"Ganja pirates?"

"Oh yes, today de pirates are here," he said, giving her the mystic eye. "Right here too, at de Grand Strand, where I and I sing my song today."

"The hotelmen pay you to come here and play?"

Ignoring the question, he grinned, thumped his drum. "And maybe I and I a sometime ganja pirate, too, you see?" He gave her a certain look.

"No thanks, my friend, I don't smoke."

"No herb? There is no mystery to life without herb, sister. Herb lights the path to Jah."

"I beg to differ, my friend—"

"Jossie."

"What?"

"My name is Jossie, no problem. Go to Jack's, meet some pirates, then you decide about herb, okay?"

"Okay, Jossie. And my name is—"

"Lucy, all right?"

"But how did you know?"

He grinned, banged on his drum. "My friend Desmond say there's a sailor lady taking pictures, come by the hotel at noon and maybe she'll take one of you, so here I am, no problem."

She took one of him, no problem. Took several, listened to his plaintive Rasta tune, and went on her way, camera in hand, tripod and bag over her shoulder, back to the beach. To China Grill, out over the water, where the waiters were cleaning up lunch and setting up dinner early just for her. After the China Grill, she would have just one location remaining, aside from the room shots which she could do anytime in her own room after it had been cleaned up: Naked Beach.

Having cased it previously, Lucy made short photographic work of the China Grill. She left her gear in the care of a waiter, ran down the beach, and found Desmond, in his tiny swimsuit, his brown, exquisitely articulated body gleaming in the sunlight as he washed down kayaks by the sports hut. "Hey, Des," she said, "I met your friend today."

"Who's that? Oh." He grinned. "Jossie."

"Yeah, mon. Plays a mean flute. Tells a tall tale."

"He's a pretty boy, though, don't you think? I thought you might want to take his picture, eh?"

She looked him over and smiled. "You are all pretty boys around here, Desmond. But yeah, I took his picture. And now I need to take some out on the island. Can you run me out there in the motorboat?"

He shook his head. "No pictures allowed on Tower Cay, Lucy. I am—"

"Not *of* the island, Des. *From* the island."

"But cameras are not allowed. I cannot—"

"I already got permission from the big boss man, Des. Jackson Hababi himself. Check it out. It's the only way, except from up in the sky, that I can take a picture of the whole place, you see?"

He stopped the hose work. "Well, okay, if Hababi say so, but anyone out there be complainin', I got to bring you back."

"Good enough."

Lucy ran for her equipment, then met Desmond on the dock. They loaded the bag and tripod into the motorboat and headed out. "Not much wind today, eh?" Lucy said.

"Nothing. Good for waterskiing, though. You want to try it later, say around four?"

"Waterskiing? I haven't done it in ten years. Sure, why not?"

They docked at the island, Lucy climbed out of the boat, and Desmond handed her gear up. "Thanks, Des," she said.

"No problem. I'll be back in half an hour."

"No cameras allowed out here, babe," a man's voice called out, and she quickly whipped around. Oh no! There stood a pair of hotel guests, non-journalists, dripping from the hot tub, naked! "Didn't they tell you that?" He grinned. "Also, no clothes allowed."

She tried not to stare below their necks. Even without looking down she could see that the woman, pushing fifty, dressed in sunglasses and sandals and nothing else, was built like a brick shithouse, and didn't even have a tan line. Had she had her tits done? "I know, but I'm working."

"Come on, lady," said the naked, thick, and hairy man. "You can't expect us to . . . let's go, off with the clothes, honey."

The woman laughed. "Come on over and join us in the hot tub. In this heat you can lose weight just sittin' there. Have a beer and not even worry, it's great."

"No thanks, I gotta take some pictures."

"Yo, driver," said the man to Desmond. "Didn't you tell her about the rules out here? No clothes and no cameras."

"Yes, sir, I did, sir," said Desmond. He too had a smile on his face. "But Lucy explains to me that she is working."

"Hey, I'm working, too," said another naked middle-aged man, lumbering into sight, also naked and dripping. "Working on cooking my ass." He turned around. "Hey, photo lady, how's it look?"

Lucy glanced. This guy had the disappearing, shriveled rear end of an old man. "Roasted. You'd better put on some sunscreen."

"She's right, Jack," said the dame with the perfect tits. "Whyn'tchou get Angie to take care a you. I'd do it myself but I don't think Angie'd like it much."

"Hey sweetheart," Jack said to Lucy, and winked. "Maybe you'd like to give me a hand with the sunscreen, eh?" He did a little shimmy, and his flabby, fleshless, red rear end shook. He was wearing a gold chain, sandals, and nothing else, and held a cigarette in one hand and a beer in the other.

"Um, no thanks," Lucy said. "But if you don't mind, I do have a picture I want to—"

"Honey," said Jack patiently. "You don't really think it's fair for you to be out here, dressed, with a camera, taking pictures, while we're bare-ass naked? They told us there were no exceptions to the rules out here, and yer breakin' the two main rules."

"He's right, Lucy," said the naked woman. "No cameras, and no clothes, on Tower Cay."

"So what do you want me to do?" Lucy said. "Not take my pictures? Fine. I'll just come back when there's no one here."

"No, no, Lucy, that's not it. Come on," he insisted. "Have a beer." What the hell, why not? She laid her equipment down and started after him toward the tower.

"Just give me a minute, Des," she said.

"Okay, Lucy." He laughed. "Whatever you say." He turned the motor off and tied the boat to a piling. Actually, now that she was here where Angus had met his end, Lucy was glad to have the company. There were lingering vibes she didn't like. Surely these naked characters would chase them away. The guy came out a moment later and handed her a cup of beer. She had a taste. It was ice-cold Red Stripe draft, and in the hot sun it went right to her head. She hadn't eaten anything but coffee and a slice of papaya all day, she'd been up since four a.m., and it was after one. "Good beer," she said.

"Yeah." He sipped at his. "So anyways, it seems to me we can make a deal here. Tell ya what. I know you got a job to do, but hey, how do you think I feel, standin' here naked in my goddamn sandals, and you wearin' shorts and a shirt? Like an idiot, is how I feel. So how about this: you take off your clothes, and then you can take your pictures. Look"—he gestured at the hot tub—"we're all naked." There were four people in the tub and two out of it. Towels and clothes were strewn about. They were all naked except for jewelry and sunglasses, completely at ease in spite of varying degrees of fat, flabbiness, cellulite thighs, sunburn.

"I don't know if . . . I can't work naked!" she said. Christ, she was thinking, I really don't want to strip in front of these guys, with their dangling scrota and hairpieces and trashily sexy wives. But why? I've seen a chorus line of transvestite hooker junkie queens displaying ten-inch, silver-spangled dicks like they were the crown jewels on parade on an East Village stage, and a bunch of naked middle-aged tourists intimidate me?

Well, yes, as a matter of fact. People like this aren't supposed to go naked in public!

"Sure you can, honey," said she of the perfect breasts, subtly thrusting them forward. "Just relax. Take a soak first, then take your pictures. Try it, you'll like it."

Lucy downed the rest of her beer, took heart from the icy alcoholic buzz, and five minutes later lowered herself naked into a hot tub with eight people she'd never seen before. She drank two more cups of beer, and the beer joined with the hot salty water to send her reeling out of the tub, naked like the rest of them, to fetch her camera and start firing away. Stepping carefully, if slightly astumble from the beer, she worked her way around the platforms, the trails, and the dock, and got her photographs: some nice panoramics of the entire hotel stretched along the shores of Blackwater Bay, some close-in shots of the tower and the platforms and the palm trees, and as a bonus, a bunch of utterly weird naked group portraits of the eight half-drunk tourists lolling on the edges of the hot tub. She was just about ready to pack it up and signal Desmond—there was a flag you ran up a pole when you wanted to get back to the beach, and he had split about the time she dropped her drawers—when, looking through the camera, something struck her about the way the rocks were lined up along the edge of the sunbathing platform. She went over and had a look. This one rock didn't look like it belonged there, and the dirt was stirred up around it, like it had been dug or something. She pulled at the rock a little.

Then she went for her shorts and shirt. "Been nice getting naked with you all," she called out. She bundled up her clothes, ran the flag up the pole, then gathered up her photo equipment and walked over to the dock.

5

Mushroom Madness and Monkey Business

Her driver, under a wool cap and shades, grinned as she climbed into the car, but she didn't recognize him until he took off the shades and hat. "Jossie!" she said. "You're a cab-driver?"

"Can't make no livin' playin' de flute and singin' my song," he said. "Got to have me money, and de taxi make me money. Simple as that." He whipped his chrome-splashed cab around the strutting roosters and sleeping dogs on the banana leaf back roads of Ocho Negros, delivering her to Jack's. His fast driving and easy smile appealed to her, and by the time he dropped her at Jack's, she had his phone number and he had agreed to do some private tour guiding in the next few days.

Perhaps if she hadn't been going nonstop for ten hours, she might have thought it an odd coincidence that he'd told her about "pirates at Jack's" and then conveniently showed up to take her there, but she was already in outer space from the endless day. And now, coming down off a three-beer liquid lunch, she figured she had to go for maybe ten hours more. No problem. Tomorrow she could unwind in the wind. Meanwhile, strolling into the afternoon quiet of Jack's where a parrot squawked repeatedly, "Give peace a chance, smoke ganja," she wondered what she was looking for.

Aside from the noisy, pacifistic parrot, an enormous green and yellow critter perched atop its palm thatch roof, nobody occupied the token booth, and not a soul sat at the bar. A scrawny white guy in shorts washed glasses, and the Gipsy Kings came on low over the stereo. The ocean, framed in the palms that fringed the cliff, lay still. At a white wrought-iron table two men huddled in conversation. One looked familiar: the white video boy from the night before, displaying his spray of blond dreads and the same white disco suit, but today barefoot and shirtless. The other man was a bearded black fellow in an immaculate green suit over a white shirt and tie, possessed of an elegant bearing. He too looked familiar, although for the moment she couldn't place him. She slipped her shades on as she hit the daylit patio. "Hey, photo woman," Dreadlocks said pleasantly as she approached the table, "You want a beer, darlin'?"

They were drinking mineral water. "No, thanks. I'm fine."

"Water then. You want to sit down?"

She looked at him. "I guess. I mean, why am I . . ." She stopped and waited. They looked up at her, not unfriendly.

"I tried to video you the other night," Dreadlocks went on, "but you turned away." He was not a boy but a boyish man, past thirty, deeply tanned, and his eyebrows and eyelashes had been bleached nearly white by salt water and the tropical sun.

"I always ask permission before taking pictures of people," she answered. "Or I sneak shoot if I have to. But what I don't do is shove the camera in anyone's face."

"Hey, I was ten feet away, " he said.

"Yeah, with a zoom lens."

"Hey, I'm dreadfully sorry, really. I didn't mean anything. Most people start preening the second a camera's pointed at them. They—"

"Where are you from?" Lucy interrupted. "You sound like . . ."

"Africa. Kenya, actually. But school in England, and six years here." He held out a hand. "My name's Kensington. Adrian Kensington. And you're Lucy . . ."

"Ripken." She shook his hand. "Lucy Ripken."

"My pleasure," said Kensington. "Won't you join us?" He gestured at an empty seat. "Oh, I'm sorry. Lucy, this is Rackstraw Barnes." The bearded man nodded and smiled at her as she sat down and removed her sunglasses, but he didn't say a word or offer a hand to shake.

"Rackstraw Barnes? Adrian Kensington? Jesus, where am I, the House of Lords?"

"Ocho Negros, Lucy," said Kensington. "Home of the last of the lost English."

"I can dig it," she said. Then she looked at him, as if to say, again, this is very nice, but why am I here?

"You have lovely eyes," said Kensington, gazing at her out of his own pale blues.

"Thanks," she said, and smiled. And waited.

"So, you like Jamaica?" Kensington finally ventured, his tone friendly enough.

"Yeah. I mean, I'm working, photographing the hotel for an architecture story, but in my spare time I windsurf, and the trades are good. Usually." She looked out to sea. "Not today, I guess." She shrugged. "I like the people, too. I don't know why New Yorkers are so uptight about coming here."

"Ganja-crazed Rastafarian bad boys ravishing their virginal women on the golf courses and tennis courts, what else?" said Kensington, his Eton-honed public school lingo rolling mellifluously off his tongue. "There was an incident a few years back . . . a couple of tourists got hacked up."

"Yeah, I remember reading about it," said Lucy. "Tough break for them, eh?"

Kensington took on a sly look. "I heard from a mutual friend that you might be interested in some . . . herb?"

Lucy countered, "That would be Jossie, eh? Did he tell you that? No, not me. What he said was there might be some ganja pirates around, and that I should maybe come here to see what was up." She leaned back in her seat. "So here I am. You lads don't look much like pirates to me."

Kensington grinned, displaying bad upper-class English teeth. "Pirates? Goodness! What kind of tales has Jossie been telling, Rackstraw?"

Barnes shrugged, disengaged.

Kensington paused, and smiled tentatively. "Well, anyway, to get to the point, as it were, what do you want to know about pirates, Lucy?"

"Man, I don't know," she said, impatient with the obtuse conversation. "A guy died the other night at the hotel, and everybody's talking about this heart attack he's supposed to have had, and I . . . but why am I telling you this?"

"Why not? What have you got to lose, right?"

She felt light-headed from exhaustion, sun, and beer. She stood up. "Nothing, except that I don't even know who you are." She pushed her chair out, and moved back from the table. "Nice to meet you both," she said, "but I gotta get back to the hotel." She headed toward the bar.

"That's cool, Lucy," said Kensington, sounding like he had something to tell her. She stopped, waited a beat, then looked back. "But check it out: you want to see some pirates, have a look 'round Tower Cay at midnight tonight."

After staring at the man for a few seconds, she said, "Why are you telling me this?"

Kensington shrugged. Then abruptly Barnes spoke up: "Because you asked," he said, "about pirates."

There were no taxis in the Jack's roundabout. She headed down the dirt drive on foot and hit the main road in the white midafternoon heat. Had to be at least 90 degrees, the windless day merciless. Where were the trades? In a light-headed stupor she started walking along the dusty roadside, and ten minutes later turned off on a path marked by a roughly painted wooden sign that said VEGETARIAN FOOD. The words reminded her that she hadn't eaten. Perhaps some native vegetables would be good. Better that than the heavy fare they'd be dishing up back at the Grand Bland.

Fifty feet off the road, through a maze of overgrown philodendron, hibiscus, and bougainvillea, she came upon a little building constructed of driftwood and cast-off lumber. A crooked open doorframe formed the entrance, and the menu had been scrawled next to it. "Specialty omelets, vegetarian pies, Red Stripe beer, fresh fruits. If you want to be jerk eat your jerk pork at the next stand please, we do not serve flesh here! Praise Jah."

She was tempted to go for some jerk pork at the next stand please but couldn't face another fifty yards on that baked road without food and drink. She slipped through the doorway into cool darkness. Smoky air. Dirt floor worn hard by feet and time. To the left, rickety tables and chairs, a few thin bright dusty sunbeams slipping through cracks in the walls and roof. A couple sat at a table in the corner, gray silhouettes in the dim ambient light. To the right, a small counter, behind it a grimy black cookstove, a ragged basket of scrap wood, a tabletop with food and condiments strewn, some shelves with dishes, and in the middle of it all a small, middle-aged, bearded Rastaman with waist-length dreads tied back with a piece of twine. He wore a dirty, frayed T-shirt with Haile Selassie and Bob Marley heads side by side on it—did they ever meet? she wondered—and old jeans held up by yellow plastic rope. The room reeked of ganja, and on the counter the butt of a huge spliff rested in a plastic boomerang-shaped ashtray from the Fontainebleau Hotel, Miami, Florida. The man smiled gently at her. "Good afternoon, sister," he said. "What can I do for you?"

"Um . . . maybe a vegetarian pie," Lucy replied, pulling up on a stool at the counter. "And some mineral water if you have it."

"Sorry, no pies today. Only omelets and Coca-Cola and beer."

"Well, I'll have . . . an omelet, then. But skip the drink." He nodded. "Just a glass of water, please."

"Um, excuse me, Miss . . . Ripken, isn't it?" She turned around. The voice, big, smooth, mellifluously radio-toned, had come from the male half of the couple in the back. Her eyes, adjusting to the faint light, made out a man and woman dressed in matching white shirts and tan pants, with straw hats placed on the table: the fabulous Strausses! Low-rent radio reporters from Philly; they'd been on the plane, at the dinner, at the opening. The wife once worked for Angus Wilson. That much she knew from Mickey.

"Yeah, Lucy Ripken. Call me Lucy, please."

"We're Jane and Jim Strauss," he said. "Gosh, I'm sorry we haven't had a chance to talk thus far."

"We saw you windsurfing the other day," Jane said. "A fascinating sport, Lucy. Simply marvelous to watch."

"Yes, well . . ."

"We just ordered a special omelet," Jim said. "If you'd like to join us, why don't you ask our friend Jacob here"—he nodded at the Rastaman behind the counter—"to throw in a couple more eggs, and have a seat here with us."

Excuses to beat this one were few. Nonexistent. "Sure, why not? Thanks." She turned back to Rastaman. "Can you . . ."

"No problem, sister. Couple more eggs, couple more mushrooms, omelet for three come up."

Lucy made her way over to the table and sat. The Strausses were in their fifties. Ruddy. Smiling. Relentlessly upbeat, Mickey'd said. "Well, imagine finding you two here in this obscure little spot."

"We always seek the obscure, little, out-of-the-way places," said Jane. Her voice had a frothy quality. "That's what makes these islands so . . . captivating."

"We like to give our listeners something different," said Jim. "That's what this business is all about." He had about him the earnest aura of a scoutmaster.

"Right," said Lucy, deciding she did want a beer. She'd felt herself falling into a role she hated, that of the novice crouched at the feet of the elders. It stemmed from some fundamental insecurity about her work. "Excuse me," she called over to the counterman. "Maybe I will have a Red Stripe after all."

"No problem," he said.

"Well," said Lucy, "Damned hot today, what?" That exquisite English accent of Adrian Kensington's lingered in her mind, polluting her sentence structure.

"Yes, but isn't this place charming?" said Jane Strauss, glancing around the dark, grungy little room.

"Oh, absolutely," said Lucy. "Entirely quaint."

There was a pause. "I gather," said Jim Strauss, weighing in now that the ladies had finished with the small talk, "that you were the unfortunate soul who discovered poor Angus the other night in the hot tub."

"Well, actually it was Allie Margolis, but yeah, I showed up right after her. God, what a night that was." She had a thought. "Who told you?"

"Oh, I have my sources," he answered, and gave her a look meant to emphasize the importance of these sources. "Not exactly an auspicious opening for the Grand Strand, I would say."

"No, not exactly. Are you going to mention it on your program?"

"Angus's heart attack? Goodness no, if we did that we'd never be invited back," said Jane.

"It has no bearing on the quality of the hotel," said Jim.

"No, I guess not," said Lucy.

"Strange thing, though," said Jim. "Gosh, I've known—I knew, I should say—Angus Wilson, may he rest in peace, for twenty years. He introduced Jane and me, God bless him. But I've seen him report on resorts all over the world, and I never once saw him get in a hot tub. Particularly one requiring nudism."

"That so?" said Lucy.

"You bet. He was an Old World kind of guy. And you know what else?" he went on. "Angus had a powerhouse ticker. He walked five miles every day, played tennis twice a week. I wouldn't have picked him to blow a valve like that."

"Omelet comin' right up," Jacob the Rastaman said, arriving with a Red Stripe.

Lucy took the bottle and hoisted it. "Well, here's to . . ."

"Angus Wilson," said Jim Strauss solemnly. They sipped their drinks.

"And, in a lighter vein, here's to a special Jamaican omelet," said Jane. Switching moods abruptly, she and her husband laughed, lifting their glasses of Coke at her. Lucy managed a smile. They drank and watched a big green wasp buzz the table. Lucy waved at it, sending it toward Jane Strauss, who cringed as it hummed past and out through a crack in the wall.

A moment later, the man brought over a round, perfectly cooked omelet divided into six wedges, and three plates.

Jim Strauss was an enthusiastic eater, devoting his concentration to the food at hand, and emitting a range of sensuous snorts to signal his enjoyment. He ate three wedges, Lucy ate two, well-dosed in local chili sauce, and the petite, slow-eating Jane one. After lingering over a second round of Cokes—and a second beer to cool Lucy's hot sauce burn—they complimented Jacob on his fine cookery, paid the bill, and headed out into the hot, still afternoon. Lucy felt sated and sleepy but strangely alert, considering all the beer she'd sucked up.

"God, these flowers are so beautiful," Jane said, as they picked their way through the tangled gardens back toward the road. "Just look—I mean look—at that orange," she added, pointing out a particularly brilliant burst of bougainvillea.

"Yes, dear," said Jim. "Very nice. Ahem," he cleared his throat, then, "Ahem," did it again.

Lucy, following behind, had a minor revelation: these Strausses in their matched safari outfits and hats were an amusing pair. She giggled, brushing aside a pothos leaf the size and shape of an elephant's ear, and observed that Jim Strauss had certain elephant-like mannerisms, although he was neither particularly large or elephantine. It was more a matter of . . . ponderousness.

They stopped at the roadside to get their bearings. The air was still and hot. A truck blasted past, a wooden-gated pickup full of standing workmen who waved and whistled as they drove by, raising a dust cloud. Jim Strauss, attempting to clear his throat of dust, let out an unintended snorting roar, then said, "Pardon me, I'mmmmm, um, I don't know." They stood stock still, Lucy facing the two of them. The moment had a peculiar bright, luminous, yet frozen quality to it. It felt, Lucy recalled later, as if a dam was about to break, or the earth to quake. Then the Strausses' faces abruptly took on a cartoonish quality. She quickly looked away; her stomach lurched, and she knew. God, could it be?

Here came Jossie, with perfect timing, cruising in Lucy's very own taxi, headed east. She stepped across the road, waving him down.

"Hallo, Miss Lucy," he said. "I went to looking for you at Jack's, and they said you had left, so I came this way. I thought you might need a ride back, no problem, so here I am, see?" Another magical coincidence.

She leaned in the front window and admired the interior. On the first ride, she hadn't really appreciated the graphic brilliance of the checkerboard dashboard, or the black dice with green dots hanging from the mirror, or the fake zebra skin seat cover. Jossie wasn't a Rasta-hippie, he was a Caribbean lowrider! The colors simply throbbed! You could travel to the stars with style in this thing! "Yeah, sure," she said, testing her voice, which seemed to be coming from somewhere so far down in her body she didn't know where it was. It worked! "I could definitely use a ride, and my friends too, if that's okay."

"No problem. You ride in front, yes, and—"

"Hop in the back, folks," she said. "This is my friend Jossie, and he's going to take us back to the hotel."

"The hotel," Jim Strauss said, as if he had never heard the word before. "Ho . . . tel." He laughed, and opened the back door of the cab. "The light is really incredible here, isn't it, dear?" He grinned at his wife. She took off her sunglasses

and rubbed her eyes with her clenched hands. "It's like . . .
pulsating."

"Jim, I think I need to lie down," Jane croaked. "I really
think I should."

"Hop in de cab, please," said Jossie, "And I will take you."

They all climbed in. Lucy felt like she had just boarded a
new ride at Disneyland, and she wasn't sure what to expect.
As they drove through town, things sparkled, broke up in the
heat, rearranged themselves. They drove past a gas station,
glowing in the afternoon sun. It struck her as an architectural
and technological wonder. What a marvel is a building! she
thought. What marvels men make, everywhere, every day.
What marvelously simplistic insights you have, every day, she
added to herself, a less impressionable interior voice bringing her back to earth.

"So tell me, my friends," said Jossie, "are you enjoying
your stay here in Ocho Negros?" He glanced into the rearview. There was no answer. Lucy turned around.

The Strausses were glued together on the left side of the
backseat, Jim hard against the door and Jane stuck to him.
Their mouths hung open, and they ate dust from the open window as they stared out, dumbfounded expressions evident even
behind the shades, under the hats. They looked like mummies.
No, they looked like her parents. No, like greenhorn tourists.
Tourists on drugs! "Are you guys okay?" Lucy asked.

Jim's mouth abruptly shut, and he took off his sunglasses very slowly with one hand and gave Lucy a strange

grin. He leaned forward conspiratorially, his eyes wide open and unblinking, and whispered, "I can see the molecules."

"What?" Lucy asked.

"Atoms," he replied, reaching out with a slow-moving hand, and waving at her face. She leaned back, he missed. "I can see the atoms . . . in your face, in the car . . . in the sky!" he said. "Every single darn molecule! Jane, can you see them?"

"Only when I open my eyes," she said in a tiny little voice. "But my stomach goes somersaulting when I do, so I can't . . . Ohhh, what did we . . . what kind of omelet did that man make for us?" she asked, as Jim fell back next to her.

Jossie looked over at Lucy. "You have Rastafarian specialty omelet?" he asked in a low tone.

"Yeah, we did. At that stand right by where you picked us up. Guy name of Jacob."

He lowered his voice even further. "Mushrooms, mon?"

"That's what the man said."

"You know what kind of mushrooms a Rastaman put in his omelet, Miss Lucy?"

She swallowed, and felt a ripple of rubies wash down her throat. She blinked, and the windshield broke into diamonds; then a birdcall somewhere out there echoed like a flute through the emerald canyon that ran down the middle of her mind. "I didn't at the time, but I think I do now."

"Ever since the hippies come here, it been very popular. But people like this . . ." He glanced in the rearview. "I don't know. Well, here's the hotel, so good luck."

They had arrived at the gatehouse, where Jossie pulled up and turned off his engine. "Can't you take us in?" Lucy said. "The driveway's so long."

"Sorry, Miss Lucy, I'm not one of their contract cabbies, so they will insist on search de whole car before lettin' me in."

"Since when have they been doing that?" she said, amazed, even as the words came out, that she could hold a regular conversation while all around her the fundamental mysterious structure of the universe hinted that it might just reveal itself. The leaves danced though the wind did not blow, and in the movement Lucy recognized . . . what did she see there? She could not name it, but she understood, past language, that it was very important. But why? The questions echoed, a cry in the brain. The brain—her brain—felt far far away. Perhaps she'd better head on out there, to where her brain had gone, lest it get lost.

"Here's some money," said Jim Strauss, his radio-smooth tone reduced to a cracked whisper. He thrust a ten-dollar bill over the seat. "You get the change, okay, Lucy? We've got to go." He flung the door open, dragged himself and his wife out, said, "We're guests," toward the plumed gatekeepers, then the two of them staggered off down the driveway.

Lucy and Jossie watched them go, then he looked at her. "You all right, Lucy?"

"Me?" She swallowed, and grinned. "You want to know if me . . . if I'm all right, Mr. Jossie? Well, yeah, as a matter of fact." She smiled and handed him the ten bucks. "Silly . . . psilocybin agrees with me. You ever try it, my friend?"

"Magic mushroom? No, mon, I stick to ganja. Enough mystery in that for me. Maybe a beer sometime when it really hot."

Lucy giggled. "But you see, Joss," she said, waving at the trees outside, which waved back at her. "The world keeps changing, all the time, from one scene to another, one reality to another, like a movie. Sometimes it's fun to track it. Shit," she said, as Angus Wilson, dead in a hot tub, floated into view, a toxic vision smogging up the reaches of her mind. "I don't think I like this movie." Abruptly, she opened the car door, and the image was gone. "Well, I've got your number. If I can't reach you I'll . . . send my pigeon." She laughed, then remembered that she was on the case. "Oh, like I was asking before, since when do they stop you from driving in here any old time?"

"Just a few days ago. I figured it was security for Dexter coming here the other day, and that's okay, but now the opening happen and still they want to search me 'fore I come in."

"Hmmm," said Lucy, intrigued by an image of herself with the pipe, hat, and cloak of Sherlock Holmes, on the job. All the people call him Dexter, like he's their personal friend. That's where she'd seen the dapper Rackstraw Barnes before! He was in Hanley's entourage at the Grand Opening. She got out of the car and closed the door. "Talk to you soon. Maybe tomorrow, maybe the next day, okay?"

"No problem." He drove off. Lucy wiped the glazed look off her face, put on her shades, and strolled through the entry gateway past the stone-faced, plume-headed gatekeepers, whose stoic expressions reminded her, at that moment, of masks she'd seen at a show at the Museum of Folk Art a few months back. She'd gone to that show with her friend Delia, and afterward they'd taxied downtown to Lucky Strike on Grand Street for steak frites and Beaujolais Nouveau, and then had drunk French cognac till four a.m. with two Italians she'd never seen before and would never see again. The Italians had been handsome, charming, intelligent, articulate in English, and she had walked home alone at dawn. Why? she wondered, strolling down the lushly planted driveway toward the hotel's porte cochere. Above her, the beautiful red fruit of the ackee trees dangled, jewel-like. She dared herself to pick one and bite it, thinking, how could that lovely red thing kill me? No way.

No way you're going to find out is more like it, sister, said an inner voice, a more practical one of the many voices rising up within her. The pitch of these voices had intensified, and now threatened to blow her away with a cacaphonous, chaotic blast. Shut up, she shouted to herself silently, and it worked, for a minute, as quiet fell across the interior terrain.

She slipped into the lobby and through without seeing anyone she knew. By the time she'd made it back to her room, her watch had sprouted wings, and it was definitely time for a swim. The room had been cleaned and had the look of a place she'd never seen before. She walked around, touching furniture, forcing herself to whisper, as she touched each thing, what it was: "Chair. Desk. Closet. Bed. Good, Lucy," she spoke aloud, mocking herself. "That's really good." Her voice sounded hollow and strange in the large, neat, completely foreign hotel room. But the psilocybin did shift things around on a fundamental level, and you had to get your bearings. Naming things was one way to do that. The names of even the simplest things had power, and to say them out loud tapped in to that power and made it hers. Or at least reminded her that she was a human being in a room full of things somewhere in the real world, and not just a bundle of sensations wired together in a frail little body by accident, stuck in the void, adrift for a reason she would never know until she was dead and then it wouldn't matter, would it? Ah, the wondrous things psychedelics bring to mind.

She took her clothes off, and then, en route to the head to put on her bathing suit, she remembered her pictures. She went to the desk, sat down, and had a look at the architectural test shots on the digital camera. Gazing intently into each image, she conjured up the shoot, and understood how the pictures would work. She had done her job well, and this filled her with a certain satisfaction that she could feel, now, high on the magic mushrooms, like a physical thing, a happy little creature nestling in her body. She looked down at her body. Her body, naked, seated, had rolls of fat on the belly. She could see them there, rude reality. She sat up straight and they went away. Bad fat, bad!

Next she shifted farther back into the digital files, seeking out the greenish images from Angus's death scene and other moments from that night, and started clicking rapidly through them. The green darkness roiled right up out of the images and filled the room around her, swirling like a swarm of flies, but she ignored it for what it was, the drug working on her own fear and negativity. At that moment, someone rapped softly on her patio door, startling her out of the deep, dark green swampy reverie into which she was sinking. That's right, the human race is out there! "Lucy, Lucy, you in there?" It was Desmond. "Ski time, Lucy."

"Um . . . just a second. Yeah, Des. Just lemme . . ." She put the camera down, jumped up, and ran into the bathroom to put on her one-piece. She threw it on then went over to the patio doors, drew the curtains, and opened the door. There he stood, all six foot two inches of perfect dark chocolate manhood, with a smile on his face. She could tell—what was it, the smell? The eyes? The vibes!—that he was genuinely glad to see her. "Hi," she whispered, and swallowed, returning to earth.

He looked into her eyes for a moment. "Lucy," he said in a low voice. "You been smokin'?" He grinned.

"Smoking? What, ganja? No, Desmond. No reefer for me." This was true, wasn't it?

"Well, you look a little bit . . ."

"I'm fine," she said, and abandoned all thoughts of death-scene photography as she stepped out onto the sun-stippled patio. The cigarette-style ski boat floated just offshore, out front of her room. Leroy, Desmond's assistant, sat in the back, and Harold Ipswich stood on the beach in trunks and a life jacket, holding a pair of waterskis and looking out onto the bay. His pose was effortlessly elegant, a good sign, she thought. The water was glass, reflecting a porcelain, pale blue sky, and the seabirds flying across left trails that wove, in her eyes, a dancing web of their own. Lucy followed the exquisite form of Desmond across the grass and onto the heat of Blackwater Beach, where the sand crunched like diamonds between her toes.

She negotiated Harold, whose thoughts of lust and longing danced like little sprites on the surface of his face, without giving herself away. The sprites were clearly benign, and when he applied sunscreen to her back, at her request, and she discovered that he had incredibly delicate and supple hands, she decided she might have to have him this very day. Then she jumped in the boat with Desmond, whose lithe figure moved like an exotic animal, an erotic oversized cat, through the webs of reality and non-reality spinning and intertwining in her brain, while Harold, frizzed hair flying, pulled to his feet and skiied successfully across Blackwater Bay on the first try in his life.

Now, floating on her back twenty yards behind the speedboat, skis on her feet and a handle in her right hand, she waved at Leroy, and he told Desmond to get it moving. Lucy grabbed hold of the handle with both hands and prepared for psychedelic waterskiing.

She took a deep breath as the rope went taut, their speed picked up, and away she went. She wobbled for an instant, forced her legs into line, and found her balance and her feet at the same time. She was up and racing! Racing very fast, except that everything moved in slow motion, which made it easy. Harold waved as she cut down the center of the wake. Desmond picked up the pace, and Lucy cut over the wake with a flex of her knees and steered herself out to the side of the boat. She focused on her form and balance, then lifted her right foot, kicked off the ski, and quickly planted it behind her left foot on the other ski. She whipped a few turns, banking off the little wake waves, jumping and bouncing, and then, in a wild instant, hit an unexpected bump and went flying, tumbling, crashing, her ski flew off and she was dragging through the water, gripping the rope and racing, a dolphin, a whale, a submarine on the move. She kept her head down and felt the ocean splitting around her, the underwater jetstream flashing past in waves of power until she realized she wasn't breathing. She uncurled her hands and let go, slowed to a stop, and came up gasping as Desmond circled around to pick her up. They found her lolling on her back, grinning at the sky. Her arms felt nine feet long, but she didn't mind. "What a rush!" she said, laughing up at the men in the boat. "That was a gas!"

"You did great, Luce," said Harold. "Looked like a champ."

"You want to go again, Lucy?" Desmond asked.

"No, I don't think so, Des. Once was enough. I . . . Harold, you want to go out to the island with me? I think I could do with some hot tub time. My arms are wasted." She held them up limply—they felt like overcooked linguini—then swam over and climbed up the little ladder into the boat. She rubbed her head briefly with a towel and sat down. "Whew! I'd forgotten how fast you go!"

"Sure, I'll go to the island with you, Luce, but are you ready to . . . I mean, that's where you found Awful Angoose, isn't it? Right in that damned tub."

"Yeah. But so what!" She was buzzed off the ski run, and felt invulnerable. "I mean, it's not like he . . . well, what's to be afraid of?"

"Nothing. So let's go," said Harold with a shrug, and five minutes later they pulled up to the Tower Cay dock. They climbed up the ladder and stood on the dock in their swimsuits, clutching towels. Desmond cranked the boat around and raced off.

The physical effort involved in keeping her feet on waterskis had taken her past the psychedelic peak; now the magic had settled into a lovely and completely manageable intensification of color and sensation. The afternoon sun had edged down far enough toward the horizon to let the air begin cooling. A faint breeze had picked up, and stirred the palm fronds overhead.

Lucy suddenly realized that she and Harold were supposed to strip. Well, now. She had a look at him, he had a look at her, and they burst out laughing. "Luce, I'll leave it up to you."

"Harold, I don't know, I mean . . ." She blushed, and touched his arm. "Hey, tell you what, let's go over to the tub and sort of ease into the water and out of our suits at the same time."

"Sounds good to me," he said, and headed over. Following him, she pictured his buns through the bathing suit. He was no Desmond, but then, being white and 40-odd years old, that was not surprising. Actually, he didn't look bad, some muscle definition in the back and shoulders, good posture, nice legs. The only problem a bit of a pot, but nobody's perfect. "You want a beer?" he said, stopping at the door to the tower.

"Yeah, sure," she said. "What harm's one more brew gonna do?"

He disappeared into the tower, and she went on to the hot tub platform. In a fit of modesty, she quickly stripped off her suit, threw it down with her towel, and lowered herself into the steamy, bubbly water, on the far side, so she could watch his approach. Only problem was, sitting there, she remembered how Angus Wilson had been sitting opposite from where she was, naked and dead, just a few nights past. She stared at the spot, then closed her eyes and watched her memory of him sitting there dead. She opened her eyes

and turned around to have a look at the rocks along the platform edge.

"Hey, you're already in there," Harold said. "What's the
deal?" Angus went away. She shrugged, lifted her right foot
delicately out of the water, and waved it at him. He came
around the tub and crouched to hand her a cup of beer.
"Here you go." She took it, sipped, and smiled at him. He
put his own beer down, then straightened up. With his hands
on the top of his trunks, he paused. She liked the way he
looked up there.

Now was the time! Lucy spoke impulsively, her voice
gone sultry with intent: "Come on in, Harold. I'll take yours
off for you." He gave her a look, then stepped into the tub
and slid down next to her.

"Aaaah," he said. "That's nice."

Lucy was panting. She reached over and slipped her hand
in the back of his trunks and felt his rear end. He lifted himself a little, and she tugged the shorts off his butt. Then she
slipped her hand around to the front, and pulled them loose
there too. Once they'd gotten down around his hips, he
reached down and slipped them off the rest of the way. Lust-
inspired Lucy put her hand on him, felt him grow. She pulled
herself over to him as he threw his arms around her and their
mouths met in an open, searching kiss. Her intuition had
been right: his hands, all over her, were good, as was his
tongue. Lucy felt herself melting away, driven by longing and
dammed-up need, into the empire of the senses.

Moments later, Harold hoisted her up out of the hot,

swirling water onto the edge of the tub, spread her legs, and first, after pausing, looking into her eyes, and pulling her down for a last kiss on the mouth, he lowered himself into the tub, lifted her legs out of the water, and kissed the soft insteps of her feet. He sucked her toes, licked her ankles, worked his mouth up and down the backs of her calves. She watched, and though she knew and understood it was him, she felt his tongue, his hands, his lips like a small busy horde of autonomous sex creatures working on her, devoted to nothing except bringing her pleasure. They were her slaves, the parts of his body. Then he moved his mouth upward along the inside of her left knee, slowly, nibbling gently with his teeth. She felt his beard rasping along her inner thigh, pleasure in that soft scraping pain, and then his tongue driving, searching, touching her. Eyes closed, she held his head, she moaned, opened herself wide, falling back onto the deck, letting go, entirely letting go. She opened her eyes, saw nothing but sky, blue and embracing.

After a few moments it was his turn. She slipped into the water and urged him out, opened his legs, put herself between them, came down onto him with her mouth open, her eyes closed, gave herself to giving him pleasure. After a time he stopped her, pulled her up, moving together in rhythm they quickly spread out the towels and made ready to make love right there on the hot tub platform, sun sliding lower and the breeze picking up, they were groping and kissing and ready to fuse when the sound of the motorboat zooming up to the dock came through loud and clear.

"Fuck," Harold barked, a loud frustrated whisper.

"Unfortunately, not right now," she said, jumping up, the motor-buzz shocking her back to earth. He too jumped to his feet, and they stood naked, bewildered, as the sound of voices came from the dock. What now? Normally in a situation like this you grab for your clothes. But on Naked Beach, what to do? She slipped back into the tub, and Harold followed, becoming detumescent at record speed. Well, they'd have to finish later. Right now, the thing to do was get it under control. They settled into the tub, Harold picked up his beer and had a sip.

Joey Ruskin and Maria Verde, naked, came into view, carrying bundles of clothes and towels. Joey was built like a Roman sculpture, except that no fig leaf would ever suffice to cover that piece of anatomy, wouldn't you know it, and Maria, droopy Maria, comported herself in the manner of a serious exhibitionist, nipples on parade, a heap of large, cheap jewels placed to enhance the clothes that were not there.

They demonstrated no surprise at finding the hot tub occupied. "Hi, Lucy," said the naked Maria, all bubbly-like. She'd apparently forgiven and forgotten their earlier run-in. "Hello, Harold. How's the water?" She threw her stuff down.

"S'fine, Maria," he said.

"Joey, you comin' in?" said Maria with an inquiring glance his way. He hardly looked at her as she slipped into the tub with a grunt.

"In a minute," he said, and sat on the bench opposite

Lucy and Harold. Lighting an unfiltered English cigarette, one of the snooty variety that came from a flat, elegant box, he left his legs casually open. He dangled, looming large in their line of vision. "I trust you're having a good vacation, Lucy," he said. "I know you had some trouble the other night, and I hope it hasn't spoiled our lovely island for you."

"Everything's fine," Lucy said. "Right, Maria?" Lucy pushed herself across the tub, and turned her back on Joey. "Except that the sun was in my eyes over there." Now she faced Harold, at whom she smiled. "This is much better."

Maria giggled, thirty-nine going on seventeen. "These water jets are just so . . . insistent," she said, looking at Harold. "Don't they simply make you want to . . . squirm?"

He stared at her deadpan. "No." He looked at Lucy. "Hey, you know what, I think I'm ready to head back now. I'm getting boiled, know what I mean?"

"Oh, don't let us drive you away," said Maria.

"Yeah, let's go," Lucy said. Keeping her back to Ruskin, she climbed out and slipped into her suit.

"Could you raise the flag, Harold?" Lucy asked, heading to the tower. "I want to climb up in here and have a look around."

"Sure, Lucy," Harold said, gathering their things. Joey Ruskin and Maria Verde watched.

"Careful up there," said Joey, as Lucy entered the tower. "Those stairs can be tricky."

Lucy stepped inside, passed the little beer bar, and headed up the stone stair that wound around and up. She counted twelve steps and arrived on the second level, where light entered from two windows carved into the seaward side of the tower. Aside from a great view out to sea straight north to Cuba, there was nothing there except a stone floor, a couple of sunning mats from down below, and an empty beer cup. The stairs started up again on the other side of the room. Twelve more steps. The third level was the same only narrower, and the two arched windows faced landward, forming the "eyes" in the face seen from shore. Lucy stepped across the cool stone floor and leaned out one of the windows. Across the bay, the white hotel complex gleamed in the late afternoon light, and she could see a volleyball game in progress on the beach. Bits of music drifted past, and laughter. She leaned farther out through the stone arch of the window and looked down. On her right, Harold stood on the dock watching for the motorboat. She looked to the left, and gasped: Joey Ruskin lolled on the edge of the tub, with Maria Verde in the water crouched between his legs, head in his crotch. He was looking right up at Lucy. He grinned. She pulled back into the tower, shaken. Mickey was right about this one. What a major creep!

Then she saw it. Wedged into a little crack between stones where the floor met the wall. She bent down to have a better look, and pulled it out. It was a cigarette butt, from a fancy filterless English cigarette. Shit! She dropped it on the floor and charged down the stairs, hitting the dock as Desmond arrived in the motorboat. "Whatsamatter?" Harold asked as she dashed up breathlessly. "You look all shook up."

"Um . . . nothing. I'll tell you later. Let's beat it to the beach, eh? I've had enough of this place."

They jumped in the boat and Desmond raced them away. "Hey, Des," Lucy said, as soon as she'd gotten her breath under control. "Two questions before we hit the beach."

"Shoot," he said.

"One, when will my transparency film be ready?"

"I don't know, like I say, that large format he ship to Kingston. Tomorrow okay?"

"Yeah, sure. And two, when you brought Joey and Maria out to the island just now, did you tell them we were there already?"

"Joey? I bring no Joey, Lucy. I just brought Maria."

She landed on the beach with the image of Joey Ruskin, smoking a cigarette and gazing down from the tower at her sprawled out naked with Harold's head between her legs.

Back in her room, back at the desk, back on the job, yet again she studied Angus, dead in the tub. The lighting wasn't great, but it was obvious from the tilt of his head: he had a broken neck. The marks she'd seen were the surface manifestation of a disaster that had happened beneath his skin.

The phone rang. "Hi, you ready?" Harold.

"Ready? For what?"

"You already forgot? Cruise time, Luce, remember? Sunset, the yacht, another gathering of the fun squad?"

"Christ, do I . . . do we have to do this one?"

"Hey, it's a nice boat, they'll give us champagne and caviar, we watch the sun go down and come back."

"I know, but I've been up since four. I'm a zombie, Harold."

"Call me Harry. Let's just go. We'll come back and skip dinner, and I'll give you a massage you'll never forget."

She liked the sound of that. "All right, give me ten minutes . . . Harry."

"They're shuttling people out in the ski boat. Meet you at the dock in fifteen."

"Sounds good." Actually, an hour on a yacht with the scribe squad sounded like torture in her presently wasted state of mind, but Harold—Harry—would be there. What a nice basic name. She called room service and asked for a pot of coffee, rush it, please, then jumped in the shower. This was the longest day she had been through in years, and there was still much to do.

Twenty minutes later, feeling semi-refreshed and semi-wired from a double dose of afternoon Blue Mountain, she headed out to the dock, struggling to conjure up, out of her psychedelic fade, another blast of social energy to carry her to sea. She wore the finest in New York yachting garb: pink pedal pushers and a black sleeveless turtleneck, huge silver hoop earrings, and pointy black high heels.

Lucy motored out with Harold and Mickey, the fashionably late trio last to board before the yacht headed out for the sunset cruise. In the launch on the way out, Mickey gave her the lowdown on the Strausses, who'd left for New York just an hour ago because "Poor Jane apparently went for a nude swim in the pool, which was sort of okay, then strolled naked up to the bar and ordered a martini, which was marginally okay; then after drinking the martini she dashed through the lobby, still nude, and began to climb an ackee tree in the driveway in order to snack on some fruit. That was not okay. Now," said Mickey with a grin, "I heard you had lunch with them today in town. What happened? I mean, Jane Strauss has never been my candidate for Lunatic of the Month."

Lucy shrugged. "A mushroom omelet. What can I say?" She grinned. "Did she actually eat an ackee?"

"No. Herr Husband, baying like the Hound from Hell, chased after her and pulled her out of the tree before she could get her hands on any."

"Well, thank God for that," said Harold. "What a loss to the world of radio journalism that would have been."

"Hey, isn't one dead hack enough for the week, Harold?" said Mickey.

"I guess. Damn, that Ruskin sure gets around," he added, aside to Lucy, as they pulled up next to the yacht. Joey Ruskin, in yet another snazzy lightweight suit, appeared at the ladder and offered a hand to help the ladies up. Lucy effortlessly avoided his offer as she stepped onto the ladder. Harold's hand on her rear end, pushing up, made it easy.

The yacht, called *Esmeralda*, had previously belonged to a Lebanese merchant who made his fortune dealing arms in the international marketplace. Almost 100 feet long, possessed of four cabins, two sitting rooms, a screening room, and several decks, *Esmeralda* embodied a whorish sort of elegance, a mix of art deco and Oriental black lacquer inside, the usual gleaming brass and teak out on deck. Money had been spent, not necessarily well, to insure that it was clear that money had been spent.

Lucy found a seat on the upper deck, grabbed a glass of champagne off a passing tray, and settled back to watch the party happen. Jefferson Hababi acted as host, and Jefferson's mom, Mrs. Hababi, was rumored to be on board as hostess although for the moment she was ensconced in her private quarters and not quite ready to make a public appearance.

"God, isn't this boat super?" said Susie Adams, dashing over to park herself by Lucy. They sat on the upper deck, on a cushioned banquette that ran along both sides.

"Yeah, it's nice," said Lucy. She looked Susie over. As usual, the girl had missed the fashion boat. She wore a sort of sailor outfit, and looked like she belonged in a Busby Berkeley chorus line. "Too bad about Mrs. Strauss, eh?"

"Oh, you heard?" said Susie. "Yes, she apparently became indisposed from some town food, and they went home early."

Lucy looked at her. "Right. Indisposed." Lucy downed her champagne, liked the buzz, and waved at a waiter to bring another glass over. "So, other than that, and the dead guy the other night, everything going all right?"

"Wonderfully," Susie said, sliding past the irony. "Did you meet the guys from the Travel Channel? They're downstairs videotaping the Hababis' private quarters at the mo-

ment. They're gonna do a whole segment on the Grand
Strand next week. Talk about publicity to die for."

Joey Ruskin approached, arm-in-arm with Louise Rousseau. "Hi, Lucy," said Louise. "How's it goin'? Hi, Susie. Lucy,
I love your outfit. It's so . . . defiantly non-seaworthy."

"Thanks," said Lucy. "I guess that was the intent. You're
looking good, too, kiddo," she added, although in truth
Louise would probably do better not wearing skintight silver
jumpsuits like the one she had on at the moment. Too much
hip spread.

"So tell me, Louise," Susie said, all smiles, sucking on a
long cigarette. "Have you found your locations?"

"Oh, yes, there's some marvelous scenes here. The boys
from the mag will do just fine. And I think I'm going to get
Joey to model, too." She looked at him adoringly. He
grinned.

"Isn't that nice," said Lucy.

Susie stood up. "If you'll excuse me, I've got to go down
and see how the video's coming along." She dashed off. Joey
and Louise slithered down on the banquette a few feet
from her.

They were outside the bay now, and headed west. Maria
Verde popped into view at the top of the stair. "Hi, everybody," she said, and bounded onto the deck in yellow shorts
and a flowered halter top, followed by Mike Nack in white
polyester pants, a brass-buttoned blue blazer, and a white
shirt with ascot and captain's hat.

"They're serving caviar down below," Mike Nack announced. "It's Iranian. Really expensive. You might want to have a taste." He and Maria sat down across from Lucy. Then Maria sighed, relaxed, and lolled against Nack, glancing over at Joey. "God, is this beautiful," she said.

"Yes, it is," Lucy said, jumping up and moving to the rail for a look back at the hotel. Mostly what she wanted was a view that didn't contain Joey Ruskin. But Louise followed her to the railing, and he trailed after Louise.

"Look at the mist up on the mountains," said Louise, pointing at the green hills that sloped up behind the string of beachfront hotels that hugged the shore. "I bet it's a whole different world up there. And look, there's the tower out on the island, sticking up over the point. Can you see it there? It looks like the turret on a castle, doesn't it? We'll have to shoot something out there!"

"Yes," said Joey. "You should see the views from up there in the tower, Louise. They're wonderful." He looked at Lucy. "Don't you think so, Lucy?"

He had her frozen with his handsome snake stare. "Fuck you, Ruskin," she said softly. She handed her glass to Louise, who took it, a dumbfounded look on her face. Lucy strode across the deck, pushing Mike Nack aside, and descended the ladder. Below, she found Mickey and Harold eating caviar like they were running a race, with a video crew taping every move. She grabbed another glass of champagne and joined them.

Two hours later, as they walked back to her room, she and Harold reviewed the general weirdness of the yacht cruise. They agreed that the highlight had been the wobbly appearance on deck of Mrs. Hababi, a raven-haired, white-skinned, valium zombie with the heavily made-up look of a badly aging minor film star of the1960s. Just as they came about a hundred yards offshore from Jack's Joint, she had emerged from her quarters to bestow memorial Grand Strand brass paperweight models of the *Esmeralda* on each member of the press. The members of the press thanked her and applauded, and she disappeared back into her quarters as the sun went down.

Lucy told Harold what she'd seen from the island tower, and what had happened since. He bristled like an angry dog, ready to go after Joey Ruskin on the spot—"I'll dismantle the motherfucker," he growled—but she convinced him to hold off.

"After all," she reminded him about the time they arrived back at her door, "at the moment there is the matter of the massage you promised me."

It took them about two minutes to get back to where they'd left off that afternoon, aching on the edge of a great first fuck. But then, with Lucy open and yearning for him, moaning for him, Harry stopped, and turned her over. He poured oil on her back, rubbed it down her ass and her legs, and slowly, with deep, delicate force, he massaged her from the bottoms of her feet to the top of her head, and then worked his way down her back. About the time she had achieved total sensory meltdown, he seized her by the hips, turned her over, stretched himself out on top of her, and slid smoothly inside her. Just as he did so she remembered to worry, and had a look. Such a responsible man! Somewhere in the midst of all that foreplay Harry had managed to slip on a condom, that essential tool of casual sex in the new millennium.

The massage had lasted fifteen minutes, and the love-making lasted fifteen mostly furious minutes more, until they came, almost together but Lucy beat him by a minute or so, and then they collapsed, glued together with sweat and sweet massage oil.

They flopped over sideways and slept that way, until Lucy awakened with a start and checked her clock. Almost 11:30. Shit! "Harold, wake up," she said softly. "Let's go for a swim."

"Swim? What?" he muttered. "Sleep time, Lucy. Forget it."

Lucy lay there a minute, swirling in the stream of her exhaustion, the endless day, the investigation she was trying to jump-start. The drug had left her with a stomachache and a kind of hallucinatory afterburn, causing what she saw to linger in her eyes for a split second after she moved her eyes away from it; the beer and champagne contributed a headache; the waterskiing added arm, shoulder, and lower back aches. Did she have the energy to pursue this? She had no choice. She sighed, leaned over, and kissed Harold on the lips. Then she turned the bedside light on. He blinked his eyes open, out of focus. Who was this guy, anyway? "Hey, Harry," she whispered, "you ready to hit the surf? It's almost midnight."

"Damn, that's right!" he said, instantly awake. "Time to play *Seahunt*." He jumped out of bed. "The only problem is, I don't have my trunks."

"Well, what the hell." She grinned, looking him over. "We're going to Naked Beach, right?"

Lucy put on a one-piece, and Harry slipped into his boxer shorts. She grabbed the masks, snorkels, underwater flashlight, and fins she'd borrowed from the watersports hut earlier, and turned off the light. She led the way to the beach.

Clouds covered the moon. The tide was fairly low, Lucy noted as they walked to the water's edge. They'd have to watch out for coral. "Okay," she said softly, "This is the plan: we swim straight out till we're parallel with the island, then work our way over toward it. When we get to the coral I'll use the light to find a passage through."

"What are we looking for, Luce?"

"I don't know. Pirates. A boat. Something."

"Don't sharks feed at night?"

"Yeah, but not on us. Not in these waters," she lied. Actually, she had no idea what kind of sharks patrolled the north coast, or what such sharks might like to eat. As long as she and Harry didn't scrape themselves on the coral and bleed, she figured they'd be all right.

"I'll take your word for it," he said. "Let's do it." She flashed the light on him for a second and had to laugh. In red boxer shorts, fins, a snorkel, and a mask, Harry looked less than dashing. "All right, so I'm not Lloyd Bridges," he said, backing into the water.

"But you can swim that far, right?" she asked.

"Can of corn," he replied, then slipped his snorkel into his mouth and dove in. She followed, swam a few strokes underwater, then surfaced and blew her snorkel clear. The flashlight dangled from a loop around her left wrist.

They sidestroked steadily, quietly moving out to sea, and moments later stopped close together in the still, silvery water. "God, it's so warm," she whispered.

"Yeah. So what now, Luce?" he whispered back. "You ready to head over toward the island?" They could see the glow from the low lights around the tub and tower.

"Yes. Let me lead the way so I can check for coral."

They swam silently for two minutes, then stopped. She put her snorkel in her mouth, adjusted her mask, and went under. Turning on the light, she caught a flash of a pair of long dark shadows dodging out of the beam, spotted a solid wall of twisted and shadowy coral, then turned off the light. Better not to look at that weirdness. "We have to move around to the seaward side," she whispered. "There's no way through here. Follow me." They moved out a few dozen yards farther, then continued west. Directly offshore from the looming tower, they stopped and treaded water for a minute.

"Now what?" Harold hissed. "I'm gettin' tired, Luce."

"Just a sec," she said, and flashed the light on underwater for an instant. There! A break in the coral. "This way," she whispered. "Stay right behind me, and don't make any moves to either side." She flashed the light on for another second to double-check the passage, then dove and slipped through. Harold followed close behind.

They surfaced inside the coral barrier and got their bearings. The water was shallow enough to stand on the rocky bottom, and the fins protected their feet from urchins. "Listen," Lucy whispered urgently, and they held still. The low faint hum of a small outboard electric motor drifted over the water, growing louder as they waited.

The motor abruptly stopped. A flashlight came on, stabbing out of the darkness, and a voice hissed, "It's over here, mon." The light was quickly turned off. Then oars splashed softly in the water as the boat moved toward the passage through the coral. Lucy tugged Harold by the waistband of his boxer shorts, and they moved slowly backward, away from the channel, and waited. After a moment, they could make out the shape of a rubber dinghy, with one person in front navigating, a second in the back rowing the boat toward the island, now just a few yards away.

A flashlight blinked twice on the island. "There he is," said the navigator. "Pull to the right a little." Lucy knew the voice, but couldn't quite place it.

"Yeah, mon," said the rower. "No problem." The voice was unusually high-pitched, but definitely native.

"Keep it down, Rudy!" said the navigator.

"Yeah, mon," said Rudy, the volume dropped a little. "No problem."

"Hey," came a voice softly from the island. "Ruskin?" Another voice she knew but couldn't place.

"Yeah, everything's okay," said the navigator, none other than the ubiquitous Joey Ruskin! Lucy could feel Harold tense. She tightened her grip on his waistband.

"You got the goods?" said the island voice, and Lucy suddenly placed it, too: Mike Nack. God, what—or who—next?

"Yeah. You ready?"

"Uh-huh. Just hurry up, will you? A place like this, you never know when some chump's gonna decide he wants a hot tub in the middle of the night." Yes, that was definitely Mike Nack. The boat bumped up against the rocky shore. She could make out their silhouettes, Nack standing onshore, Ruskin seated in the boat.

"Don't worry. There's nothing to worry about."

"So what happened the other night, then?" Nack snapped back. They were passing parcels from boat to shore.

"An unfortunate coincidence, followed by a tragic accident," said Joey coolly.

"I'll say," said Nack as he took the last parcel. "That all of it?"

"Yeah, mon. Ten bricks."

"I still don't know why you couldn't just bring the shit in through the gate. They're not gonna search Mr. JTA." These two might be doing business, but the sneering tone didn't suggest much affection between them.

"I told you, Nack," Joey said. "They've got people everywhere, including on staff at the hotel. Plus that Ripken chick is sniffing around like a bitch in heat. Just put it in the ground with the other stuff and we'll get it out of here in a day or two, when things have calmed down."

"Don't worry about Ripken. She's just looking to get laid."

"Heeheehee. You're probably right. I wouldn't mind a taste myself," said Joey.

"Me either," said Nack. "Like to rear end the bitch, with that muscular ass of hers."

"No shit, mon, she's a ripe little mango," said Joey. "All right, just stay cool now, Mike. Hang loose for a day or two, then we'll make our move."

"Okay, Ruskin. It's your call."

"Just keep that ten grand in mind, Mike."

Harold held her arm softly, caressingly, drawing out the venom of the ugly words. "Okay, Rudy, let's go," said Joey. Nack gave a shove to the boat, and Rudy started paddling. They passed through the channel, and a few seconds later Lucy and Harold heard the motor click on as the boat whirred away.

After ten minutes they swam over and climbed over the rocks onto the island. "Wait here," Harold whispered. "Let me make sure he's gone."

"Careful of your feet," she said, as he took off the fins. "The coral's like broken glass."

He tiptoed onto the platform and disappeared. A moment later, he called out, "All clear." Lucy picked a path over to the platform. Harold was waiting.

"That was Mike Nack, wasn't it?" he said, still whispering.

"Definitely. Who would have thought a goon like that could get involved in—"

"Dope smuggling. What a great scene that was," he said. "Like a fucking movie."

"Yeah, except that was a real dead guy the other night."

"What does that have to do with this?"

"That's the mystery, Harry, know what I mean?"

"I guess. But where's the dope is the mystery now, right?"

"Nope." She walked over to the rocks lining the edge of the platform. "It's right here, under this rock." She pointed. Harold came over, and together they knelt down. He dug into the sand a little and then pried up one end, and she pointed the light underneath. It illuminated a brick-shaped package, wrapped in tin foil and sealed in a clear plastic bag.

"How'd you know that?" he said.

"Female intuition, dude. No, actually, I took a picture, and then the rock moved. Why, I asked myself?"

Harold pried the rock up farther, and Lucy worked the package out. There were others stacked underneath. She hefted the one in her hand. "Probably two pounds," she said. Harold took it.

"Used to be they measured grass in kilos," he said. "A kilo is two point two pounds." He grinned. "A lot of dope."

"Yeah, so what're you gonna do, Harry, take it home and smoke it?"

"I don't think so. Jamaican pot is too rich for my blood. There's probably eight or nine more of these suckers in there," he said. "What should we do?"

Lucy didn't even hesitate. "Take 'em."

"Take the shit? Then what?"

"I don't know. I'll figure something out, Harry. Main thing is, we have this"—she grabbed the package from him, and held it up—"we have some leverage, right?"

"I guess. But we also . . . I mean, you heard those assholes. They know you're onto something, Luce, so . . ."

"So we'll stash it in your room for now, Harry. How's that?"

"My room!" he squawked, and then sighed. "Shit, all I wanted was a little romance, and look what I get," he complained, but he didn't look at all displeased.

"A real-life adventure," Lucy said. "And something interesting to write about."

"So let's move the shit off the lot," he said, pulling the rock all the way aside. "How do you propose we get it back to the beach, Luce?"

6

A Dangerous Hike and a Dance

At six-thirty Lucy woke to the sound of Harold dressing in the dark. "Good morning," she murmured, tasting salt, watching his body move in the pale light. She felt a slight, sweet soreness between her legs. God, she'd had good *sex*! Twice in one night! It could still happen in this life.

"Hi, Luce," he whispered. "How are you doin'? I'm gonna go change and check on things. Meet you at breakfast in an hour." He bent down, kissed her on the lips, then slipped out the patio door.

Lucy lay still for a few moments. As the early light infused the walls of her room with delicate pastels, her body filed a report: sore crotch, psilocybin headache with hallucinatory afterburn, stiff, ski-strained arms and lower back, a coral cut on her left calf from the return trip. All this and sunburn, too. They'd paddled in on their backs in the dark, trailing shark-tempting blood, leg-kicking with five foil-wrapped

ganja bricks balanced on each of their stomachs. She ached
all over, but so what! Sex, skullduggery, and sleep—even a
scant four hours' worth—worked wonders for a girl. They
had stashed the twenty-two pounds of dope in Harold's
room. The next move would come from someone on the
other side.

Showered, groomed, and wrapped in a bright yellow
sundress, Lucy headed off to breakfast at seven-thirty. She
found Harold at a table on the seaward side of La Terrazzo
Grande, where he had a cup of hot Blue Mountain coffee
waiting for her. "You look great," he said, checking out her
dress and her body right through it, his lasciviousness leav-
ened with a grin.

"Thanks," she said, a little tingly in spite of herself. The
sight of him didn't even give her the post-fuck blues. Another
good sign. "Everything okay?" she asked with a glance
around.

"Yeah." He lowered his voice. "Just so you know . . . I
took the light fixture out of the bathroom ceiling and put it
up there."

"Sounds good. Better than under the bed, that's for sure."
She scanned the terrace. "Hey, it looks like the food line's
open. You wanna get some breakfast? I'm starved."

"Yeah, but Lucy . . ." He covered her hand with his.
"What next?"

"I don't know." She pulled her hand free as Maria Verde,
bearing a laden breakfast tray, arrived at their table. She wore

a multi-colored jumpsuit that resembled a clown costume, and her signature goon grin. She'd seen their joined hands.

"Hi, Maria," Lucy said.

"Good morning," Maria said, her grin widening to a kewpie doll smile. "Do you mind if I join you?"

"Hell, why not?" Harold said. "Sit down and enlighten us, Maria, as to the ultimate meaning of the Grand Strand."

She sat. Her tray held two plates, one piled with fruit, the other with bacon and toast. "Thanks. Harold, there's no need to be hostile."

"Hey, forget it, Maria," said Lucy. "Harold's just sick of the song and dance is all."

"But this hotel is so . . . happening," said Maria, folding a piece of undercooked bacon into her mouth.

"That must be why Allie Margolis decided to stick around," said Lucy sarcastically.

"Oh, Lucy, why don't you just forget about all that," said Maria. "Allie's gone."

"I'm gonna get some eats," said Harold, pushing his chair back and standing abruptly. "Lucy, you coming?"

"In a minute, Harold," she said. He headed off to the counter. The two women watched him go. Then Maria grinned complicitously at Lucy.

"He's a cutie," Maria said. "You two seem to be . . . hitting it off."

"Something like that," Lucy said, and watched Maria stuff her face for a moment. "Speaking of hitting, is there anyone on the circuit—besides me, Harold, and possibly the deranged Mrs. Jane Strauss—that Joey Ruskin hasn't screwed?"

"Oh, I don't know," said Maria, and now her grin turned devilish, an awesome sight given that her mouth was crammed with half-chewed bread. "But he's a wonder, let me tell you."

"Actually, I'd rather you didn't, Maria. Hey, Mick," said Lucy, standing quickly as she spotted her pal. "Let's get some eats, huh?" She grabbed Mickey by the arm and steered her away from the table.

"So how's it going?" Mickey grinned. "Are you and Harold getting on—that is, getting *it* on, as they used to say in the bad old days?"

Lucy laughed. "So far, so good, Mick. Good call, matching us up. God, look at this! Pork Universe!" The overloaded counter stretched out before them. They grabbed trays and got in line. "So what're you up to today?"

"I don't know, I guess the falls hike. I've managed to avoid it all these years. You goin'?"

"I suppose. I hear it's pretty scenic. Hey, by the way, those are inspired shorts," she added, viewing Mickey's baggies, black with clusters of bright yellow bananas.

"Thanks. They distract from the rear view, as intended. Speaking of views, scenic or no, we're gonna need a major hike after this feeding event," Mickey said, flourishing a loaded plate of bacon and French toast. "Otherwise we'll be shipped home in hogsheads. Hey, Harry," she added, as Harold passed by.

"I can't eat with that Verde woman sitting there, Lucy," he said. "I'm gonna park at one of those tables on the beach. I'll catch up with you later."

"Okay," said Lucy. "You gonna take the hike this morning?"

"No, I think I'll stick around here, know what I mean?"

"Why so quiet, toots?" Mickey asked her.

"Oh, I'm just contemplating the scenery." From the bus window they gazed upon the vista of a two-pump gas station, a fruit stand, a pharmacy, a sundries shop, a funeral parlor, and a hardware store, all in a row, linked by a crooked sidewalk mobbed with people dodging among honking, smoking automobiles, trucks, buses, bicycles, and motorcycles. Each building had once been painted its own shade of pastel, but a layer of dust had turned them all vaguely, dirtily pink. Downtown Ocho Negros. How it had glowed yesterday, in mushroom light!

"It is exotic, isn't it?" said Mickey as a trio of roadside workmen looked up at them and waved, big grins on their faces. "Hey, I didn't get a chance to ask you at the morning glut," she added after a minute. "How's your work going? And how about 'the case'?"

"Do I hear ironic quotes around that, Mick?" Lucy said. "Suggesting a degree of disbelief as to the usefulness of my investigation? Well, let me just say," she added loudly, "that the plot has considerably thickened. And I shall tell you more later." She could feel Mike Nack's eyes on the back of her neck.

She pictured the scene yet again. Still excited about the architectural photographs—Desmond had delivered them as she ate her eggs, and each and every one had turned out precisely right—she had walked back to her room to change her clothes after breakfast and found a chambermaid halfway into the closet, rooting around in her photography equipment. What was to clean in there? Not much, unless you were looking for some ganja bricks. On the other hand, the chambermaid had not seemed rattled at all when Lucy walked in on her. She'd merely backed out of the closet and said, "Straightening your things, ma'am." She wore a black and white uniform with the pink Grand Strand logo stitched over her breast, and a black nameplate with gold lettering identifying her as Prudence Fallowsmith.

Lucy had watched from the patio while Prudence Fallowsmith finished with her room. Then Prudence had left and Lucy had changed into her black shorts and a green T-shirt and some sensible shoes—well, perhaps sleek, low-rise, black leather hiking boots were not all that sensible, but they looked sharp as hell—grabbed a camera, and headed out. Now a busload of Grand Stranders were headed for the Green River Falls and its world-famous hike.

Soon they left Ocho Negros behind and followed the coastal road back toward the airport for fifteen minutes before cranking a left into the hills. "Oh, Christ," Mickey groaned a moment later as their Grand Strand bus swung around an uphill turn and entered the official Green River Falls Hike parking lot, "I didn't think it would be this bad." There were at least thirty buses lined up in the fenced asphalt parking lot, most with engines running, scenting the air with diesel exhaust. The drivers, mostly stout, middle-aged black men in short-sleeved shirts, gathered in groups, smoking and chatting. To the right, a wooden booth controlled foot traffic down to the beach at the bottom of the falls, where the hike commenced. Straight ahead, the falls lay in a gorge hidden beyond the wall of idling buses, fences, and a thicket of banana, bamboo, and ferns. You could almost hear the roar of the water, except that the fleet of buses roared with more volume. To the left, a steady stream of damp tourists flowed off the trail that delivered them from the end of the hike back to their waiting buses—through the gauntlet of a "Jamaican Village" of shacks and pushcart peddlers selling T-shirts, postcards, beer, baskets, and a selection of elongated wood carvings of giraffes, Bob Marleys, and long-legged waterbirds. Along the edges of the "village" and the parking lot, a dozen shifty-eyed dudes loitered skittishly, maneuvering to interest the honkies in ganja.

Mickey, Lucy, and the other Grand Stranders filed past the booth and plodded down a well-worn trail to the beach, where more dozens of tourists milled, and seven or eight rastas offered boat rides and whispered drug options. Three driftwood huts perched on the bank of the river advertised beer, jerk pork, and grilled fish.

The scene was lovely in spite of the commercial and tourist overload. The river emerged from a ferny green grotto laced with delicate yellow and white flowers to meet the sea between low banks of white sand. Lucy and Mickey edged away from the Grand Strand gang and headed toward the trail. Lucy took a few pictures of people taking pictures and then stuck her camera in her pocket. There would be plenty of postcards available up top to document the hike.

They paused at the bottom of the hiking trail, where the amusement park quality of the event became evident. As far as they could see up the falls—several hundred yards— single-file lines of tourists, their hands linked to form human chains, trudged upward, back and forth across the ragged, photogenic rock formations over which spilled the multi- layered, mist-shrouded falls. Clearly, hiking the Green River Falls was One of the Things You Do in Jamaica.

Lucy and Mickey stepped aside to make room as another gang of sunburned, camera-bedecked hikers hit the trail. They were followed by the Grand Strand squad and their guide, who introduced himself as Robert. He organized them into a single line and told them to join hands to help each other on the steep parts. Suddenly Maria Verde appeared, dashing off the bottom of the trail and across the beach. Wearing bright green, skintight bicycle shorts and an electric blue sleeveless T-shirt and no bra, she rushed up breathlessly to join them. "Hi, everybody," she said. "Sorry I'm late. Had some business to take care of." Lucy glanced up, and there was Joey Ruskin in a white linen suit over a black T-shirt, looking way too much like the other guy on that ancient, once-upon-a-time hipster TV show, *Miami Vice.* A long time ago, when she was about twelve years old, Lucy had considered those guys kind of cool. Leaning over the railing halfway back up the access trail, Joey waved at Lucy. She didn't wave back. Mike Nack appeared at her side and grabbed her hand in his clammy mitt. With Mickey on her other side, the four of them—Mickey, Lucy, Nack, and Verde—formed the tail end of the Grand Strand hiking chain. They started off.

They moved upward, back and forth across the gorge, hopping from rock to rock to fallen tree among the pools and falls and drifting mist. It was beautiful in spite of the mobs. The roaring of the falls nearly drowned out the sound of obnoxious shrieking, idiot laughter, and the rest of the tourist racket. Lucy fell into a reverie in spite of being joined at the wrist to the noxious paw of Mike Nack.

The trail steepened and idle conversation fell away beneath the overpowering roar of the waterfalls. They had reached a difficult point in the climb, where each person depended on the one ahead in line to haul them over the lip of a large rock. You had to edge out as far as you could on one rock, then the person in front took your hand, and as you lunged into space he or she hauled upward and got your weight over the edge of the next rock—or you could slip and fall forty feet.

Mickey waited below her, and Mike was poised atop the upper rock, his hand out to her. He hadn't been a bad hiking partner so far. He'd kept his mouth shut and observed the scenery, including the skintight shorts–clad, oversized butt of Maria Verde, clambering upward in front of them. Admittedly obsessive about ridding her own butt of cellulite, Lucy wondered how a flabby-ass girl like that found the nerve to wear those tight pants. She wondered if Mike Nack would consider such a sack of fat sexy. She wondered why she cared. She turned her attention back to the matter at hand—getting from this rock to the next. For a moment, she would have to put her life into the moist mitts of Mike Nack as she committed her weight over the edge.

She leaned, he grabbed, she scrambled. He stopped hauling and held her there, hanging. "Where is it?" he hissed. One Lucy foot dangled, the other had toe purchase on an inch-wide ledge.

"What?" She clutched his wrists more tightly. "Pull me up, you dumb—"

"The ganja, dammit, Lucy. Where is it?" he snapped quickly.

"What the hell are you . . ." She dropped all her weight onto her toes on the rock ledge, bent at the knee, pushed up, and more or less flung herself over the lip of the rock, landing with a scramble on top of Nack, nearly knocking him down. She quickly found her feet and turned on him. ". . . talking about, you motherfucker?" she said. "Try threatening me like that again, I'll—"

"Lucy, I wasn't gonna . . . I wasn't really gonna . . ." he whined, throwing his hands up as she raised her fists.

"Yo, Luce," Mickey called out from below, "You gonna give me a hand?"

"Damn. Just a minute, Mick," she called out, then turned back to Mike Nack. "Now what are you babbling about?"

"Lucy, you've gotta . . . you can't . . . just tell me where it is, dammit! What did you do with it?" he pleaded.

"Tell you where what is?"

He was talking fast, his tone desperate. "Come on, Lucy. The pot. The bricks. I know you took it, and it's . . . it's . . . not yours to take."

"Hey, Mike," Maria Verde called out, her head popping into sight over a rock. "Everything going okay down there?"

"Yeah, yeah, Maria, no problem. I'll catch up in a minute."

"So you're missing some . . . what'd you call it, ganja?" Lucy asked.

"Look, I don't know why you think you need to be in-volved in this thing, but—"

She decided to take the plunge. "I wasn't planning on getting involved in this thing, as you call it, Mike, until I ran into a dead guy the other night."

"That doesn't have anything to do with—"

"Oh, bullshit. You don't really believe that, do you, Nack? How well do you know Joey Ruskin, Mike?" He blanched. "And who the hell knows what Angus stumbled onto that night?"

"Angus had a fucking heart attack, Lucy. Why can't you

give up this . . . this . . . Look, let me tell you how it works."
His eyes were darting around. He was in a panic, talking a
mile a minute. "Why should I bullshit you? Hear me out,
then you can decide what you want to do. You're a writer,
you get paid shit just like I do. So this is the deal. There's
a million people like us up in New York, Boston, Philly,
wherever, who would still like to smoke the occasional
joint, only all the dope's moved to the ghetto and nobody
has any connections anymore. So Joey's trying to set up a
separate network that bypasses the Kingston posses and
makes reefer available to people like us. You can't tell me
you find smoking pot immoral, Lucy, or is it just that you
want a cut?"

She said, "No, I don't. But . . . a cut of what? What's in it
for you?"

"Use your head, Lucy. You know how it goes when we get
back. The PR bimbo hustles us through customs, there's no
way they're gonna inconvenience important travel editors
like us, so we sail on past."

"With your bricks in your bags."

"You got it. All wrapped up nice and tight and odor-free.
Joey's got it figured out. I meet a guy at the airport, he takes
my bag and gives me a lot of cash, and that's that."

She considered. Actually, it sounded like a pretty good
scam, as far as these things went. "Well, there's still the little
matter of Angus Wilson and his so-called heart attack."

"It wasn't so-called, dammit."

"Come on, Mike, do you really believe that—"

"Hey, Luce," Mickey called up. "There are packs of wild tourists baying at my rear. Get me outta here."

"You got it, Mick," she said, hanging over the rock for a look down at her.

"So where's the dope, Lucy?" Nack hissed.

"I don't know," Lucy tossed off. "Maybe ask me later and I'll remember. Here you go, Mick," she added, leaning over and reaching down.

"You have got to come up with my dope, Lucy," Nack whined. "Or . . . or . . ."

"Accidents can happen," Maria Verde said softly. She arrived on the rock just as Lucy hauled Mickey over the edge. Mickey landed on her feet, and suddenly the four of them stood eyeball to eyeball.

"Well, no use taking a meeting here," said Mickey cheerfully, a few seconds later. "Let's waltz up another rockpile."

"I think Mickey and I will go solo from here on," Lucy said. "We'll catch up to you later."

Nack had a long look at her. "Okay, Lucy, but just remember what I said."

Maria grinned, and this time the malevolence welled up onto the shifty surface of her face. "And what I said," she added, and scrambled away, Nack trailing behind.

"What was that all about?" Mickey asked after Nack had climbed out of sight.

"You don't want to know," Lucy said.

When Mickey answered, "Oh, yes I do," Lucy decided to tell her. After all, there was strength in numbers. Particularly in the face of a threat.

Half an hour later she had brought Mickey up to speed on the goings-on, and Mickey had enlightened her as to what she, Mickey, had won that long-ago day when she'd drunk an entire bottle of 151 to win a bet. Over three other travel writers, two women and one gay man, she'd won the chance to attempt seduction of Joey Ruskin, and she had succeeded.

They completed the hike, then took a stroll through the instant Jamaican village of Green River Falls, where entrepreneurial natives of the Magic Island sold their wares. Lucy bought a T-shirt with a black, big-hipped lady dancing across the chest in bright native garb, and a bottle of ginger beer. When the Grand Strand gang climbed on the bus a few moments later to head back to the hotel, neither Mike Nack nor Maria Verde was anywhere to be found, and so they left without them.

"So you want to come over to Harold's room and help make a plan, Mick?" she asked as they climbed off the bus back at the hotel.

"No, I don't think so," Mickey said. "I'm gonna take a tennis lesson from the pro. He looks like Denzel Washington and talks like Hugh Grant, so . . . I'm sure you can handle it—whatever it may turn out to be—with Harry's help."

"Yeah, yeah," Lucy said. "Catch you later."

"No doubt. Tonight's the big do at Hababi's."

"Oh, God, that's right. You gonna dress up?"

"Sorta. But it's beachfront casual, so . . ."

"The zombie wife'll probably be wearing Versace."

"Yeah, well, that's her problem," Mickey said.

Five minutes later Lucy rapped on the door of Harold's room. When no one answered, she knocked again. Nothing. She circled the building, located his patio, and approached. The door was locked and the curtains drawn. She couldn't see a thing. She returned to the back of the building, rapped loudly on the door, and called out, "Yo, Harold, you in there? Harold, open up."

"Can I help you, miss?" came from somewhere above. Lucy stepped back for a look. A chambermaid—not Prudence Fallowsmith this time—looked down from the second-story balcony railing.

"Um, yeah," Lucy said. "I left my purse in my friend's room and he's not here and I really need it. Think you might let me in for a minute?"

"Well I don't know, ma'am, I'm not supposed to—"

"His name's Harold Ipswich and he and I are good friends," Lucy said. "You can take my word for it. His room's right here, we're both on the press trip. Hey, go in with me. I just wanna take a quick look."

"Well, all right, ma'am, hold on a minute." She disappeared, and emerged a moment later from the stairwell. "Please don't say anything about this to my boss."

"Not to worry," said Lucy. "My lips are sealed." The girl, whose name tag ID'ed her as Jane Arlington, pulled out a fat ring of keys, picked one out, and unlocked the door. Lucy pulled it halfway open. "Harold," she said softly, and when there was no answer she pulled it all the way open and had a look. "Jesus Christ," she gasped on seeing the room, for it had been torn to pieces: drawers pulled out, clothes strewn all over, blankets and sheets tangled in a heap on the floor. Ransacked.

"My goodness," said the maid. "I cleaned this room not two hours ago," she said. "This fella some kind of wild man?"

"You're sure it was this room you cleaned?"

"I did all of the ground floor in this wing first, ma'am," she said with certainty. "Well, I'd best get my cart and do it again," she sighed, and turned to go.

"Hey, wait," Lucy said. "You've got enough to do, you shouldn't have to do the same room twice. I'll take care of this. What can I say, Harry's a slob."

"No, ma'am, I—"

"I insist," Lucy said, and pressed a twenty-dollar bill into Jane's hand. "Now you just go ahead and do what you have to do. I'll lock the door when I leave."

"I can't take this . . . we're not allowed to . . ."

"Just take it, Jane, honey. I know you can use it." She did.

As soon as she was alone behind a locked door Lucy turned off the lights, then dragged a chair into the bathroom, climbed up, and began dismantling the light fixture, a glass globe with an ornamental brass fitting that screwed into a bracket above the ceiling. A moment later, she had it loose. She pushed the wires and the dangling socket and bulb aside and reached up into the round black hole. After a few seconds of groping she pulled one of the ganja bricks down. She tossed it down and reached up for another one.

When she'd brought them all down, she replaced the light fixture, returned the chair to its place amidst the chaos of the bedroom, then went back into the bathroom to gather the bricks into a plastic laundry bag. She turned off the bathroom light and was halfway across the bedroom headed for the patio door, bag in hand, when she heard the sound of a locked door being tried.

She slipped from the semi-dark room into the darker closet, pulled the slatted wood door halfway shut, and crouched, holding her breath.

"Oh my God, look at dis!" A woman's voice, hissing.

"Jesus X. Christ." A man, whispering. Harold? She couldn't be sure, as the lights came on and she cowered in the closet. "What a mess!" Definitely Harold.

"I will help you to clean up, Harry," said the woman, whose voice sounded faintly familiar.

"Nah, forget it, Pru, I'll take care of it. Just let me check on this." Lucy could hear him moving the chair into the bathroom, climbing up on it, and dismantling the light fixture. "Shit, it's gone!"

"What's that?" said Pru.

"The pot. I'd stuck it up here. No one knew but Lucy, and there's no way she would have moved it unless . . . oh, hell," he said, and Lucy heard him jump down and rush to the phone. He dialed a number and waited. "She's not in her room. Damn!" He slammed down the phone. "Listen, you get back over there and see what's up, okay? I'm gonna see if there's anything in here that might tell me who . . . visited."

"No problem, Harry," said Pru, and suddenly Lucy knew the voice: Prudence Fallowsmith, the woman who cleaned her room. What the fuck? Her room! Christ, what if they tore hers up, too! What if they took her transparencies!

Lucy heard the door close. She waited as Harold picked up the phone. "Hello, operator. Have you got any messages for me? Right, Harold Ipswich. Nothing? Nothing from Lucy Ripken? Are the people from the Green River Hike back? . . . Half an hour ago? Thanks." He put the phone down. "Damn," he said. She heard him sit down on the bed.

She stood up, slid the door open, and walked out of his closet, bag of bricks in hand.

"Hi, Harold," she said. He jumped. "It's right here," she added, displaying the bag. "I was—"

"Jesus, Luce," he said, rushing to her. "You scared the shit out of me. What the hell are you doing in there?"

"I came by a little while ago and talked the maid into letting me in since you weren't here and I was worried about this." She waved the bag at him. "But it's all here. When I saw how they'd wrecked your room I figured I'd better move them."

"Who did it?"

"I don't know, Harry. The maid said she'd cleaned up two hours ago, so your guess is as good as mine."

"Yeah, well, we both know who that would be, don't we? But how did they know to look for it here? Who let you in?"

"The maid. Her name was Jane. Jane Arlington. But Harry, who the hell is Pru?"

"Pru?" He looked like a guilty boy, grinning awkwardly. "What do you mean?"

"Come on, man, don't bullshit me. Someone named Pru was here just a—"

"Ohhh, that Pru. Prudence. She's a maid, too. An employee here."

Lucy waited for more. It didn't come. "Yeah, I know. I discovered her cleaning the inside of my closet the other day. So why are you and Pru on such intimate terms, if I might ask, Harry?"

"Intimate? Hardly, Lucy." He looked . . . conspiratorial. "Listen, Luce, I can't tell you now, but trust me. She's all right."

"All right? What does that mean? We've got a twenty-pound sack of illegal dope, my life was just threatened, and I'm supposed to trust a hotel maid to be in on the deal?"

"Whaddaya mean, your life was threatened? Did you go to the Falls? What happened?"

She paused, wondering whom to trust, and decided if she couldn't trust Harry, she was sunk anyway. She told him about the hike.

"Criminy," he said when she'd finished. "The plot thickens. So now what?"

She stood. "So now I need to get over to my room and

see what sort of havoc got wreaked, know what I mean? But for starters I'd like to get rid of this," she said, picking up the bag and shaking it at him. "Leverage is one thing, but—"

"No, we can't do that now, Luce," he said quickly. "Not a good idea."

"But I thought that's what you wanted to do. I'm sure as hell not gonna stash it in my room. Not with that slimeball Nack lurking about."

"Let's take it down the beach after dark and bury it."

"Harry, this is getting seriously sticky. Besides, we have to go to the Hababi event tonight."

"Right. Perfect. We'll go late. After we're sure all our pals have already headed out, we'll do the dirty work."

Either Prudence had cleaned up, or they hadn't hit her room. It was like she'd left it, right down to the architectural transparencies still sitting in the desk drawer and the digital images of Angus, dead, still in the camera.

Shepherded by Jefferson Hababi, the busload of press invitees, including Joey Ruskin, Maria Verde, and Mike Nack, took off as darkness fell, and shortly thereafter Lucy and Harold sneaked their sack of pot down the beach and buried it beneath some rocks above the high tide line about halfway to the mansion on the bluff. Back in her room, Lucy showered, then slipped into bikini underwear and a very short black linen dress, put on her face, and met Harold in the lobby. They arrived by cab at the beachfront home of Jackson Hababi about an hour late.

"Well whoop-de-do," said Harold, as they stepped out of the cab and paused for a look at the house: two stories of sprawling pink stucco stretched into the darkness of the manicured jungle in both directions. An enormous Georgian fanlight window, lit from within by a crystal chandelier, glowed above the front door. Parrots squawked in the rustling palms, and the sound of steel drums drifted faintly from the other side of the house, which faced the sea.

"Let's do it, Harry," said Lucy, taking his arm as they approached the front door.

Harold hefted the big brass knocker and rapped twice. A few seconds later the door swung open, and a tuxedo-clad, white-gloved butler ushered them in. They strolled through the glittering, brightly lit entry hall into an enormous, marble-floored living room furnished with throw rugs, Oriental vases filled with flower arrangements, and expensive wicker. A life-size, full-body portrait of Mr. and Mrs. Hababi in evening clothes dominated one wall. Opposite it, four open pairs of French doors let onto a torchlit verandah. They followed the butler across the living room and onto the verandah, where the revelers had gathered.

On the far side of the crowded verandah, a barbecue cooking line was going full blast, and three white-toqued chefs manned the grills and smokers. Lucy smelled burning pork, beef, chicken, fish, and, mingling with the different meat odors, the piquant aroma of jerk sauce. The steel band, banging melodiously on their metal drums, had set up under the palms down closer to the water. Spotlights stuck among the coconuts cast the three drummers in a blue and red glow. Another food line offered salads, vegetables, and breads. Two bartenders mixed drinks. Clusters of partygoers stirred it up on the tiled verandah, the lawn, and the beach.

She and Harold got Red Stripes and stood at the edge of the verandah, where they could see in both directions. The first face she recognized belonged to Sandy Rollins, in a blue spotlight, hovering near the band. In a red dress, Sandy swayed, and the way she swayed conveyed a simple truth that Lucy had not considered about Sandy Rollins prior to that moment: she loved to screw black men. Or was it musicians? In any case, drink in hand, hips grinding, Rollins offered herself to the three steel drum players, who were currently beating out a tropical version of "You Are the Sunshine of My Life."

There were plenty of white girls who came to the islands to get laid by the local talent for a week or two. But Lucy had not figured Sandy Rollins, longtime Haitian resident and racist extraordinaire, for one of them. Maybe she had a load of liquor on, and the sexual repression that underpinned her racism was overcome by gin. Who could understand such twisted things? Surely not the bibulous Dave Mullins, clutching a tall glass of something blue as he sashayed up to Rollins with an elephant-samba move, and began to dance. Effortlessly she shifted her body more directly at the musicians, stranding the Dancing Dave Bear with his blue drink in a blue spotlight. Then he spotted Harry and Lucy across the lawn and slipped into a cha-cha-cha maneuver as he headed their way, a merry grin plastered across his round, sunburned face. "Here comes the party animal," Harold murmured. "And he looks positively enlightened."

"Hey, kids," bellowed Dave. "Yer late! What happened, miss the bus? What a great pad, eh?" He hoisted his blue cocktail high, then killed it.

"You got it, Dave," Lucy said. "How's the barbecue?"

"Excellent," he said, ogling her dress. "Particularly the pork. Hey, Lucy, you wanna cha cha cha?" he added, wriggling his hips.

"Nah, I don't think so, Dave. I gotta eat. Maybe Harry'll dance with you," she said, and grinned.

"I think," said Harold drily, "that Maria Verde would be a better partner for Big Dave, don't you, Luce?"

"Absolutely," Lucy said. "Dave, track that Verde honey down, *immédiatement*. She'll samba you right to paradise, I reckon."

"She's not here, or I would," he said. " 'Cuz I like the way she shakes her thang." He grinned. "But she got off the bus right outside the hotel gates. Said she forgot her lipstick. She come with you maybe?"

Lucy and Harold looked at each other. "Oh, shit," he said.

"Should we go back?" she said.

"It's too late," he said. "If she saw us, she's already got it. If she didn't, she might tear your room up this time but she'll never find it anyways."

They needn't have worried. At that moment a loud, tangoesque flourish on the steel drums sent the crowd scattering to the edges of the verandah, clearing the center into which now tangoed Maria Verde and Jackson Hababi, followed by Joey Ruskin and Mrs. Jackson Hababi, and last by Louise Rousseau and Mike Nack. The three couples swirled about for a moment, during which time Joey Ruskin, tonight wearing black, demonstrated his effortless mastery of the tango. They stopped to a smattering of applause. "Good evening, my friends," said Jackson Hababi, in a white linen suit. "And welcome to my home. I hope you've all had a chance to enjoy the barbecue, and had several drinks as well, because now it is time to tango. Boys," he shouted out to the band, "something lively now, eh?"

The band responded with a driving calypso tune, and the verandah, now a dance floor, quickly filled. "I'm gonna get something to eat before they shut down the pork line. You want to join me?" Lucy asked Harold.

"No, I think I'll hang here and check out the dance moves," he said. "I'll catch up in a minute."

Lucy skirted the dancers and made her way to the barbecue. She approached the cook in the middle. "What can I do for you, ma'am?" he asked, his voice high-pitched and somehow familiar.

"Jerk pork, please," she said. "And some potatoes." She pointed at the fries. "Looks great!"

"Only the best, ma'am," he said. "Best jerk on de island right here tonight." Jesus, that voice! The third voice on the midnight run!

"And how are you tonight, Lucy Ripken?" said Joey Ruskin, sauntering up. "Your appetite is good, it seems," he added, eyeing her loaded plate.

"Hello, Joey," she said, giving him an even look, not easy with a mouthful of barbecued pork, but she sure as hell wasn't going to let this smooth operator cramp her eating style.

"Did you enjoy the Falls today, Lucy?" he asked smoothly. "Maria said you had a bit of a scare."

"Cut to the chase, Ruskin," she said as soon as she'd swallowed. "What do you want?"

He grinned, his golden cat eyes flickering. "I think you know what I want, Lucy. The question is, what do you want?"

She took another bite of jerk pork. "God, this stuff is great," she said. "You eat much of it, Joey?"

"Not for me," he said. "My job requires a good appearance, and jerk pork can be dangerous." He patted himself on his flat stomach.

"No doubt." She wiped her mouth and watched him.

"So, Lucy, you spoke with Mr. Nack today. I understand that you are . . . interested in participating in our little . . . business venture."

"Did he say that?" She pulled on her beer bottle. "I don't recall ever saying anything like that."

"I think you should reconsider, Lucy. I am prepared to . . . Mr. Nack has indicated his willingness to split his proceeds with you fifty-fifty, should you be interested in participation.

And I am willing to throw in another, shall we say, five thousand dollars, as a good faith bonus, if you demonstrate your willingness to participate by noon tomorrow at the latest."

Lucy ate a few fries. "What sort of demonstration did you have in mind, Joey?"

"I would like to see half of the shipment in Nack's room at that time. We can work out the details from there."

"Hey, Lucy Ripken," said Michelle Stedman, appearing suddenly at her side. "Enjoying yourself tonight?" She held a glass of white wine. "Good evening, Joseph, how are you?"

"Fine, Michelle," said Joey. "Looks like Jackson's done it again tonight."

"Yeah, he's the life of the party," Michelle said flatly. "Right, Lucy?"

"You got it, Michelle," Lucy said, not missing the dry, ironic undertone. She smiled at Michelle, whose short green dress appeared to be made of silk. "That is one gorgeous dress, girl."

"Thanks, Lucy. Fortunately, looking trendy is a job requirement."

"I didn't say trendy, Michelle. You're way past that."

"Excuse me, Miss Ripken," said Joey, "but I've got to talk to Mr. Hababi." He started away, then glanced back. "Just remember, Lucy, you can't take it with you," he said. "Noon tomorrow."

He had a point. But that was tomorrow, this was tonight, and Harold over there looked like he wanted to dance. Lucy hadn't felt so much like dancing in years, it seemed. "I'll see ya, Michelle," she said. "Mr. Harold Ipswich is about to rock my boat."

Lucy did the samba, she did the mambo, she did the tango, she did the cha cha cha. She did the shake, the bake, and the break down snake. She did the watusi, the mashed potatoes, and the bus stop shuffle. She led a conga line that flirted with the surf. She did the locomotion till the stars ran for cover. In the end, at three a.m., clutching a final cold beer, with the bus loaded and the motor running, she finally had a personal word with Jackson Hababi.

"Hey, Jackson," she said. "Great bash. Thanks for everything. The hotel's charming."

"I'm so glad you've enjoyed yourself, Miss Ripken," he said, smiling. They had danced the tango together. He was a graceful gentleman, old-world charm, probably slept in pyjamas.

"Yes, the trip's been lovely. You've worked hospitality wonders . . . especially considering what happened to Angus Wilson the other night."

He just kept smiling. "Yes, that was unfortunate. Truly unfortunate timing, don't you think? The poor man."

"Whatever did you do with his body, Jackson? I mean, what's the procedure here, anyways?"

"Procedure? Same as yours in the States, I imagine. Doctor Babcock officially confirmed the cause of death as a heart attack, we informed his wife by long distance call—I handled that myself, naturally—and she requested that he be cremated.

We took care of that through the mortuary here in Ocho Negros. She's coming for the ashes tomorrow, as a matter of fact."

"I see. And that's that, eh?"

"Well, yes. But why, Lucy? Why do you ask?"

She shook her head. "Nothing, Jackson." She glanced over at the waiting bus. "Thanks again for the party. I had a wonderful time. The hotel looks splendid—the architect did a marvelous job."

"Yes, William does have a touch, doesn't he? Well . . ." he held out a hand. "In case I don't see you again, Lucy Ripken"—they shook hands—"*arrivederci.*"

Lucy stepped on the bus and waved good-bye as the door closed.

7

The Wind Cries Lucy

She sensed it first subconsciously, and sat up with a jolt. Instantly wide awake, she had a look around. The day was well on its way, Harold was out cold at her side under the sheet, and beneath it all, driving through every layer of her awareness, came the wind. She heard palm branches rattling, the skitter of a lawn chair tumbling across the beach, the elemental rush of atmospheric pressure releasing. As she jumped up and quickly suited up, she knew what she had to do to get some perspective on her current dilemma: windsurf!

"Oh, maaan," moaned Harold, throwing an arm over his face as she drew open the curtain for a look at the thrashing, white-chopped sea. "Is it already tomorrow?" He cracked an eyelid for a squinty look at her.

"I'm going sailboarding, Harry," she said, slapping sunscreen on her shoulders. "It's blasting out there, and I gotta hit it. It's nearly ten, I should be ready for a lunch break around one. Meet me at the feed line." She came over and kissed him. "See you then, loverboy," she added softly, then drew the curtain shut. Harold waved a hand and rolled over as she headed out. They'd only done it once last night, but it had been long, slow, and profoundly sweet, passion submerged in gentle exploration, discovering the secret landscapes of each other's bodies. Harry was a patient lover.

The beach was empty, but down toward the dock a couple of guys attempted to launch a Sunfish into the onshore blast of north wind, which had stirred up a swell. Three-foot waves tumbled over each other and crashed onto the hardpacked sand, awash with coconuts, palm branches, driftwood, and a motley array of lobster buoys and mooring markers that had broken loose and blown ashore in the wind-driven surf. She could hear gear clanking on the yachts moored in the bay and flags snapping atop the buildings and the boats; the palms were bent like drunkards in the blow. Ankle-stinging sand whooshed off the beach and whipped across the lawn, while the gulls, pointing north, hovered in place, black keening silhouettes against a thin white sky smeared with pale, blue-yellow light. The sea churned with tumbling whitecaps.

As she headed down the beach toward the surf hut, leaning into the wind and hyperventilating with nervous anticipation, she watched the two guys in the Sunfish get turned around, caught in a gust, and capsize. The sailors crawled out of the waves a few seconds later. Leroy and Desmond ran down into the water and dragged the boat up out of the chop while the pair of would-be sailors, surf-bedraggled and tangled in their lifejackets, stood on shore watching. Once, she would have hated a day at the beach like this, with sand in the sandwiches and raging swells on the sea. Now, as she reached the hut her heart pounded with excitement and fear. This was well over a 30-knot blow. She'd never sailed anything quite so intense. It would be a test.

"You been out there yet, Des?" she said after he'd collected the lifejackets from the sailors, a couple of guys from the Travel Channel video crew. Sheepishly they headed back up the beach toward the terrazzo.

He jerked his head at the sailboard rack, where a short board with footstraps lay on the sand in a semi-rigged state, loose sail flapping madly. "No, Miss Lucy, I was just getting ready when these fellahs tell me they want to sail a Sunfish. I tell them no way it will work in this blow, but they insist. They guests, you know, so I let they try." He shrugged. "At least they didn't break any my gear." He grinned. "Don't tell me you want come out wit me, Lucy. Very much wind out dere today for a woman to ride, sister. Dis be a northern blow, and it don't stop till the storm come." He pointed north. In the distance, a bank of heavy-looking clouds hugged the horizon.

"Don't give me this 'for a woman' jive. Just rig me up. You'll need some company out there, Des. Only set me up with the smallest sail you got, okay?"

"I'm riding a 4.0 today, so 3.2 should do right by you," he said. "Leroy, don't stand there like a space dog, rig the lady with de eight-foot wavejumper. You'll have to do water starts today, honey," he went on, as Leroy, who never said anything, ran for the rack. "No way I'm going to send you out there on one a dose long logs. Oh, Lucy, by de way, before you go out dere, you might want to talk to de lady was lookin' for you earlier 'round the breakfast line."

"Hey, I don't want to talk, I want to sail. Who was she?"

"Said her name be Wilson. Daisy Wilson. She been askin' for you. I think she married to de man what died de other night on de island. Here to pick up de ashes, you know."

"Angus Wilson's wife?" she blurted, throwing down her harness. "Give me a minute, Des. I'll be back, I promise. I want to get out there," she said over her shoulder as she headed toward the terrace, her eyes cast seaward.

"No problem, Luce," he called after her. "I'll take a run, get a taste. Catch you on the way back."

Lucy scrambled up the stairs and checked out the terrace. They'd unrolled a row of blue-and-white-striped canvas canopies from the edge of the roof to the floor along the seaward side, effectively blocking the wind. Sheltered behind the canopies, the guests had taken beach deprivation in stride and segued from breakfast right into Bloody Marys, mimosas, beers, and screwdrivers. Up on stage a man dressed in white played a guitar and sang a calypso tune softly. Before Bob Marley, there was Harry Belafonte, also born in Jamaica. Lucy picked her way through the busy tables, regretting having only her swimsuit on as she looked about for someone who might be looking for her. She was a modest girl at heart and hated the way the men cased her body. Although last time she'd checked it hadn't looked bad at all. Harry certainly had no complaints.

She greeted the nudists from the island, gathered at a table in a cloud of cigarette smoke. They played gin and drank vodka. Grinning, the men looked right through her suit; but then, they'd already seen her without it, so she didn't care. At another table, the video crew, among them the two drowned rat sailors, sipped coffee; at another sat Dave Mullins, Michelle Stedman, and Susie Adams. Press and PR, gathered together. Was there any difference? She approached. " 'Morning, gang," she said. "How is everybody today?"

Mullins groaned and made a hangover face. "Not too bad, considering," he said.

Michelle eyed Lucy's suit. "Are you actually going swimming out there, Lucy?"

"Sailing, honey. With Desmond. You know Desmond, the boat guy? He and I are going windsurfing. It's howling out there. Perfect conditions."

"Looks nasty to me, but then, I've never much liked the wind."

"I love it. But that figures, since I'm a windsurfer, so . . . hey, Susie, I hear tell Mrs. Wilson's arrived to pick up the . . . remains of Angus."

Susie squirmed. Lucy wondered if she'd been told not to talk to her. "That's right, Lucy. Came in late last night. We sent the limo to pick her up. She's leaving today, I'm af—"

"Where is she now, do you know?"

Susie waxed diplomatic. "Well, naturally in light of what happened we've given her the presidential suite, but Mr. Hababi left explicit instructions that no one was to disturb her while she is here. She's kinda of freaked out, you know?"

"Of course," said Lucy. "Well, see you guys later," she added with a wave, and headed next over to the hot tub on the deck, where she grabbed a towel off the neatly folded stack, wrapped it around her waist, and went over to the bar. "Can I use the phone please, Jeremiah?" she asked the bartender.

"Sure, Miss," he said, setting it on the bartop. "Can I fix you a drink?"

"Just some coffee, please," she said, picking up the phone. "Hello, front desk? Could you please connect me with Mrs. Wilson in the presidential suite? Yes. I know what Mr. Hababi said, but this is Mrs. Hababi's assistant, and I need to talk to her. Yes, immediately. Thank you." She smiled at the bartender, who'd heard her lie as he served her coffee. "Thanks. Hello, Mrs. Wilson? Yes. This is Lucy Rip—yes. I heard you were looking for me this morning. Fine. Perfect. Did you notice the waterwheel in the lobby? Yes. Five minutes." She put down the phone and picked up the coffee. "Maybe you'd better give me a taste of—" she scanned the bottles arrayed on the barback—"that," she said, pointing at the Kahlua. "I think I'm gonna need a little something extra today." He shot some into her cup, and she slugged it down. It went right to her head and brought a buzz on as she took off for the lobby.

A thin, small, middle-aged woman with black hair in a bun, wearing flat shoes and a plain black dress, stood by the waterwheel clutching a box, about a foot square and six inches deep, wrapped in white paper and tied with a string. Her pale, drawn face was devoid of makeup. "Mrs. Wilson?" Lucy said, approaching her. The woman eyeballed her outfit. "Hi, I'm Lucy Ripken. Forgive my . . . I was just about to go windsurfing when—"

"That's fine," she said, holding out a hand. Lucy shook it. "Daisy Wilson. Thank you for calling."

"I had to trick the switchboard to reach you. The front desk said you weren't taking any calls."

"That was not my doing, Miss Ripken, but I'm not surprised. You simply would not believe some of the things that the management of this hotel has done since Mr. . . . since Angus . . ." She shook the box at Lucy, and tears came to her eyes. The stuff inside rattled. "This . . . this is my husband! I fly down here and they give me a . . . a box of . . . God, I don't even know what's in here, and . . ."

"I'm sorry, Mrs. Wilson. I'm really sorry. I didn't know Angus, but . . ."

"Oh, you don't have to make excuses. I know that most of his colleagues hated him," she said. "But he preferred it that way. He always said not cronying about with other journalists made it easier for him to avoid becoming cynical about his work."

"Yes, that makes sense," said Lucy. "We do tend to get jaded. But, I'm sorry, Mrs. Wilson, but why did you want to talk to me? Do you want to sit down? Can I get you some coffee?"

"No, that's all right, nothing. I don't want anything from this place. I had a call from someone in New York. A woman . . . a girl, really . . . named . . . Alice? Allie. Allie Maginn . . . Marg . . ."

"Margolis?"

"That's it! Allie Margolis. She said that if anything . . . that I should call you if I wanted to find out about what really happened to Angus."

"Yes. She found Angus, and then I—"

"I know. Let me explain." She drew herself up. "When Jackson Hababi—Angus has . . . had . . . known him for years, by the way—called and told me that Angus had died of a heart attack, I was horribly shocked and upset, of course, but I was also surprised. Angus was very healthy, and had his annual physical not six weeks past. But at his age, well . . . okay, he had a heart attack. I could believe that. But then when I asked Jackson Hababi to see about doing an autopsy and then storing the body until I could get down here to bring him home—we have a family plot in the best cemetery in Philadelphia, and Angus wanted to be buried there—Hababi told me they had to cremate Angus immediately due to the weather and the problems with—*conditions* was the word he used—on this side of the island. He made it sound like, well, I've been here before, Jamaica is a poor country, but it's not darkest Africa, for God's sake. They have doctors and coroners and funeral parlors and . . . anyway, I was so upset I didn't question him at the time, but then I called the Jamaican consul the next day, and he told me there was absolutely no reason in the world they couldn't do what I'd asked, and of course I could come down here and take Angus home, and"—she began to sniffle again—"so I called Hababi back to tell him, and he told me Angus had already been cremated. So when Al . . . Miss Margolis called the same night, of course I was curious. And now I come here and they hand me this, and tell me they're sorry." She shook the box of ashes and bits of rattly bone. "The bastards!" She burst into tears.

"Jesus," said Lucy. This poor woman. "What did Allie tell you, Mrs. Wilson?"

"Only that, like I said, that if I wanted to find out what really happened when Angus died, I should talk to you. What did she mean, Miss Ripken? What do you know?"

Lucy stood on the beach facing into the 30-knot blow. Desmond and his yellow-and-purple-striped sail rode the wind toward her, and watching him leap the waves, she put Mrs. Wilson's question out of her mind. She and the lady had exchanged information. During the exchange, Lucy realized she'd been distracted by the dope she'd heisted, and the sense of power it had given her. The real issue was not dope but death. One of the people with whom she'd been hanging out, more or less, had killed Angus Wilson. She was sure of it. How could she treat it like a game?

Strange—usually the wind slowed with a dropping tide.

Not this time. It was almost 11:30, low tide was 12:17 according to the chalkboard on the surfhut, and this particular norther just kept coming, jetstreaming on down from Fidelville.

Desmond slipped his harness line free, sculpted a flawless jibe, dropped the sail, and stepped off into shallow water in front of Lucy. Close to shore, the waves had dropped with the tide, even if the wind hadn't. He was grinning. "Man, is it blowing, Lucy. You ready to hit it?"

"Ready as I'll ever be," she said, checking her harness lines one last time, and breathing deeply. "Let's go." She picked up the tail of her board with one hand and the mast with the other and guided the rig into the water. She held the mast with one hand, letting the taut, yellow and blue sail point downwind while positioning the board in the water. She simultaneously stepped into the footstraps and took hold of the boom with both hands. She swung the harness line onto the hook and took off, pointed northwest between Naked Beach and the point. Within seconds she was ripping along, blowing past Naked Beach before she even had her bearings.

This was different than what she knew of boardsailing. Driven by the powerful wind, the board was out of the water more than in it, flying from swell to swell, slapping down with bone-jarring impact. The slightest adjustments in her knees or arms caused radical turns. Even with the harness shifting much of the work from her arms down to her hips, the pull on her shoulders was intense from the taut little

3.2 meter sail. Basically, she was hanging on for dear life, for a few minutes on that first tack, anyway.

Then she began to get a feel for the maneuverability and the amazing, skittish speed, and the impact every time she landed from a jump. About the time Desmond caught up to her, flying past with a gleeful shout, she was ready to try her first high-speed power jibe. She cranked the board 90 degrees with the slightest rail-pressure, then took a flying tumble as she tried to flip the sail. "Damn," she said, popping up from underwater and immediately getting slapped in the face with a warm, salty wave. She quickly swam to the board, worked it around into a downwind point, and then positioned herself under the sail, boom in hands, feet on board. She pushed up, lifting the tip of the sail out of the water. As the wind lifted her she quickly found her foot straps, hooked into the harness line, and took off, headed east now on a tack parallel to the beach. She worked the tack, jumping waves and carving turns while watching the scenery. She passed the mansion on the hill and discovered, beyond that point, another bay stretching into the distance. There were no hotels or houses on this next skein of beach, but two little deserted-looking islands beckoned at the other end of the virgin bay. She blew past the mansion, came about, and headed back toward Naked Beach, and once inside the bay turned the board farther downwind. Desmond rocketed past, heading back to the hotel beach for a break, and she risked a quick hand wave, then re-gripped the boom as she zoomed toward the beach, airborne from whitecap to wave like a flying fish.

A few seconds later she stepped off the board in shallow water and dropped the sail. She had landed well down the beach from the hotel. She looked around. In this fierce wind not a soul walked the shoreline. She headed toward the palm trees lined up along the edge of the sand. It took her just a moment to find the spot where they'd buried the dope. She moved the rock markers and began to dig.

Get rid of the shit. That was her new plan. It would surely bring the bad boys out of the woodwork. Unfortunate about the lost leverage, Harry, she mused to herself as she threw the stash over her shoulder, but this is what I have to do. He would understand. The two pillowcases were knotted together, with five foil-wrapped bricks in plastic laundry bags inside each one. She walked back to the water's edge, turned the board around, and positioned the sail. She slung one bag over each shoulder, so the weight rested on her back, then picked up the mast, stepped into her footstraps, and headed out for a dope burial at sea.

She tacked as far upwind as she could, then came about and headed east toward the deserted islands and beach as soon as she'd cleared the point under the mansion. The intensity of the speed remained the same, but she felt more comfortable with it now. She used the swell-chop to launch herself, banking off one wave and flying up the face of another to propel herself into the air. All this with twenty-two pounds of ganja in a pair of sacks bouncing off her back.

Flying along on a crosswind tack, she couldn't hear a thing except the howling wind, the sound of water, her board cutting and slashing through it. Still a good half mile from the islands, where she had decided to dump the dope, she glanced back to get her bearings and saw—just as she lost control and crashed into the sea—the hotel's speedboat, the cigarette cruiser she'd been skiing behind just the other day, headed full throttle in her direction, engine roar audible above the wind as it banged over the waves.

She quickly groped to the surface, fighting the tangle of pillowcases and harness lines and booms to get into position. The boat blasted by six feet from her head, whipping a turn so the driver could get a better look at her. It was Ruskin, in designer sunglasses, of course!

She hurriedly positioned herself for a water start as Joey circled the boat around for another run at her. This time, he would probably not waste time just looking. As he charged, she could feel the sacks of pot swirling around her head; then the wind lifted the sail free and she followed, bursting clear of the water, hanging on to the booms. The weight of the dope and water in the bags pulled her back. But the wind was her savior, and it got her free and flying out of harm's way as Ruskin roared past.

Lucy leaned back, pulling the sail in tight, and pointed on a faster tack that took her straight at the two islands ahead. The boat engine raced again, buzzing like a deranged wasp as he turned it around. She chanced another glance back: Joey was bearing down directly on her once more! She was going incredibly fast, blasting over the waves, but all she had was the wind, and the damn boat probably had

500 horsepower! She concentrated on the near island, a few hundred yards away now. Another look back. He was closing in! She whipped a few turns, zigzagging through the chop, to throw him off, but he stayed right on her tail, engine roaring as she homed in on the island just ahead.

With the downsurge of a swell she saw the island's jagged surrounding coral reef, exposed by low tide, just a few seconds before she was on it—those few seconds long enough for her to bank off a wave, plane up another, take to the air, and fly over the exposed coral to land on the water beyond and keep moving. Joey didn't even see the reef. She had ten yards on him, and glanced back just as the cigarette boat hit the reef she'd just flown over at full throttle. The bow rammed into the reef, sending the stern up into the air and catapulting Joey Ruskin into the water inside the reef just ahead of the boat, which flipped forward to land on top of him before exploding in a gas tank fireball. Lucy was fifty yards away, yet the shockwave from the explosion knocked her off her board. Underwater, in a semi-panic, this time she tore off the bags of pot dragging at her and let them sink as she struggled to the surface. The flaming ruins of the boat sent a cloud of black smoke streaming into the wind; chunks of smoldering hull bobbed in the chop nearby, her sailboard drifted away, and still the norther ripped and howled around her.

Half-stunned, she swam over and pulled herself onto the sailboard. The island was just twenty yards away. She popped the mast loose from the board, released the sail, and belly-paddled herself to a little leeward beach, dragging sail, mast, and booms behind. Panting, she crawled up on shore, sat down, and, feeling an urge to burst into tears, instead started deep breathing and seized control of herself. After a moment she stood up and walked over to the end of the island nearest the explosion. The fire had burned itself out quickly, reducing the cigarette boat to a smoldering, ruined butt. "Joey?" she called out plaintively. "Joey, are you there?"

She wandered back to her sailboard and looked out to sea. The clouds were closer now, and she could see roiling, stormy movement on their dark undersides. There was nothing but wind-torn water and cloudy sky all the way to the horizon, and for a moment she forgot about Jamaica at her back and felt as if she'd just landed on a deserted island. She was all alone. Down below, inside the reef, the bags of dope drifted on the bottom of the sea. She wondered, almost idly, if they might find it in the course of cleaning up this nightmare. She wondered if she ought to dive for it, take it out past the reef, and do a better job of burying it. Too late for that now—the buzz of an approaching speedboat became audible. A moment later, it arrived. On board were two members of the Jamaican Coast Guard and Jefferson Hababi.

"So I said I was out sailing, and Joey came blasting along in the speedboat. I told them I guessed he was just showing off and didn't see the reef."

"And they believed you?"

"Why shouldn't they? Junior Hababi wasn't about to

question my story in front of them. I mean, maybe they're bought and paid for by daddy, and maybe they're not, but he wasn't in any position to—"

"Right," said Harold, abruptly. She resented his tone and the way he interrupted her. "So tell me again . . . what were you doing with the stuff out there, Lucy? I don't understand."

"I told you, Harold. After I talked to Mrs. Wilson, I just wanted to concentrate on what happened to Angus Wilson, and the . . . shit, why are you so worried about the damned dope anyway, Harry? I made a man die today, I almost got killed myself, and you're grilling me, for God's sake! What are you, some kind of—"

"Hey, I'm sorry, Luce." He took her hands. They were in a taxi, headed into Ocho Negros for dinner. Lucy had insisted on off-campus dining. She didn't want to see any of the gang on this particular evening. "You didn't make him die. You saved your own life. Incredible, jumping the reef." He paused. "But I have to admit I'm sorry you unilaterally decided to get rid of our evidage. I mean leverence. Leverage. God, I've been talking too much patois. Starting to get to me, mon." He smiled. "Anyway, forgive me. I'll say no more about the pot. So you wanna hit Jack's for dinner?"

"Nah, something a little quieter, Harry. I'm kind of wiped out. Not every day I dodge an exploding attack speedboat."

"No shit. Poor baby." He stroked her cheek gently. "Hey, I know this really good local place up on the hill behind Ochi. Authentic island cooking. Wanna check it out?"

"Sounds good, as long as there aren't any Grand Stranders around."

"I'm sure it's on the list of forbidden places. It's pretty funky up there." He leaned forward in the cab. "Hey, mon, take us up to Round Hill Road. You know the Green Dolphin?"

"Yeah, mon." The cabbie nodded. "Bit out of the way, eh?"

"That's right," said Harold. "Just what we're lookin' for."

Fifteen minutes up a winding road, from Ocho's American neon to sporadic residential lights, and finally into near total darkness, brought them to the Green Dolphin Restaurant, a low, dark, handmade wooden building buried in a bower of banana trees. "You want I wait?" said the cabbie as he stopped by the front door, marked with a wooden sign with a green dolphin painted on it. "Won't be no cab up here later."

"No use wasting your time. We'll figure something out," said Harold, handing him money.

"Okay, mon." They climbed out and he took off. They stood in the road for a few seconds, and when the motor noise faded they were bathed in the overpowering music of the night: birds, insects, frogs, the warm wind, soft now, blowing through the dark canyons and the hills above them. Stars glittered between the clouds—the tail end of the storm that had soaked the coast for three hours before moving over the mountains and down to Kingston. The low throb of a reggae bassline lulled them, pulled them down three wooden stairs to the front door of the Green Dolphin. Harold opened the door for her, and they went in.

The room glowed darkly, lit only by candles on the table-tops, and was heavily scented with cooking smells mixed with tobacco and ganja smoke. They could hear the soft babble of patois, Marley on the system. The voices slowed as they walked in, and as her eyes adjusted Lucy knew why: they were the only white people there. But the smile of the dread-locked man who led them to a table and the way the other guests casually resumed eating, drinking, and carrying on reminded her of what she had known ever since the first time she'd been on the island: black Jamaicans were friendly, non-racist people.

Harold knew the owner, Sonny Mance, and he knew the local dishes, so they got a taste of most everything on the menu. They sampled bammy, cho-cho, sprats, curried goat, callaloo, hot jerk pork, and briny escoveitched fish. They tasted pepperpot soup, pumpkin soup, and hard dough bread. They drank Red Stripe, Dragon Stout, and fish tea, and passed on the mushroom tea that was offered as an after-dinner pick-me-up. She was bloated to the max, but didn't let that stop her—she worked on a Matrimony fruit salad while waiting for her Irish Moss and a final nip of ortanique liqueur.

Afterward, Harold paid the bill, they jived with Sonny a little, and then went outside. No cab in sight. They went back in to ask him to call a cab. The phone wasn't working. They decided to walk. Sonny said he'd try to find them a ride. They thanked him and took off down the hill. Probably six miles in the dark to Ocho Negros, and then five more down the waterfront to the hotel, but no matter. Lucy's terrors of the day receded as they strolled through the darkness, the road faintly gleaming in starlight before them. Dogs barked in the distance. They walked for fifteen minutes, passed a few houses, not a single car went by in either direction. She was falling in love with this odd man who exhibited such a cynical zest for life, who played the fool one minute and demonstrated such competence the next. Who would have imagined, seeing him in the airport and remembering him from Dan's Tavern on East Seventh Street, that Harold Ipswich would know Sonny Mance and everything on his menu?

Exhausted from her sail, her escape, the afternoon with the Coast Guard, the major food and beer event of the evening, after half an hour trudging downhill, Lucy abruptly ran out of gas. She took Harry by the arm and wandered to the edge of a turnout. Ocho Negros twinkled below, the curved bays laced with hotel lights, the dark sea stretching away to meet the stars. She slipped her arm around his waist. "Harry, I'm a wreck. I can't walk any farther. Will you carry me down there?"

"Five miles? No problem, doll," he said. "Climb aboard," he added, presenting his back. She leapt on, and off they staggered, laughing madly as he wove back and forth. They stopped after a moment and he let go of her legs. She kept her arms around his neck, legs dangling, body pressed against his back, simply feeling him, feeling, at the moment, that she truly wanted, in fact needed, to drag him into the bushes at the side of the road and have her way with him. Instead, the sound of a cranky unmuffled engine descending the road above them jarred her back from the land of lust to the reality of roadside. An old truck ground around the turn above them, one dim headlight enhanced with what appeared to be a flashlight held out the window on the passenger side, and rattled down to halt where they waited.

And so they trundled down into Ocho Rios with six friendly goats in the back of the truck, which had been dispensed by Sonny and which belonged to his brother-in-law, Ferguson Rainey, who was driving. Not wanting to chance a run-in with the ticket-writing gendarmes downtown, Ferguson dropped them on a corner a couple of blocks up the hill. On foot once again, they started down toward the coast road, where the cabs would be roaming.

Half a block downhill, in and out of storefront light, hand in hand they strolled. Two men stepped out from the darkness of trees at the side of the road and stopped in front of them. They were Rastas, one short and thick, the other tall, both with long dreads stuffed into knit caps, scruffy beards, sandals, jeans, T-shirts. The tall one said, "Excuse me, mon," but didn't get out of the way.

Harold said, "Yeah, okay." They waited a few seconds, then tried to pass. The man sidestepped, staying in the way. Lucy gripped Harold's hand. "What can I do for you, gentlemen?" Harold said calmly.

"What can you do for us is tell me where is de herb which you take de other night, mon? It is not belong to you, see, and there is very much concern that de rightful owners be havin' dere ganja."

"And who might these rightful owners be?" Harold went on, seemingly not at all afraid. Lucy didn't understand it. The dudes radiated menace. She was fighting an impulse to run for it, but Harold was hanging on tight.

"Dis is not your busyness, my friend," said the tall dread.

"So why is it yours?" Harold said, still entirely calm. He let Lucy's hand go.

"Because it is, mon," Dread Man answered, and with that, the shorter guy suddenly flourished a knife. "So be talkin' now, or we be—"

Harold simultaneously kicked the tall one in the crotch and slammed the other one on the shoulder with the edge of his hand, sending the knife flying, then he followed with a punch in the stomach. The fat Rasta folded over like his friend, who was half-crouched, groaning, holding his balls with both hands. Harold grabbed them and banged their heads together, then dragged them into the dark trees off the side of the road. "Let's get outta here, Lucy," he said, grabbing her hand and hustling down the road toward the bright lights of downtown Ocho Negros. "There may be a few more of those boys lurking."

The whole thing had taken maybe fifteen seconds. And now it all added up. Prudence. Fumbling over a word. The third degree in the car. Now this display of elegant brutality.

She let him lead the way for a block and a half, to a local knockoff of an American icon: Kingston Fried Chicken, it said on the big neon sign, which featured a black Rastafarian version of the colonel grinning down on the streets of Ocho Negros. There was enough light inside to ward off an army of drug-crazed bad boys, and a policeman directing traffic at the intersection twenty yards away. Lucy dragged him in and turned on him. "You're a cop, aren't you?" she said furiously. "You're no travel writer, you're a fucking po-liceman, Harold."

"Hey, calm down, Lucy." He took her hands. She shook loose.

"A goddamn cop. What in the hell are you doing here, Harry? You shit. I . . ." She felt the tears rising, and fought them down. "I can't believe it. You've been using me like a patsy. What the hell's going on, Harry, goddammit? Tell me it isn't true. Fuck," she said, and the tears came. "Fuck fuck fuck," she spit the curses out, sobbing. A large black woman with two small children eating chicken wings took the kids by their free hands and led them away, a frown on her face, shaking her head at the disgusting language of the American tourists.

"It's not like it seems," Harry said. "Look, let's get back to the hotel where it's safe, and—"

"What's not like it seems, Harry? You're not a cop? Tell me it's true, Harry. Tell me you learned self-defense in your idle hours on East Ninth Street, so you could kick ass when the chance arose. Tell me Prudence Fallowsmith is your mother's housekeeper's cousin. Tell me, Harry, tell me how much you love me." She grabbed him by the lapels of his linen jacket. "Tell me the truth, Harry."

"Let's go outside. There's a bar around the corner. Lot of Americans hang there. It'll be safe."

"Fine," she said, snapping into control. "You lead the way." He did, into the Conch Cafe, two doors down, where Jimmy Buffett's "Margaritaville" blasted from the jukebox and a whole lot of tourists watched each other, waiting for something to happen. Harry led her to a booth in the back, and they sat opposite each other. "So what the—" He held up a hand, and she shut up as the waitress approached.

"Two beers," Harry said.

"One beer," Lucy said. "For him. I'll have a double . . . you have any Stolichnaya?"

"Absolut, ma'am," said the waitress.

"Fine. A double. On ice." She leaned back and looked across the table at the man she'd been in love with fifteen minutes earlier. His eyes pleaded. She felt hard, betrayed. "So, Harry Ipswich, what's your fucking story?" she snapped, unable to contain the bitterness in her voice.

"My 'fucking story' is I love you, Lucy," he said. "So why don't you let me tell the rest before you make your mind up that you hate me because you feel it's your duty to hate cops."

"So you are a cop then?"

He swallowed. "I can't lie to you. DEA. Special agent."

"DEA. You're a narc? I can't believe it. I'm fucking a narc?"

"Jesus, Lucy, do you have to be so crude? I'm still the same person you—"

"No you're not, Harry. That person wasn't a liar, or a narc, or . . . Christ, I don't know what you are."

"Lucy, what's with you? Are you some kind of legal drug crusader? This isn't the sixties, babe. Wise up. It ain't fun stuff anymore. You know that. I didn't exactly see you sucking up the reefer the way some of the writers do."

The waitress arrived with their drinks. Lucy paid for hers, Harry for his. She insisted. She took a big hit and put it down. She felt hostile, aggressive. "So what's your story, huh? What's your excuse?"

"Excuse?" Now he was angry, too. "I don't have to make any excuse. My older brother died of a heroin overdose nine years ago, Lucy. I was strung out with him, and I got high with him one night. I was so loaded I didn't even know what was happening, and I left him there, nice and high, I thought, and went out to a nightclub. I didn't even know he was dead until the next day. That was my last shot, see? So after that I went through a rehab program, and I wrote a piece about the whole thing for *New York Magazine*. Then these DEA guys approached me, and I signed up. Weird way of recruiting, but it sure worked on me. Guess I was trying to atone for the sin of that night Terry died, and . . . I don't know, but I thought I'd be chasing heroin dealers. Instead they put me on the Caribbean beat since I was established as a travel writer. What the hell, these days the Kingston pot dealers are just as bad as the Colombian coke dealers and the

Chinese heroin dealers, let me tell you. Lucy . . ." He stopped and reached for her hands. She pulled them off the table, and took another sip of vodka. The ice had half-melted and it was cold and clear and good going down, sharpening her sense of herself, at least for the moment.

"That's a fine story, Harry, and I'm sure every word is true. I guess if you want to be a cop that's no business of mine. But why did you decide to involve . . . Christ, what am I doing here with you? You've been using me, Harry, for God's sake! I thought I was making choices, but you've been directing the whole show. Sleeping with me, whispering this romantic shit in my ears, Jesus, I haven't felt like this about anybody in years, and now I find out that—"

"Hey, wait a minute, Lucy! I didn't arrange for you to stumble across the body of Angus Wilson. Nor did I plan for you to get obsessed with his death. And I didn't plan to . . ." He stared at the tabletop. ". . . to fall in love with you." He looked up at her. "Which I have done, and it's made the last couple days the happiest I've had in years." He leaned forward, and lowered his voice. "Now, let me tell you what's going on here. Then you can decide if you want to hate me, or . . . whatever."

She leaned back, folded her arms across, and watched him talk. She knew he was telling the truth, but she didn't know if that mattered anymore.

"You have no idea how tangled up the politics, the money, and the dope smuggling is on this island, but you walked right into the whole mess when you began sniffing around Wilson's death. I'm not sure about all the players, but I can tell you this much. Joey Ruskin was successfully setting up a new network up here on the north coast, and it seems that he had recruited some writers to mule for him. I came on this trip pretty much to see what was shaking with his deal, see who he was using, and so on. My instructions were not to make a bust this time, but see if I could trail the stuff back from him. Obviously, the death of Angus Wilson complicated matters for me as well as Joey, his cronies, the hotel people—and you, of course. But besides all that, some of the Kingston posses weren't at all happy with the competition—or so it would seem from the appearance of our two friends tonight."

"So tell me something I don't know," Lucy said. "Like how you could let me play along with these people for so long, when you knew what—"

"Play along! It was your idea to take the dope, remember? And it seemed like a good one at the time. I didn't think they'd go after you, Lucy. I really didn't. Ruskin was an amateur. He just knew some people who knew some growers, and thought he'd go into business. He had no idea how dangerous these people can be. I was actually planning to bust him, as a matter of fact—or rather, have Prudence bust him."

"She's Jamaican police?"

"A local fed. Undercover. When you suggested we take the pot it seemed like a perfect way to bring Ruskin's suppliers out of the woods. I admit that I . . . used you . . . as a smokescreen to some extent, but I had no idea you'd take matters further in your own hands the way you did. Really."

"Why was Prudence searching my room?"

"I had to make sure you were clean, Lucy. It was hard enough, falling for you. If you'd had any drugs, or maybe had joined that idiot Nack in Joey's little conspiracy, I would have been in a terrible position."

"You asshole. You had me checked out to make sure I made the grade, so you could sleep with me?"

"Come on, Lucy, look at it from my angle. I would have hated to have to bust you."

They sat for a moment without speaking. Lucy killed her drink. "Christ," she finally said. "Jesus Christ."

"Look, now Ruskin's dead, and it's starting to look like the hotel people might be involved, at least in the Wilson coverup. I think things are gonna get nasty in the next few days. Maybe you should think about—"

"The next few days? What about today? I almost get killed by a lunatic in a boat, we almost get mugged on the street, and you turn out to be a cop. That's enough nasty for me, Harry."

"Come on, stop with the cop talk, Lucy. You've been playing cop yourself all week. Why fight me?"

"Don't you get it, Harry? It's not that you're a cop, it's that you're not who you pretended to be. You lied! Our whole tiny, fragile little three days' worth of relationship is built on a foundation of lies."

"Don't be such a moralist, girl. I am who I am, for God's sake. That's not a lie."

She finished her drink and stood up. "Maybe so. I don't know. Let's get out of here." He followed her out the door. They found a cab and headed back to the hotel without speaking again. He tried a few times, and each time she shushed him. They separated in the lobby with a formal "good night." His face was anguished. Lucy went to her room, locked herself in, looked in the mirror for a moment, and checked the clock. It was nearly midnight. She called Mickey's room.

"Mick?"

"What? Who's this, it's nearly—"

"Lucy. So did you know?"

"Know what? What are you talking about?"

"About Harold."

"What?"

"He's a cop."

"*What?*"

"DEA. A narc. Our own little Harry. Listen. We need to talk. Can I come up?"

"To my room? God, it's a . . . sure, why not? Should I call for cocktail delivery?"

"No, nothing for me. My nerves are fried, Mick, but I don't dare drink anymore. I don't know what the hell I'm doing right now. I thought Harry . . . I . . . shit, I feel like . . ."

"C'mon up, Luce. Right now. Harry a narc! Criminy!"

Half an hour later, Lucy felt calmer, and Harry was forgiven, more or less. As Mickey pointed out, reinforcing what Harry'd said, he hadn't planned to use her, or to fall in love with her. Lucy had pushed herself into the drug scam because of Angus Wilson; she'd fallen in love with Harry because of who he was, and that hadn't changed. "Besides, romance ain't easy to find these days, honey, so take it when it comes," Mickey added.

Not too much later, Lucy went back to her room relatively calm, utterly weary, and ready to forgive him. She locked herself in and called his room. She let it ring many times, and while it rang, she wondered about Jackson Hababi, Adrian Kensington, Rackstraw Barnes, and a cook with a high-pitched voice. Who were all these people? There was no answer, and she finally hung up. She contemplated searching the hotel for him, but instead she took off her dress, brushed her teeth, and went to bed.

8

In the Mountains She Finds the Truth

Lucy woke to a flurry of conflicting emotions. First, as she reached for Harry in her half-sleep, an almost infantile sense of well-being and security washed over her, simply from knowing there was a body beside her, then she felt a visceral wave of sadness and loss as her arm swept across the bed, discovering the emptiness; this was followed by fury as she recalled the course of the night before; last came a sense of relief. After all, she had forgiven him, even if he didn't know it yet.

All this in ten seconds, after just three days! Damn. Shaking her head, she climbed out of bed remembering why she hadn't had a real, serious lover in, what was it, three years now? It was complicated, much more than a hump and a hand to hold.

Instead of calling Harold to find out where they stood, she put him out of mind and went to work. She dressed in shorts and a T-shirt, sunscreened her face and arms, gathered her notebook, tape recorder, and pens in a bag, put on her flojos and shades, and headed off to La Terrazzo Grande for her interview with Jefferson Hababi. It had been scheduled two weeks earlier by Susie Adams, and Lucy had confirmed with Jefferson yesterday in the midst of her exploding boat aftermath to-do with the Coast Guard. She'd caught Jefferson by surprise, bringing up the interview at that stressful moment as they stood on the little island surrounded by smoldering wreckage, and he had obliged her with a flustered agreement to meet over breakfast. The subject was to be Grand Strand food operations as they related to space planning. No problem. As she'd figured, in spite of the tense circumstances Jefferson was flattered by the attention.

She paused by the bar overlooking the terrace. Guests had been trickling in for a few days, and the open air pavilion was half full. She liked the look of the place with more bodies, clothes, and color. The human element brought William Evans's architecture to life, as should happen in a public dining area. She spotted Jefferson, casual in short sleeves, sitting with Michelle Stedman at a table near the long service counters. Lucy strolled down and picked her way through the tables to the line. She snagged a plate, loaded it with papaya and cantaloupe slices and a wedge of lime, then went to join them. "Miss Ripley," Jefferson Hababi said, nearly knocking his chair over as he leaped to his feet. "Good morning, and how are you?" He offered a hand. "I hope you're feeling better after yesterday's—"

"Ripken, Jefferson. The name is Ripken," she said with a disarming grin as she shook his hand. "I'm fine. Considering. Good morning, Michelle. How are you?"

"I'm good, Luce," she answered, and looked out to sea. "I gather you had a pretty wild session out there yesterday."

"That's an understatement, honey," Lucy said. "It was unbelievable. I mean one minute I'm having a nice intense little sail and the next, all hell breaks loose."

"Poor Joey," Michelle cut in. "That boy just never knew when to stop showing off."

"Is that what he was doing?" Lucy said, remembering the sight of the boat bearing down on her like some giant crazed shark. She took a seat and squirted lime juice over her papaya.

Michelle got up. "I hate to miss this but I've got to run. I'll leave you two to your business." She walked away.

Lucy eyed him. "Well, Jefferson, it looks like business is picking up."

"Yes, we're sixty-three percent booked for March," said Jefferson. "We hadn't projected numbers like that until next Christmas. Things are off to a wonderful start."

"Except for Angus and Joey—and your ski boat, of course."

"The insurance will take care of the boat," said Jefferson. "Can you imagine? Two accidental deaths in a week. What a terrible coincidence! My stepfather said he'd never seen anything like it in thirty years in the hotel business."

"No kidding," said Lucy. "Oh, and that reminds me," she

added. "What was Joey doing racing around in the hotel boat anyway? It's not like he works for you guys. Who gave him the keys? Won't your insurance people want to know why he—"

"Are we here to discuss Joey or the hotel?" said Jefferson, a note of exasperation entering his voice. "I already went over all that stuff with the Coast Guard."

"I was just curious," Lucy said. "It's not like you let just anyone drive that boat, right?"

"I'm sure he didn't have my keys," Jefferson responded impatiently. "But the policy covered him. He used the boat all the time, took groups of travel agents out and that sort of thing. That was his job, and it's part of my job to help him do his, you see?"

"I sure do, Jefferson," Lucy said, and pulled out a notebook. Time to shift back to paying work. After all, she did have a story to write. She turned on her tape recorder, uncapped a pen, and said, "So tell me how the building runs, Jeff."

They spent the next twenty minutes talking hotel biz. A few operational facts usually tied in to the design side of the story, demonstrating the architect's awareness of back-of-house as well as front-of-house functional requirements. Jeff knew his stuff when it came to operations, she had to admit. And she could tell he was happy to talk hotel business rather than monkey business. He gave her what she needed on how four restaurants and room service operated out of a single huge prep kitchen.

She sat back and sighed as the waiter refilled her coffee cup. Time to unsheathe her blade, and cut. The sun sparkled on the turquoise sea, the guests wandered contentedly from breakfast to beach, and the warm air was still and heavy. "Well, Jeff," she said. "It's been a great week, in spite of the—"

"We're so glad you've enjoyed your stay. We're looking forward to the article, Lucy."

She leaned forward, bearing down a little. "But I still don't understand why Harold's room got torn up the other day. Do you?"

"Harold's room? Harold who? What are you—"

"Harold Ipswich, Jefferson. He's part of the press group. The other day when we went on the hike, his room was ransacked. Who did it? What were they looking for?"

"What are you talking about? I don't know what you're—"

"I'm talking about a big bag of ganja, Jeff, and a really stupid plan to sneak it into the United States. Come on, Jeff, don't play dumb, I know you know what I'm talking about. I'm sure your father would—"

"My stepfather has nothing to do with . . . with whatever it is you're talking about. Just leave him out of it," he said fiercely. "He knows nothing about . . ." he stopped.

"About what, Jefferson?" she asked.

"About . . . nothing." He stood. "Look, I have to go. I have work to—"

"Where is your key to the speedboat, Jefferson? Is it on your key ring? Can you show it to me?" she asked. "Or should I ask your father?"

"I told you he's not my father. My father is . . ." he faltered, and sat down again.

"Yes. Go on. Who is your father?" Lucy asked quietly.

"He's . . . he's dead," Jefferson said sadly, angrily. "He died, and my mother married Jackson Hababi three months later. I was twelve years old, and they—he—made me change my name. My name is Adjami Hajjar," he said. "Not Jefferson Hababi." He crossed his arms, and looked out to sea. He sighed. "You're right, I did lend Joey my boat keys yesterday. He told me he was going to take the video crew out to film the hotel from the bay."

"And you believed him?"

"Why shouldn't I? He's been doing it for months."

"Because you knew damn well about the pot, and what happened to Angus."

"I don't know what you're talking about, Lucy," he said.

"C'mon, Jeff, give it up. I've already heard from Adrian Kensington how—"

"Adrian Kensington? That . . . what did he . . . he doesn't have anything to do with . . . with . . ."

"With the deal? No, of course not. But he did put me onto Mike Nack and Ruskin the other night. I think Kensington and his friends—rivals in the business, I suspect—were trying to stop Joey's little operation before it started."

"Who told you to talk to Kensington?" he demanded.

"A little bird," she said. "Look, Jeff, I'm not really interested in your smuggling scam. Although I think it's pretty stupid for someone with the future you've obviously got here"—she gestured at the surroundings—"to fuck it up with some small-time dope deal."

"Believe me, Lucy," he said vehemently, "I didn't expect any of these complications. When Joey first approached me I told him absolutely not, never, but then . . ." He stopped.

"What?"

"Look, you can't tell my stepfather any of this, understand? If he found out I would be . . ."

"Why would I tell him? Don't worry, Jefferson. I just want to know what happened is all. What happened to Angus Wilson?"

"I don't know what happened. I wasn't around that night. The night Wilson died. I had too much wine at dinner . . . I do that often at the official dinners." He smiled bitterly. "Then I went to my room and fell asleep. I only came back when the barman called."

"The PR dinners are difficult for you?"

"Hateful. Jackson pretends everything is so rosy, and that he likes everybody so much, but the truth is, this hotel almost went bankrupt before it opened. Jackson is seriously overextended in this deal. We can hardly pay our employees. Not that he gives a bloody damn if anyone ever gets paid."

"Did Wilson know any of this?"

"Angus Wilson? I don't have any idea, but I doubt it. For all his grins and greetings, Jackson simply loathes you press people, so no one ever mentions them around him unless it's absolutely necessary. He certainly wouldn't have told Wilson. Look, the whole thing—the whole company—is in a mess. Has been since Hanley took office and started legislating higher wages and raising luxury room taxes at the same time. Jackson is crazy with the pressure from the banks, and he's hard enough on me in the best of times, so when Joey offered me a chance to make some money on my own so I wouldn't have to keep working here, for Jackson, it sounded like a good idea."

Lucy paused. "I guess I can understand that, Jefferson. But that doesn't change the fact that you are an accessory to murder."

"Bloody hell I am, Lucy Ripken! I may have gotten into a mess with helping Ruskin set up this idiotic smuggling thing, but I don't know a thing about murder. Angus Wilson fell, damnit!"

"Fell? I thought he had a heart attack."

"He did. And then he fell into the hot tub."

"But he was sitting in the tub when Allie Margolis found him. I saw him, too. How did he fall?"

"Why don't you ask Allie Margolis?"

"I would have if you hadn't sent her home." He didn't respond. "Look, Jefferson, I'm sorry this is the way it is for you. I'll do my best to keep your part in this foolish scam a secret. But you have to level with me. You can't tell me you didn't know what Joey was up to yesterday. Just what was your part in the deal, anyway, Jeff?"

He pushed the chair back and stood up. "I don't see why

you need to know that, Lucy. It has nothing to do with Angus Wilson, or you. And no, I didn't ask Joey what he was doing yesterday, and he didn't tell me. Now he's dead, and so is the deal—thanks to you. So just leave me out of it!" he snapped, and stalked away.

Now what? Now where was that Harry Ipswich when she needed him? She went to the bar phone and called his room. No answer. She called the front desk and checked for messages. Nothing. She pulled a card out of her wallet and called her friend Jossie the cabby. He agreed to pick her up in half an hour. She went back to her room, got out her digital camera, tried Harry again, tried Mickey, got no answer, then headed for the lobby. Whatever happened, she was on her own. She snagged a *USA Today* off a table, put her shades on, and sat in the lobby lounge for a surveillance. Five minutes later the phone rang at the reception counter. Lucy looked up. The clerk answered, then looked over at her and said, "Excuse me, ma'am, are you Lucy Ripken? There's a call for you from the gatehouse. You can take it over there." She nodded at a courtesy phone. Lucy walked over and picked it up.

"Yes?"

"Yah, Lucy, it's Jossie here. Like I said before the man won't let me in so—" Maria Verde dashed through the lobby in a purple dress and big sunglasses, jewels jangling. Lucy followed with her eyes as Maria hurriedly strolled out from under the porte cochere and jumped into a yellow Jeep convertible in the parking lot. Lucy couldn't believe her luck. If that's what it was.

"That's okay, Joss, I'll be there in a moment. There's a red-haired lady coming through in a Jeep. See which way she goes. We got to follow, okay?"

"No problem." Lucy hung up, lingering till Maria Verde had backed out and started down the driveway. Then she ran for it. Jossie was waiting in his cab.

"She went thataway," he said with a grin, pointing east away from Ocho Negros.

"Let's roll," said Lucy, jumping in. "Don't lose her, but don't let her know we're following, okay, Joss?"

"You are talkin' to a professional driver, darlin'," he said, grinning into the mirror as they lit out, headed east toward Port Antonio.

Five minutes later they left the hotel zone. As they came around a turn out of a thicket and into the sun, Lucy caught sight of the yellow Jeep across a small bay. "There she is!" she cried.

"You want to catch up now?" said Jossie.

"No, this is fine. Long as we keep her in sight. But where does this road go?"

"Along the coast all the way to de east end, by way of Port Antonio."

"What's between here and there?"

"Just what you see: beach on the left, cane fields then hills on the right. Up high in the hills be cockpit country."

"Cockpit country?"

"Yah, mon. The Maroons be their own country up there. People say it cockpit country. Lotta ganja grow up there in the secret valleys and such. Maroons, Rastas, all tribal shit goin' down, you see?"

"I guess. But what are Maroons?"

"They a tribe come from runaway slaves long ago. Keep to theirself up there."

"Why are they called Maroons?"

"Don't know, mon. Always been they name."

They came onto a straightaway along a stretch of narrow roadside beach. Local people walked horses, donkeys, cows along the edge of the road. People paused to watch Jossie's flashy cab go past. "No hotels around here, eh?"

"No chance. Dexter not allow any development here. Too far from the airport, anyway."

"Good point."

"Hey, look, Lucy, she be turnin'. Headin' for the hills." Two hundred yards ahead, Maria cranked a right. Half a minute later Jossie slowed at the intersection, and turned after her. They could see a plume of dust rising from her tires up ahead, where the road began its climb out of the level coastal fields, into the jungle-clad hills.

Jossie kept it slow, dodging potholes as they trailed the yellow Jeep along the dirt and gravel road into the foothills of the Blue Mountains. The road soon steepened and grew narrower and darker as they entered the jungle. "What's up here?" Lucy said, whispering in the eerie rain forest light. Aside from the sound of Jossie's cab, only the cries of parrots and other jungle birds broke the silence.

"Not much," Jossie said. "Little village now and then.

Mostly farmers back in here. Won't see them from the road, though. Not with the herb growing." They came onto a flat, sunlit stretch of road and passed a dozen or so shabby cinderblock houses with tin roofs and dark open doorways framed in banana branches. TV antennas, a neon beer sign in a window, and a truck lacking front wheels located the hamlet in the 21st century. A scrawny mongrel ran out of a pink house and barked at them. Two small children peeked from an empty window. The road turned shadowy again as they plunged back into the jungle. They went on, drawn by the sound of Maria Verde's Jeep.

And then the sound stopped. Jossie eased to a halt. "Let's go up a little farther," Lucy said softly. "Around that corner." They edged around the bend. Jossie jerked to a stop. A hundred yards ahead, just before the next turn, the yellow Jeep was parked at the side of the road. Maria Verde was nowhere in sight.

"What you want to do, Lucy?" Jossie whispered. "She's gone into the jungle."

"I want to follow her. Maybe you should go back to the village and wait."

"No way, Lucy. You can't go into the bush up here alone. I put the cab in there"—he pointed at a thicket—"and I will accompany you on your hike."

"Thanks, Joss, but . . ."

"No buts, Lucy. Woman alone in this jungle is not safe woman, understand me now?"

"What about her?" Lucy nodded toward the Jeep as they jumped back in the cab and Jossie eased it off the road and into the trees.

"Don't know about her, Lucy. She must know what she doin' up here, don't you think? She know exactly where she goin', eh?"

"Looks that way, Joss." They ran down the road to the Jeep, had a look around, and found the path leading into the jungle. Lucy took a picture of the Jeep, complete with license plate, and then they headed up the trail.

Jossie led the way. They walked in silence, halting frequently to listen ahead. They heard nothing but birds and flowing water as they crept softly through the green vale. The light brightened, indicating a clearing ahead. A few seconds later Jossie threw an arm up to halt her, and silently pulled her off the trail into the ferns. "Up there," he whispered. "The lady, and two Rastas. Be careful now." They crept up a few yards, and Lucy had a look.

Maria stood at the edge of a clearing talking with two shirtless, dreadlocked Rastamen, both of whom carried machetes. They were too far off to hear, but the subject under discussion was clear since Maria had her bag open, and handed them American money. In spite of the money, or maybe because of the amount, the Rastas did not look happy as they counted it. The clearing contained rows of ten-to-fifteen-foot-tall ganja plants sparkling in the light, the unique leaf configuration unmistakable. A blind man would have recognized them as easily as Lucy did, however. After all, the odor of ripe cannabis was so powerful even thirty yards away she could feel a high coming on. At least a hundred plants occupied the clearing, and every single one stood tall, bushy, vigorously healthy. An herbal wonderland.

The sun threw light on the green-golden pot plants. Lucy seized the perfect photo opportunity. After the money changed hands, Maria wandered among the plants for a moment, admiring them. Then she turned her attention back to the Rastamen. With scarcely controlled lust she gazed upon their knotty, muscular physiques, shirtless, gleaming like ebony in the sun.

Lucy shot a dozen pictures, then she and Jossie high-tailed it out of there and beat it back to the car. Hidden in the bushes in the cab, they peered through the branches, waiting. Soon Maria emerged, alone, smoking a huge spliff. She threw it down, still burning, climbed in the Jeep, turned it around, and headed right at them. They dropped onto their respective seats as she passed, and so couldn't tell if she saw them or not. Either way, she didn't stop. Jossie gave it a minute, then pulled out of the bush, whipped around, and headed down the mountain.

Two minutes later they arrived back at the edge of the little village. Jossie stopped. Ahead they saw the yellow Jeep parked behind the dead truck in front of the building with the neon beer sign in the window. A vintage MG convertible was parked beyond the truck. Lucy knew that car, for she had seen it in the parking lot at the Grand Strand Hotel, and elsewhere: the pride and joy of Jefferson Hababi. "What now, Lucy?"

"I don't know, but I'd sure like to know what they're talkin' about in there. Damn."

"Hey, that lady don't know me, I go listen, no problem. It's just a little bar, I just a local man. But who she meetin'? Who drive that fancy set of wheels?"

"Jefferson Hababi. His daddy runs the hotel. He's just a kid. You been here before?"

"One or two time, darlin'. I get around, see." He grinned, and opened the door.

"Wait!" Lucy said. She pulled her tape recorder out of her bag, pushed the red record button, and handed it to him. "It's running. You don't have to touch a thing. There's proba-bly twenty minutes of tape on this side. I have no idea if it'll pick anything up, sitting in your pocket, but let's give it a try."

He put it in his shirt pocket. "No problem, Lucy. I just check it out long enough to have a Striper, then come back. They come out first you just duck, okay?"

Lucy sat for five minutes in the backseat of the taxicab, sweating in the stifling heat, watching the door of the bar. A woman stepped out of a house across the road, stared at Lucy while she shook out a rug, then went back in. Two chickens scratched their way along the roadside. Lucy decided to get some fresh air, try to calm herself down. She opened the car door and was abruptly grabbed by two men, so quickly she had no chance to struggle. One covered her mouth and eyes, the other grabbed her arms. They were strong and firm, but gentle enough that she knew they meant not to hurt her. At least not for the moment.

They quickly marched her a few yards and eased her into the backseat of a car, then tied her hands loosely in her lap. The doors closed, the motor started, and the man right next to her said, "I am going to take my hand off your eyes and then put a blindfold on you. I want you to close your eyes until I have the blindfold in place. I won't hurt you. I will use both of my hands, so please do not cry out." Lucy did as she was told. As scared as she was, there was something calm and reassuring about the way these—kidnappers?—handled her. She felt threatened, of course, but they were taking care to scare her as little as possible, and to hurt her not at all. Once the blindfold was in place, the man said, "Okay, sister, you can—"

"What the hell do you think you're doing? Where are you taking me?" Lucy cried out, but not loudly.

"You will see in a few moments, Miss Ripken," the man at her side said mildly. "Just remain calm, please. My name is Jacob. Lucien is driving. We are taking you to see a friend, and it is important that you do not know the way."

After ten minutes of bumping and winding uphill, they came to a halt. Lucy's hands were untied and her eyes uncovered.

She was in the backseat of a sixties' Chevy. A bearded Rasta with sunbleached, waist-long dreads sat on her left; another, with shorter, darker dreads, sat behind the wheel. They had parked at the side of a potholed dirt road, in a setting of pastoral poverty: a couple of painted cinderblock houses, scattered dead cars and trucks, dogs, chickens, children running about. Mango, papaya, and banana trees grew everywhere. A woman in a bright yellow dress tended a fire over which a big black pot had been suspended between three sticks. Encircling everything, the jungle. The soft-spoken Jacob said, "I'm very sorry about the manner in which we accomplish this, Lucy Ripken, but we have to surprise you or you never come."

She shrugged, rubbing her wrists, shaking blood into her hands. "I guess. So why am I here?"

He opened the door. "Bernard wants to talk to you."

"Bernard?" she said, following him out of the car.

"Yah, mon. He de elder," said Jacob. "Right this way."

She followed him around the back of a house. They passed a well-tended vegetable garden in a clearing, went through a thicket, and then Jacob opened a gate and they stepped onto a path that led into the bush. Two minutes later, they came upon another clearing, occupied by a forest of pot plants, with a wooden shack on one side. They approached the shack. "Hallo, Bernard," Jacob called out.

A wooden door swung open. An older Rastaman stuck his head out in a cloud of pungent ganja smoke. With his gray beard and dreads, he looked like an Afro-Jamaican version of the Maharishi Mahesh Yogi, whom Lucy had followed briefly once upon a time. He grinned at Lucy. "Lucy

Ripken. I and I so glad you could make it, sister," he said. He took a hit on a huge spliff he was holding, and offered it to her.

"Like I had a choice," she answered, declining the joint with a shake of her head. Jacob took the spliff from Bernard and puffed on it.

"Have some herb, sister," he said. "Bernard wants to talk to you. Good to get some herb in your head. Besides, so much smoke in he shack you get high anyway." He grinned. Shrugging, she took the spliff from Jacob, had a puff, and coughed.

Bernard laughed. "Come in, come in, Lucy," he said. "Sound like you out of practice."

"It's been a while," she gasped, coughing as she handed him the giant joint and stepped into the darkness. Sunlight filtered through cracks. A table, a couple of chairs, a bed, a few implements, Haile Selassie on the wall in full dress uniform, Jah, Ras, the Lion of Judah. The pot hit her as her eyes adjusted to the smoky dim light. The first thing the high brought was an intensified awareness of the man living here. Bernard's psychic as well as physical scent, his essence, was infused into the walls and floors and air. He was peaceful, radiant, and it all came through him from that image on the wall. She briefly studied the little emperor, long ago typecast by those in the Western world as a corrupt despot, not the messiah the Rastafarians considered him to be.

"So, Lucy, you must be wanting to know why you are here," said Bernard. "Why don't you sit down. I and I tell."

He handed her the spliff and waved at a wooden chair. She took a puff and sat. The floor was dirt, worn hard as tile from years of living.

"Yeah, as a matter of fact," she said, handing back the spliff. She felt very, very high. This was a good sign. The last few times she'd smoked dope her most compelling urge had been to run and hide, review and hate her entire life, take a valium, and pray for sleep. But now she felt . . . luminous in the dark little wood hut. Bernard's eyes glowed. He took another hit, then put out the spliff in a bowl on the table between them.

"You want some tea or water?"

"Water. Water sounds wonderful," she said. "Cool, clear water." He poured her a glass from an earthen pitcher, and she drank. "Now then, Bernard. What's with the hijinks on the highway? There I was, peacefully minding my own business, spying on some people from the backseat of a taxi cab, when suddenly I find myself waylaid, bound and gagged, dragged like a hostage into the bush."

"Jacob did not hurt you, I hope?" Bernard said.

"Well, no, but—"

"The people you were spying on—the woman Maria Verde, and the young hotelman Hababi—you know what they are doing?"

"Well, yes, sort of."

"Let me tell you a story, Lucy," he said. "But first, I and I want to show you something." He stood up, walked through a doorway into the other room of the shack, and reappeared a moment later. He held up a foil-wrapped brick. Ganja. From the sea, where she'd thrown it.

"Jesus," she gasped. "Where did you . . . how did you . . ."

"In a moment." He put the brick on the table between them and sat down. "Now for my story. Here in these northern hills we have been smoking the herb for many years, like many brothers and sisters all over Jamaica, you see? Now, down in the south near the city, for twenty years the brothers have been making a lot of money smuggling, selling ganja to the Americans, taking much of the herb off the island and turning it into a commodity. It is of very great value up there, I understand. But the Americans do not understand how it is to be used. They do not understand the spiritual values, see, because they do not understand how the herb brings I and I closer to Jah." He smiled at the portrait on the wall. "I know, a little dead African emperor man . . . but it is the idea that matters. There is no idea in the head of the boy in Brooklyn who sells the ganja on the street, except the idea of money. And all that drug money has been very bad for Jamaica. We are poor, but in these hills we are rich in the things that count to us. We do not eat flesh. We can grow what we need to eat, the weather treats us well, and we have no need for televisions, and fancy cars, and all the other American things. But tell that to the boys down in Kingston town, and they laugh in your face and call you country man, spirit man, like it some kind of insult. That no insult. I and I been a country man and a spirit man all my life.

"And so up here on the north coast we see the hotels

coming in, and we think the drug dealers and the posses come behind them. Sure enough they do. Already one smuggler ring happening, some people way close to Dexter Hanley. Then these boys in the tourist business try start up another one. We want to stop them, see? We want to keep our herb up here where it belong. We don't want the guns, and the televisions, and the fast cars running over our goats and our dogs like they do down in Kingston town.

"So we watching very careful like, and see what you people at the hotel be doing, think maybe you up to try smuggling some yourself. But then when you take the ganja out and throw it in the sea, we realize that not the case."

"How did you know what I was doing?"

"Our man at the Grand Strand. Your friend Desmond."

"Desmond is . . . is one of you?"

"Sacrificed his dreads for Jah. A painful moment for him, but then, all kinds of violent brothers be wearing dreads these days, so you never know who be what anymore. Besides, Desmond love the wind, eh, just like you. The hotel job is good for him. But you see, we try to get the gangs disputing with each other, so waste they energy with that, so my boy Jossie put you on to the other gang—he part of them but he really with us up here—so you learn from them how Joey Ruskin planning to send the pot back, and—"

"Wait. Wait a minute. So Jossie the taxi-man works for you, but he's in the rival gang?"

"Not work, sister. He with us." He grinned. "We not a gang, but we country man pretty smart, you see?"

"I'm beginning to. So Jossie led me to one gang who tried to use me to break up the other gang and get their dope."

"Those two bad boys who hit on you and your DEA friend the other night, they work for Adrian Kensington. He work for Racky Barnes. Racky Barnes work for . . . I don't know. That's the other gang."

"How did you know about those guys that attacked us, and how did you know Harold was DEA?"

He just grinned. "Eyes of Jah, sister, eyes of Jah."

"So why bring me up here and tell me all this, Bernard?"

"Because Desmond ask me to. After he see you dump the ganja and know you not looking for to make money off the herb, he says to me that you need to be informed about these matters."

"I suppose it was Desmond who brought you this," she said, putting a hand on the brick.

"He dive for it soon as the Coast Guard go that day. Took him five minutes to find it."

"And now you can sell it and make your own money."

"No, we don't sell. We trade with our neighbors, we smoke, I and I keep to ourself. No money dealing."

"That's very nice. But what do you want from me, Bernard?"

"Tell you beware. You have done your job for us, like it or no, so we responsible for you. Some of the men that Joey Ruskin worked with here are very angry about their missing ganja. They have no idea we have taken it back. They think maybe you fake them out. Then the other boys angry at your friend for kicking they butt. You got everybody angry. You best get back to USA, I and I believing."

"I'm going tomorrow."

"That is good. So now you know, and you can go. Be careful until you go, please. Jacob will take you back to the village." Without another word he showed her out the door of his hut.

During the ten-minute, stoned, blindfolded car ride back down the mountain, Lucy bounced ideas about the players around in her head and came up with some loose ends: the big boys. Jackson Hababi and Rackstraw Barnes. Was Hababi Junior protecting Hababi Senior? Not likely, with all that bad blood between them. On the other side, could the trail lead from Adrian Kensington to Rackstraw Barnes and from there right into the office of the PM? Jesus, what had she stumbled onto? She longed for Harold, for a good sail, for a way down off the pot so as to de-intensify the anxiety that possessed her.

They removed her blindfold. The cab, the Jeep, and the MG had left the village. She and Jacob went into the bar. She had a quick look around. Nothing to see. Jacob drove her back down the mountain, all the way to the hotel, and dropped her at the guardhouse by the gate. The cruise down the mountain and the passage of time had brought her back to a near normal state of mind. She headed down the Grand Strand driveway ready for a post-ganja feeding frenzy, as it was lunch hour on La Terrazzo Grande.

She stopped for messages at the front desk. There was one, to call Harry in his room, urgent, immediately. She hurried to the house phone and rang him. "Lucy, is that you?" he barked, halfway into the first ring. "God, I was so worried about you. I—"

"Yeah, it's me, I'm fine," she said. "Just going to lunch."

"Wait. I mean, I'll come with you. But come over here first, okay? I've got something to show you."

"Be there in five minutes."

En route, glancing over the terrace as she passed by, she saw Mike Nack and Jefferson Hababi having lunch together.

Harold opened the door before she had a chance to knock, and enveloped her in a hug that she instantly, instinctively, reciprocated. She held him, then found his lips with hers. The kiss quickly turned passionate. When at last they broke apart and looked at each other, they knew the fight had passed: the relationship was back on course. "Goddamn, Luce," he said, "Where have you been? You wouldn't believe what—"

"I've been up in cockpit country, mon, breaking the law with the Rastamen."

"Cockpit country? You went up there? What the . . . hey, listen, this thing is really getting out of hand. I was walking down the beach this morning, down toward the mansion, you know, and guess what I found wadded in the high tide sand?"

"What?"

"This." He held up an empty Grand Strand pillowcase. "What you sank the dope in."

She laughed. "Imagine that. Sorry, Harry, but I'm way ahead of you."

"Whaddaya mean?"

She gave him the lowdown on her trip, holding nothing back. Afterward, he said, "Jesus, what a tangled tale. Well, I guess my revelation that Rackstraw Barnes owns the mansion doesn't mean much, does it?"

"The mansion down the bay? Barnes? Really?"

"Yeah. And I hear tell when Hababi started planning this hotel, Barnes threatened to bring him down. He wasn't too happy about tourists treading on his private sand."

"But where did he get the money to buy a pad like that?"

"Let's talk about it over lunch," Harry said. "I seem to recall, from my dope smoking days, that one gets a little hungry. I'll bet you're starved."

"You might say so, Harry," she said. "But you know what?" she added, suddenly, acutely, hungry for something else. "I think lunch can wait another half an hour. I've got this urge—this irresistible, undeniable urge—to . . ." She smiled, took him by the collar of his shirt, and led him back across the room ". . . take your clothes off, Mr. DEA Man."

When they finished an hour later the lunch hour had ended, so instead they slipped into bathing suits and out onto the beach with room service burgers and Red Stripes. They sat beneath an umbrella, ate, and watched the sea. "You know," said Lucy. "I could teach you to windsurf today. It's perfect out there." A light chop stirred the water outside Naked Beach, where they could just make out an array of nudists.

"Forget it, Luce," Harry said. "Save it for another life. Let's just hang here, and figure out what the hell we're gonna do tonight."

"Tonight? What's so special about tonight?"

"We are out of here tomorrow, kid. Anyone gonna make a move, tonight's the night."

She contemplated the possibility. "Yeah, I guess so. So what do we do?"

"How about I buy you dinner at the Pasta Piazza, or whatever the hell they call it?"

"You're so generous."

"To a fault."

"Meanwhile, I do want to take a little sail. But you should check out the photos I shot today. Wait'll you see Maria, in her purple dress, frolicking among the marijuana trees."

She got up, killed her beer, and wandered down the beach past the prone bodies of Susie Adams and Louise Rousseau and Dave Mullins, lying in a row on the sand, unconscious as they barbecued in the hot tropical sun.

"Hey, Desmond," she said. He was washing down a kayak. "How ya doin'?"

"Okay, Lucy. How you?" He gave her a look.

"Not too bad, *mi amigo*."

"I'm sure. Oh, by the way," he said, "I have something for you."

"What's that?"

"Just this." He handed her tape machine over with a smile. "I don't know what on it but our friend Jossie say he thought you may be wantin' to hear it."

"Jeesh," she said. "You guys are amazing."

"Praise Jah," he whispered. "Now," he went on, his voice returning to normal. "You want to take one last sail, Luce? I think it going to pick up out there."

She looked out to sea. "Really? Yeah, why not? Can I stash this here?"

"I put it in my bag, give it to you after we sail." He stuck the tape recorder in his knapsack and threw it behind the counter in the hut. "Nobody go in there but me and Leroy, and Leroy sure I rip his lungs out I catch him in my stuff."

"And you would, of course."

He grinned. "I and I a peaceful man, Lucy. But long as Leroy fear my fist, think I bad boy, he not cause no trouble."

The rest of Lucy's last day at the Grand Strand proceeded uneventfully; or rather, it was full of events, but they were of the kind one would expect on a Caribbean vacation. She sailed for an hour with Desmond, and no mention was made of anything beyond the wind. Then she and Harold played three sets of tennis against Mickey Wolf and the club pro. They got thrashed. After that they drank beer with Mickey, during which time Harold's secret identity was not mentioned. Then they retired to Lucy's room to make love again, finishing the frolic in time for a sunset swim. This swim was followed by separation for showers, grooming, and dressing for dinner. Lucy felt simultaneously burned out and blissed out. She had gotten just enough sun; she had done some good windsurfing; she had her story. And she was, she thought, in love. The "case" be damned! Let Harold handle it. It was his job, after all.

Before the tennis session they had listened to the tape that Jossie had made in the little bar up in the hills. The sound was muffled and staticky, but they could just decipher, among the patois jive of the locals and the rumbling wash of Jossie's beer arriving in an empty belly, the voices of Jefferson Hababi and Maria Verde in a low-toned, controlled argument. The gist of it: Maria threatened him. Jefferson swore he didn't give her away, said he blamed Ruskin. Maria asked what that bitch wanted. Jeff said he didn't know, probably a cut of the dope money. Maria asked where was the dope, Jeff said he didn't know, she hadn't told him. Maria said he didn't know much, did he. He said he guessed not, but. She said don't give me any of your excuses you half-baked rich punk, just get me what you said you would, by tonight.

When Lucy and Harold discovered the three sauce options available at the Pasta Piazza, they decided the chef had apparently smoked several spliffs before embarking on his Caribbean version of California cuisine, for how else could one explain fettucine Alfredo with ackee and papaya, or fusilli with clam/mango olive oil, or spinach spaghetti with lobster and guineps in garlic-infused white wine? They decided to go Chinese instead, and headed out to the Grill under the pavilion on the pier. As darkness fell they held hands and strolled the promenade, caressed by the tropical air, basking in the afterglow of a day in love in the sun. For some reason—the pot, the sun, the beer—the whole murder and marijuana scenario had drifted out of focus in her mind. She had figured out a lot of stuff, but she had nowhere to go with it. Harold could use the information, but what good would it do her?

"That's why I gave up dope, Lucy," Harold said when she told him of her ambivalence. They were seated out on the pier, eating Chinese food by moonlight and candlelight. "You lose moral focus. Get lost in a relativistic swamp, know what I mean?"

"Not really, Harry," she said. "I mean, I smoked the dope this morning, for God's sake. Three hits on a spliff. It's been almost twelve hours."

"THC stays in your bloodstream for days, Lucy."

"So what, you're telling me that THC in my bloodstream has corrupted my morals? This is getting rather obtuse, Harold. If not downright irritating. What the hell do you expect me to do?"

He laughed. "Sorry. You're probably better off uninvolved, anyway, Luce. This thing could get dangerous."

"Oh, an assault with a motorboat and a kidnapping

aren't dangerous enough for you? Uninvolved? You're the cop, but I've done all the work this week. Don't patronize me, Harry."

"Hey, back off, doll. I know you've been on the case. And you've been incredible. But they know we're leaving, and there's a lot of money at stake here. They must figure we've got their dope stashed somewhere."

"Well, maybe, but I suspect this Bernard may have put out the word that the dope is back in his hands. And anyway, Mike Nack and Jefferson Hababi are not exactly heavyweights, Harry."

"No, but whoever possibly has his knife at Mike Nack's throat might be. Like those rude boys the other night. And don't underestimate Jeff Hababi. He talked too much and he knows it. He's a scared kid with a cruel father, and sometimes there's nothing . . . no one . . . more dangerous."

"But look at this, Harry," she said, gesturing expansively at the moonlit sea stretching away before them. "Does this look dangerous to you?"

He took hold of both her hands. "You're right. It's too gorgeous a night to worry. Let's go back to my room, eh? I bet you could use another massage." He stood.

"Sounds . . . inspiring."

Dropping her hands, he said, "Listen, I gotta do one thing. I'll meet you back at my room in, say, fifteen minutes."

"What are you up to, Harry?"

He paused. "Checking on our boy Mike Nack."

"Nack? That weasel isn't going to do anything, Harry.

Take my word for it. The one to watch out for around here is Maria Verde."

"I know. Prudence is on her case. But I just want to make sure little Mikey is behaving himself."

Harry took off. Lucy declined another glass of wine, which flowed endlessly, freely, in the Chinese restaurant as it did everywhere else at the hotel. She sat for a moment, watching the light on the water, composing the opening paragraph of her article on the hotel design, wondering what would happen between her and Harry back in New York. Putting that out of mind in favor of the beckoning delights of a last night on the Caribbean, enveloped in the cocoon of waterfront luxury, she rose and strolled off the restaurant pier and down the beach toward the guest room wing. A flashily dressed five-piece band held forth on stage on the terrace, thumping out that primitive, relentless, and utterly engaging reggae beat. The dance floor was crowded with sunburned, exhausted, drunk, and happy revelers, swaying now in time to a reggae version of "My Way."

Lucy slowed to watch the scene for a moment. Among the crowd she spotted Mickey in a red dress dancing with her tennis pro, and Dave Mullins with Louise Rousseau, an odd but unexpectedly well-matched pair bopping to the beat. Sandy Rollins loitered alone at the foot of the stage, eyes on the drummer. In the warm night breeze, with music throbbing and alcohol flowing, the vacationeers and their chroniclers from the travel press partied on as they had all week. A storm had crashed through, a woman had gone mad, a

smuggling operation had been exposed and blown, two people had died, and it all added up to a mere ripple of distraction in an unstoppable wave of pleasure-seeking. Lucy sighed,
ever the wine-drunk existentialist; she felt herself separate
and alone, and she contemplated that universe of aloneness
as she headed down the beach.

Strolling along with her feet in the sand washed by warm
salty water, she looked ahead to life back in New York and
decided that she and Harold would work it out, one way or
another. So he was a cop! Until this morning, she hadn't
smoked a joint in five years. She hadn't done a line of coke in
nearly as long. She didn't really hold with busting people for
drugs, but it didn't have to get between them. Drugs weren't
part of her life, one way or another. Harold had his reasons
for doing what he did, and she could respect them.

"You can stop right there," said a woman, speaking softly
as she stepped out of the shadows in front of Lucy. Maria
Verde, Lucy knew instantly. The faint light gleamed on the
weapon she pointed toward Lucy. A gun.

"Maria," she said. "I wondered where you were this
evening."

"Cut the chitchat, Ripken. You know what I want. Where
is it?"

"Where is what?"

Verde stepped closer—close enough to jam the barrel of
the pistol into Lucy's belly. "Hey, easy there, I just ate." Maria
poked harder. "Ow!"

"You know what your problem is, Ripken? You're just

too damned smart, aren't you? Think you got it all figured out, think you can just waltz in here and rip off the professionals. Well, think otherwise, bitch." She poked her again, harder. "Where is the fucking ganja?"

"At the bottom of the deep blue sea, Maria," Lucy said.

Maria hesitated just an instant. "Bullshit. I know you dumped it, but your pal Ipswich picked it up."

"No, he picked up the empty sack. It washed up on the—"

"Shut up," she hissed. "Stop with your fucking jive. What'd you do, sell it to that fuck Kensington?"

"Kensington? Who's Kensington?" Maria hit her, sort of hard, on the side of the head with the gun. "Ow. Jesus, Maria, you're hurting me." The woman's malevolence was real, and beginning to frighten Lucy. The gun had a silencer, the music was loud, the rage in Maria's voice was loudest of all.

"Fucking right I hurt you, cunt. And I will again. Don't lie to me. I know you met with Kensington. You think that little worm Jefferson Hababi can keep anything from me?"

"Jefferson Hababi? What are you talking about?" Maria hit her again, harder. "Ow, shit. Yeah, so I met with him. So what?"

"So you'd better tell me where my ganja is or you can say hello to your good friend Angus Wilson, 'cause I'm gonna do you like I did him if you don't start talking, bitch."

"*It was you?*"

"That's right, Ripken. Which means I have nothing to lose. You understand?" She shoved her with the gun, turning her around. "Let's go. Down the beach. Away from this rat fuck hotel. Then we'll talk, and you'll tell me what I want to know."

As they walked past the edge of the hotel and down the dark, empty beach, Lucy was terrified, but her head buzzed. Verde the killer. She was up in the tower, probably keeping watch for Ruskin. Angus wandering about in a fit of insomnia. The tide way out; he got his feet wet, walked to the island, climbed the tower stairs to get a view, saw the boat come in, the unloading, Maria shoved him out the window—or forced him to jump—no, she probably just got the gun this very day, that was what she demanded from Jefferson in the cafe, so she must have surprised Wilson, shoved him out the window, and then she and Joey set him up in the pool. Tough luck, Angus. Jesus, if she would do that, and she would tell me about it, she's only got one thing in mind for me. Fucking crazy woman!

"So I gather Jefferson was able to get you a gun today, then, eh, Maria?" she croaked, struggling to sound cool.

"Jefferson? Get a gun? What are you—"

"Up in the village. Your meeting. After your visit to the pot farm. I photographed you, and taped it, and—" Maria slammed her head with the gun. "Ow, fuck," said Lucy, as blood flowed down her temple. "What are you doing? Are you nuts?"

"What do you think?" Maria hissed. "What do you fucking think, you brainless bitch. You think I'm in this for my health?" She pointed the gun at Lucy. "Now, where the fuck did you stash the pot, or who did you sell it to? I want the dope, or the money. Talk."

A dark form flew out of the shadows and crashed into Maria Verde, sending the gun flying toward the water. Lucy ran for the gun as the two struggled. She found it, grabbed it, and whirled to train it on Maria. She'd never held a gun in her life. The only thing she could think was how heavy it was. Maria suddenly burst free, slammed the other person in the head with her arm, flooring him, then took off, charging into the darkness beyond the beach. She disappeared instantly. Lucy ran to her fallen savior. "Are you all right?" she said, crouching down.

"Yes, I'm fine." Prudence Fallowsmith, on the job! "I'm sorry I let her go so far with you, Lucy."

"Hey, don't worry, I thought I was a dead duck there, but you saved my life."

"I had no idea the woman was so desperate," Prudence said.

"That makes two of us. A raving fucking psycho, if you'll pardon my French."

"Let's get back," said Prudence, as Lucy helped her find her feet. "Why don't you give me that?" she added, reaching for the gun. "We'll need it for evidence."

"Evidence? Against who? What crime?"

"Try Jefferson Hababi, for starters. We have very strict gun control laws here, and we know he supplied this weapon."

"Waste of time, Pru. Popping him will get you exactly

nowhere. But let's talk to Harry about it." They hustled back to the hotel, to Harry's room, and banged on the door. He opened it, wearing nothing but a pair of bikini underwear, his glasses, and a horny grin. "Hey, Luce," he said. "I was wondering what happened to— Prudence! What's up?" He slipped modestly behind the door. With evident distaste Prudence held up the gun between thumb and forefinger, barrel pointed down, as if it was a stiff and smelly dead fish.

"A gift from Maria Verde," Prudence said.

"Jesus," said Harry. "Let me get a pair of pants on."

Prudence left an hour later, after they'd all calmed down and Harry talked her out of going to the local police with the gun to start a full-tilt investigation. Instead, he kept it. He and Lucy managed to get to bed in the middle of the night. This was the first night they slept together and didn't have sex, thanks to the malevolent ghost of Maria Verde hovering in the room. They got up at six a.m. and went for a swim together in the pink and gray-green light of dawn. The farewell breakfast for the press group was scheduled for eight a.m. on La Terrazzo Grande. After the swim, Lucy went to her room alone to pack.

After memorizing the license plate of Maria Verde's Jeep from the one image she had shot of it, Lucy packed her things, as always carefully arranging her cameras, lights, and miscellaneous gear in the bags so as to minimize the possibility of damage. She dressed in light pants and a button-down shirt for travel, left a coat out for the ride home from JFK, and headed off to Harold's to pick him up en route to breakfast.

Harold had put on his old-fashioned tropical linen suit, and looked dapper enough to eat. Lucy told him the Jeep's license plate number and he made a phone call. "They'll let me know who owns it as soon as possible," he said, hanging up the phone. "Hopefully before the breakfast is over."

Gathered at two tables on the seaward side of the terrace, the survivors swilled coffee, beer, and mimosas and compared notes. Louise Rousseau, Sandy Rollins, and Jefferson Hababi sat at one table with a couple of Grand Strand officials. At the other table, Michelle Stedman sat next to Jackson Hababi. Also at the table sat Mike Nack, looking dyspeptic, avoiding eye contact with Lucy; and Susie Adams, too tan, hungover, clutching one of her long girlish cigarettes like it was a lifeline. There were two empty seats at the second table, with Mickey Wolf, grinning a wolfish grin, poised between them. Harold and Lucy took them.

Missing from the original crew were Jim Strauss, Jane Strauss, Angus Wilson, Allie Margolis, Joey Ruskin, and Maria Verde. Dead, deranged, or disappeared. They were a much-diminished group, and after a few hits of coffee and greetings to all at the table, Lucy naturally couldn't help but saying so, to Jackson Hababi, of course. "Here's to The Incredible Shrinking Press Trip, eh, Jackson?" she said, hoisting her coffee.

He managed a little smile. "Yes, most unfortunate," he said. "Well, at least the hotel is filling up even as your ranks have been diminished."

"It's getting so trade travel writing's as dangerous as combat work," said Harold. "You'd think we were in a war zone, with all the casualties."

"Yeah," said Mickey. "I thought the worst I had to fear down here was sunburn, maybe a little gluttony and alcoholism, but noooo—we get flaming motorboat wrecks, and heart attacks, and journalists going crazy. But it's a beautiful hotel, Jackson, and it's been a gas," she added with a grin. "Right, Luce?"

"A real gas," Lucy said. "Eh, what, Mike?" she added, all innocence, smiling at him.

"Yeah, that's right, Lucy," Nack said, then went back to staring into his coffee.

"But where is the delightful Miss Verde this morning?" said Harold. "Has anybody seen her?"

Lucy watched Jackson Hababi, who didn't react. Then she glanced at Jefferson Hababi, seated at the other table. He stared at Lucy, as if trying to read in her face what had happened. She grinned at him. "Hey, Jeff," she said. "How are you doin' today?" He turned away from her. "Jefferson seems to be in a bad mood today, Jackson. What do you suppose is wrong with him?"

"I can't imagine, Miss Ripken," said Jackson. "Except that he is heartbroken to see you all going. As we all are here at the Grand Strand, of course." With that he tapped his spoon on the edge of his coffee cup.

"Here comes the combination plate," Mickey muttered. "Hogwash, bullshit, and whitewash."

"I just wanted to take a moment to tell you all how much we've enjoyed having you here as our guests," said Jackson. "I know it's been a rocky week, but hotel openings always are." Right, thought Lucy, although usually you don't have two or three attempted murders, one successful, plus an accidental death by exploding boat. "This has been an exceptionally difficult one for a lot of reasons. But all that is behind us now, the Strand is open and flourishing. As you can see"—he waved his arms to take in the expanse of La Terrazzo Grande, which was close to full—"the people are responding to our new concept, the all-inclusive luxury hotel. We are running about eleven percent ahead of our projected bookings for this month, and March looks even better." He went on, intently avoiding even a mention of Angus Wilson or Joey Ruskin. Lucy had thought he might attempt to eulogize, but no, better to just pretend they never existed. She stopped listening, turning her attention instead to the beach and the sea. She could see Desmond washing kayaks, and Leroy raking the sand smooth. The breeze riffled in the palm branches, and out on Naked Beach, the tower watched the shore with big black empty eyes. She would never come back to the Grand Strand, even if they paid her.

Jackson's speech ended, the breakfast gathering lost

focus, people rose to head back to their rooms. The bus for the airport was due to leave in an hour. "Oh, Jackson," said Lucy, "could we have a word with you, in private? A couple of final questions I need answered for my article."

"Certainly, Miss Ripken. Would you like to come to my office?"

"Well, yes . . . but could I invite Jefferson as well?" She winked at Hababi. "He could use some seasoning, as far as the press goes, don't you think?" she added quickly. "Jefferson, we're meeting in Jackson's office now, and we want you to come along," she called out to him. "I've got some operations questions I think only you can answer."

"But I . . . I've got some . . ."

"Come along now, Jeff," said Jackson. "This is their last hour here. If there's one thing you need to learn in this business, it's that you have to accommodate the press."

"Sounds good to me," said Harry. "If nobody minds, I think I'll come, too."

"That's fine," said Jackson nervously. "That's just fine," he repeated.

The four of them left the terrace and made their way back through the lobby to the administrative offices. Hababi's office was surprisingly spartan: four rattan chairs, a matching rattan table desk with a glass top, some folk art on the walls. Jackson sat behind the desk and waved at the other chairs. "Please, sit down. As you can see I'm not one for formality."

Harry sat directly facing Jackson. Lucy and Jefferson took the other seats. "Nice stuff. I love rattan," said Harry.

"Yes, it's perfect for this climate. And very cheap, of course," Jackson added with a laugh. "We spend all our money on our guests, I'm afraid." He stopped short, got down to business. "So, Miss Ripken, what can I do for you?"

"Harold?" she said. Harold pulled the gun, with its ugly silencer still attached, out of his pocket and quickly placed it on the desktop. "You could start by telling me what you know about this."

Jackson stared at the gun for a few seconds. "What in God's name is that, and why have you brought it here?" he said angrily. "I don't know what you're trying to . . ." He reached for the phone. "I think the police might be interested in this."

"Jefferson, would you like to explain where I got this gun?" Lucy said. Jackson put the phone down and looked at his stepson.

"No, I . . . I don't know anything about . . ." He stopped. "I've never seen it before," he said, summoning up enough courage to lie half-convincingly.

Lucy pulled her tape recorder out of her pocket, turned it on, and set it on the table. The muffled voices of Maria Verde and Jefferson Hababi filled the room. At the end, after Maria demanded that he get what he said he would for her tonight, Lucy turned it off. "And so you did your job, Jefferson," she said. "Maria got her gun."

"Who made that . . . where did you . . . I don't know what you're talking about," Jefferson said lamely.

"Maria Verde and you, in a bar in a little town in the Blue

Mountains, Jefferson. I followed her up there. She was driving a Jeep registered to the Grand Strand Hotel Corporation, by the way, and I have a picture of it in my camera. She met with her pot growers, and then she met with you to talk about the dope deal they were trying to put together, which had been falling apart ever since the night Angus Wilson died."

The Hababis glowered at each other. "The night Angus Wilson was murdered by Maria Verde," Lucy went on. "Angus stumbled on a dope deal going down, strictly by accident, and she pushed him out of the tower and he broke his neck. You didn't even want to think about what really happened to him out there, did you, Jackson? Not because you were involved, which is what I first thought, since Wilson might have been wise to your financial troubles and how they were affecting the hotel. But it wasn't that complicated, really. The idea that anything might get in the way of your hotel opening, what with all your money worries, just made you crazy, and so, when Jeff said he'd take care of it, you let him. Let him cover it up. Let him have the body cremated without an autopsy, against the express wishes of Mrs. Wilson—I saw her when she was here, in spite of your efforts to stop me—so that the cause of death could never be ascertained. You also let him give Joey Ruskin free rein to set up a dope ring right under your bloody nose, Mr. Jackson Hababi. One of your personal house servants—a man named Rudy— is also part of it. I guess you didn't know about it, but you sure as hell didn't look too hard, did you?" Jackson sat stock-still behind his desk and didn't say a word.

Lucy turned and said, "Jefferson, I know I told you I would keep your 'role' in this a secret, but when you provided Maria Verde with a gun that she intended to use on me, I figured all deals were off between us, my friend. And so here we are."

She sat back. After a moment, Jackson said, "So what do you want, Miss Ripken?"

Jefferson lunged for the gun, grabbed it, and waved it wildly around. "Fuck what she wants. And fuck you, too, Daddy," he snarled, then pointed the gun at his stepfather. "If you hadn't been such a bastard, none of this would have had to happen. Don't you—"

"Put the gun down, Jefferson, you idiot," Jackson said. "Just put it—"

"My name is not Jefferson, it's Adjami, goddammit," he shouted, training the gun on his stepfather. "Adjami Hajjar," he said, tears starting in his eyes.

"I told you to put the gun down, you fool," said Jackson, rising from his seat, incapable of believing that Jefferson would actually shoot him.

"I'm not a fool, you bastard," shouted Adjami, and pulled the trigger just as Harold tossed the bullets into a bowl on the table. They rattled about, then stopped.

"It's okay, Hababi," Harold said. "It's not loaded."

"Fuck you fuck you fuck . . ." Jefferson shrieked as he

flung the gun at the wall and lunged for the door. Harry leaped up and tackled him to the floor. He had him face-down and under control in seconds. Jefferson sobbed and slobbered; Jackson, frozen behind his desk, stared down at him, unable to keep the contemptuous sneer off his face.

They talked a deal. Hababi agreed, in exchange for their not contacting the police or writing anything about what they knew, to increase the wages of his employees by thirty per-cent immediately, and by another seventy percent by the end of the year. He also agreed to donate ten percent of his prof-its, scarce as they might be with all his bankers baying for payments, to a foundation that he would set up to collect money to build a new health clinic in Ocho Negros.

He also agreed to move Jefferson to another job at an-other hotel at the other end of the island, effective immedi-ately.

At the end of the meeting, Lucy pulled her backup tape recorder, borrowed from Mickey just for the occasion, out of her pocket and laid it on the table. "Just so you know: this meeting is on tape. There will be copies left with friends here. I'm sure your wife—she's the money behind FunClubs, right, Jackson?—would not be pleased to know about these sleazy dealings. On the other hand, I'm sure Mr. Dexter Hanley wouldn't mind at all having a copy of this tape, when elec-tion time comes around again. I'll be checking up on things, believe me. We are blackmailing you, Mr. Jackson Hababi, and there is absolutely nothing you can do about it." She put the recorder in her bag, and they rose and left the office.

En route to the bus Harold said he'd forgotten something and headed back toward his room. Later, Lucy realized she should have known what was up—he'd taken his suitcase with him.

He missed the bus to the airport. Waiting for him until the last possible minute, Lucy was last to board. Big Wilbert back at the wheel, they headed off to Montego Bay and a flight to New York City where the temperature hovered at thirty-six degrees, exactly fifty degrees colder than Ocho Negros. Slouched in the back, Mike Nack glowered at her. Maria Verde was nowhere to be seen. That didn't concern Lucy. After all, Harold Ipswich was not on the bus either. Instead, he was on the case, and he would surely find her.

*A preview of the next
Lucy Ripken mystery*

Mexican Booty

by J. J. Henderson

1

Photo Fakery

"Skreeeeehonnnkkkk!" The roar of a T. Rex, bellowing in frustration as it watched its dinner, a fat Brontosaurus pup, lumber across the primeval swamp to safety beneath its mother's belly, echoed through Lucy Ripken's loft and woke her with a start. Damn, she thought, denied the refuge of her dreams. Another gridlock. Will it ever end?

"Skroooonnnnnnnkkkk!" The dinosaur played a variation. Lucy muttered, "Damn," then threw the covers off. She lay naked for a moment, watching the white walls and listening to the roar that rose up from the perpetually jammed intersection of Broome and Broadway below. It was no dinosaur howling but the air horn of an eighteen-wheel behemoth, hauling garbage—New York's chief early twenty-first–century export—from Long Island to Ohio.

With a sigh Lucy swung her feet off her sleeping platform onto the cool, dirty white linoleum floor. She grabbed her frayed silk robe—the one covered with red roses and silver surfers—slipped it on, and padded over to her desk to fire up the computer. She walked to the other end of the loft, put on coffee water, did her ablutions, strolled the length of the loft snapping up the window shades, and then sat before the machine. The thing hummed softly, ready for action.

What action? That was the problem. She didn't know what to write and she didn't dare a glance at her spam-laden mailbox for fear there would be not one single item, among the daily hundreds, that actually pertained to her. Three of the six magazines that gave her regular work had folded in the last eight months, and the other three had new editors who didn't know her from Lucille Ball. The architects who usually hired her to shoot projects were laying off staff, downsizing, and scrambling to survive the dicey economic weather. It wasn't like she could just sit down and start pounding out a novel, for God's sake. There was rent to pay.

Yikes, rent! What was the date? She had a look at her calendar, pinned on the wall and still stuck in March. She tore it off and tracked down to the last Tuesday in April. The twenty-seventh. That meant she'd have to come up with $900 next week. Everybody told her how lucky she was to have a 1,300-square-foot loft in SoHo for such cheap rent, but it still represented a fair chunk of cash to her. Here it was due again. Bloody landlord. Whatever she saved in rent she paid out in legal fees, anyway. The evil-tempered little creep had been trying to evict her for seven years and still the case dragged on, the loft board shuffled its feet, the lawyers filed another round of papers, and she and her fellow tenants—there were seven living units in the four upper floors of the six-story building—dangled in limbo, immovable but not entirely legal dwellers in a building zoned for commerce only.

Where Lucy lived had once been the Cherokee Zipper Company, or so the faded sign on her front door told her. It had inspired her to call her photography business Cherokee Productions. Or, at present, Cherokee Non-Productions, since she hadn't had a paying job in three weeks, and her bank balance had reached the low three figures. Lucy sat and stared at the computer screen, fingers on the keyboard, brain blank, battling the urge to surf the Web, whose waves invariably took her to shores she did not long to walk upon. Then the coffeepot whistled and the phone rang. She looked at the clock. 8:47 a.m. Who in New York would dare call before nine? She grabbed her phone en route to the kitchen, flipped it on, and said "Hello" into a sea of static. Lower Manhattan was the land of interference, both visible and invisible.

"Hi, Lucy?"

"Yeah?" She poured hot water over the last of her Blue Mountain blend, and sucked up the fragrance of Jamaica.

"Hi, it's me. Rosa."

"Rosa! Hey, sorry I didn't recognize your voice. Why are you calling at—what is it, six a.m. out there?"

"Nah, it's nearly seven, Luce. Gotta hit the trail early, know what I mean?"

"Right. The trail." She meant it literally. Rosa Luxemburg, one of her closest friends, had fled New York for Santa Fe,

New Mexico, that adobified antique boutique for trust fund mystics and New Age artistes. Rosa had fallen in love with a dropout lawyer from California on a trek out west last summer, and now she was gone. Gone riding every day, formal English style, for that's what she'd loved to do when she wasn't throwing paint around her studio down the street: chase the foxes through the forests of Westchester and New Jersey on her horse. Only now it was Santa Fe. She'd traded in the foxes for coyotes, and the Broome Street studio for the lawyer with a little house in the high desert. He played and taught golf and wanted to write, like everybody else. Rosa rode horses and made art, cruising on cash her father had made in plumbing fixtures. Her grandparents had been Commies of the Trotskyite persuasion, but then, so had lots of Lower East Side grandparents back in the Red Old Days. Rosa, on the other hand, was rich. "So what's up, Rosita?" Lucy said, pouring coffee.

"Same old shit. Get up at dawn, ride through the desert, work in the studio. It's a tough life."

"Yeah, I bet," said Lucy, wandering back to the computer. "How's Darren?"

"Oh, he's fine," Rosa said. "I'm teaching him to ride, he's giving me golf lessons. The sex is great."

"Not surprising. You're still in the preliminary rounds." God, trust fund life was rough. But she did love the girl. "So how's your work coming along?"

"Not bad, Luce. I'm doing these cloud paintings on faded wood. Found objects. The desert's really inspiring. God, I am so glad I got out of there, I tell you. When you're in New York you think you can't ever leave, and then when you leave you can't imagine what took you so long. Know what I mean?"

"I'm glad you're working again, Rosa. You're a talented girl."

"Hey, thanks. Listen, I'm on to something I thought you might be interested in. How's business, anyway?"

"About the same as when you left. There isn't any."

"Good. I mean—not good, but you'll be happy to hear this. Look, Darren met this woman down here and she's got a couple of pre-Columbian artifacts from Mexico that she just obtained, and she's sending them with a courier up to this gallery on Madison Avenue. They're putting a catalogue together and they need someone to photograph the pieces in a rush. Darren thought you might need the work."

"Sounds good. Who do I call?" Lord have mercy, a job. "Do they have any money?"

"Let's just say you can charge a serious day rate. This stuff is extremely valuable."

"Like fifteen hundred?"

She paused. "That seems pretty steep, Luce. How about a thousand?"

"Sure, why not. It's not like I'm fighting off the clients."

"I don't care. I mean, you could charge them five thousand a day as far as I'm concerned," said Rosa, "except that the people that run the gallery are old friends of Darren's parents."

"Don't worry about it, Rosita," Lucy said. "Either way I could use the gig. So what's the place called?"

"The Desert Gallery. It's on Madison, not far from the Whitney. You know the territory. Uptown art chic. I don't have the number here but the lady you need to talk to is called Madeleine Rooney. She's majority owner and runs the place. Has the money. Husband's a Wall Street guy. Darren tells me she looks like she eats once a month. She's expecting your call. It's a rush, like I said. I think you'll probably be shooting tomorrow or the next day at the latest."

"Great. Thanks a lot, Rosa. I really need the work."

"Sure. And listen, this stuff is seriously pricey so don't be put off if she seems paranoid."

"Gotcha. She wants to skin-search me, fine."

"So how're things in New York? Finally warming up?"

"Are you kidding? They say it's gonna hit eighty today. From winter to summer with an hour of spring."

"Typical. Only now you can attribute it to global warming and not just shitty New York weather, huh?"

"I guess." Lucy sighed. "You know, Rosita, I can't believe you're actually gone. I walk past your building and want to cry sometimes. All my friends are cutting out, and I feel so stuck."

"Come here."

"And what, live with you and Darren? I can't afford to live there, Rosie, you know that. There's no work."

"So how are you and Harry doing, anyway?"

"Ipswich? Fine, fine. He's—hell, why should I lie to you?" Lucy sighed. "We were doing great, and then he started drinking."

"Drinking? I thought he was a narc."

"He is, sort of, part time. But alcohol isn't illegal, though maybe it should be." She pictured her father, immobilized in his chair, bitterly drunk. "I guess Harry's more troubled about his brother than he likes to let on."

"The one who died?"

"OD'd. Yeah. He gets on his high horse about dope, and then goes out and gets polluted on vodka and acts like it's perfectly okay."

Rosa paused. "What a drag."

"No shit. So anyway, I told him I didn't want to see him for a while." Lucy typed "Harold Ipswich" onto her screen, deleted it, then undeleted it. She stared at the name. "So how is it, not being in New York, Rosa?"

"Well, like I said, it's great not having to put on your armor every time you go outside, but there's an edge in New York. I miss it. People are nice here, but. . . ."

"Nice is not enough."

"Exactly. Still, no real regrets. The desert is so beautiful, you just can't imagine."

"Yeah, I bet. Well, listen, I better get on the phone with Madeleine Rooney, and then I gotta line up an assistant, and—"

"Oh, by the way, before you call her—I think she needs someone to write text on the pieces for the catalogue as well. You know anyone who might be interested?"

"Definitely. Beth and Quentin Washington. Remember them?"

"Your friends at the Indian museum, right?"

"Yeah. The next ones to leave Manhattan. Hannah's almost five and Beth's halfway to having another one, so they're ready to blow. But they know everything about pre-Columbian art, and they always need extra cash. I'll call them."

"Sounds good. Let me know how the shoot goes."

"Cool. Give my love to Darren."

"Right. And one of these days maybe you guys will meet and you'll see what I'm talking about."

"I sure hope so. Catch you later, Rosa."

"'Bye."

Lucy wandered into the kitchen to replenish her coffee, then threw open a window. The traffic roar got instantly louder. She leaned out and looked up and down Broadway.

Just 9:00 and already sticky hot. To the north the neo-Gothic spire of the Chrysler Building sparkled in the morning sun, and a steady stream of slow-moving cars flowed down Broadway. To the south, the Woolworth Building loomed. Five floors below, she watched her downstairs neighbor, Jane Aronstein, emerge from the building with Ross, her Labrador. The landlord popped out of his office next door a second later, in his silver-haired, weasel-like fashion, and he and Jane met on the sidewalk. Within seconds they were arguing. The elevator was probably stuck again.

Lucy pulled the window shut, went back to her desk, picked up the phone, and punched in a number.

"Museum."

"Hi. Quentin Washington, please."

"He's at the Brooklyn Annex."

"Then Beth."

"Just a minute." On hold, Lucy squeezed the phone between shoulder and ear and riffled through the phone book hunting a listing for the Desert Gallery, while her emissary roamed the dusty catacombs of the American Aboriginal Museum in search of Beth Washington.

Her incoming call signal beeped. "Damn." She switched over. "Hello. Lucy Ripken. Cherokee Productions," she added quickly.

"Hi, Lucy" came a monotone voice. "That was real professional-like. Could have fooled me."

"Who's this?"

"Simon. Simon Stevens. How's it going?"

"Simon, hey. I'm on another call, but I'm glad you called. Are you busy tomorrow?"

"Well, no, but I—"

"You want to work?"

"Yeah, I guess. What's the deal?"

"I'll call you back in ten minutes. Be there." She switched to the other line. "Hello."

"Hello?"

"Hi. Beth?"

"Yeah. Lucy! Hey, how're you doing?"

"Okay. How's it going up there? You busy?"

"Me? I'm just doing my computer thing, you know, cataloguing away. But Quentin's going nuts, they've got him— oh, never mind, you know how he is."

"The boy is tense. So how's Hannah?"

"Fine. Except that yesterday, after four months of discussion, she decided she didn't want a kid brother or sister after all."

"How nice for you."

"She'll just have to—it'll be fine. I just hope this Vermont thing works out. One kid in Manhattan is manageable. Two, I don't know."

"Any word on the Vermont gig?" Quentin was short-listed for a job curating a small Revolutionary War museum near Bennington. If he got it they were gone, from the Big City to green New England.

"They're supposed to call next week. We're told it's a done deal, but who knows?"

"Meanwhile, I've got something interesting happening. Remember Rosa, my pal that moved to Santa Fe?"

"Yeah. How does she like it down there?"

"Fine, fine. But listen." Lucy gave Beth a shorthand version of the artifacts deal.

"Sounds intriguing," said Beth when Lucy had finished.

"That's why I called, Bethy. It's a major rush, and along with your knowledge I might need some help in setting up the shots. I don't know a thing about this stuff and I don't want to miss the point, photographically speaking. It's supposed to arrive at the Desert Gallery tomorrow morning."

"The Desert Gallery! You mean that Rooney woman's in on the deal?"

"You've heard of Madeleine Rooney?"

"Sure. Everybody in this business has. She's the unholy terror of the pre-Columbian art scene. God, I don't know if Quentin's going to want to get involved with her around."

"Come on. She can't be that bad."

"I shouldn't talk so much. You'll have to see for yourself. What time are you going there?"

"You can't leave me hanging like that, Beth. Please! What's the skinny on Madeleine Rooney?"

"Oh, nothing. She's just exactly what you'd expect from an Upper East Side lady running a Native American art gallery."

"Meaning?"

"She acts like she knows everything, she doesn't give a flying fuck about the work, she buys cheap and sells high. Does it all with the most fine-tuned gall you'll ever see."

"Sounds like fun."

"What can I say? Get your money as fast as you can. Expenses upfront if possible."

"Not likely. But Rosa's fiancé is a family friend, so I figure I won't get burned."

"Hmmm. I hope you're right. So what time tomorrow? Can we come at lunch?"

"I assume the stuff will be there by ten. We'll have to unpack and start setting up, so lunchtime should be about right. It's at Madison and—"

"We've been there," Beth interrupted.

"Oh. Okay. See you tomorrow. Regards to Quent and Hannah."

"Yeah. Twelve-thirtyish, depending on the trains."

Next she called the Desert Gallery. As she'd hoped, a machine answered. She identified herself, said she was planning to come up early tomorrow to shoot the pieces, and left her number for a callback to discuss deadlines and fees. She hung up and called Simon back. Simon wasn't a great assistant, but he was a big, handsome twenty-six-year-old kid and very charming. He'd be helpful with the Rooney woman, Lucy figured. He promised to be over at eight in the morning to help load the equipment into the car. Finally, Lucy called the HoSo Car Service, and after bantering with Ari the bad boy Israeli office manager and number-one driver for a minute she lined up a car for the next morning. Once that was done she dressed and headed out in search of the *Times* and a little distraction. Which came in the form of a check in the mailbox, for $973, for a job she'd shot almost four months back. Saved! She walked down Broadway to the bank on Canal Street, practiced her Spanish with the multi-lingual ATM, then headed up Wooster to read the paper over a decaf double espresso at the Dean & DeLuca coffee bar. A check and a job. Things were definitely looking up.

Lucy and Simon sat in the backseat of a ruby-red, late-model, high-end Chrysler with white fake leather upholstery, cruising up Madison Avenue. "There," she said. "On the right. Behind that Checker cab." She did a quick fix with her lipstick as Ari swerved across two lanes of traffic to whip into the only available curb space, in front of a fire hydrant. "Simon, can you please unload while I go in and let her know we're here?" As she climbed out of the car, ran a hand through her hair, and approached the glass double doors of the Desert Gallery, Lucy felt mildly frazzled and anxious. To be expected. The Manhattan air was nearly visible, thick and hot at 8:45 a.m. in late April. Her dry cleaning hadn't been ready yesterday afternoon, and her black jumpsuit was better suited for fifty-degree weather. Inside the doors waited Madeleine Rooney. Lucy had left Rooney her message and gotten one back in return, in which the woman's hoarse, smudgy voice had okayed the shoot for today and suggested they talk fees and deadlines upon arrival. Lucy hated to make such a commitment—assistant, car, gear, haul uptown—without money matters settled, but having gotten the gig through a friend, she'd decided to play it by ear.

She tried the glass door, found it locked, and hit the bell, peering in. A long, elegant space, spotlit three-dimensional art on pedestals and stands. A wraith—a woman—rose up behind the counter in the back, and a second later the door buzzed softly. Lucy grabbed a handle and pulled it open.

She did a quick take on the room and liked what she saw. The Desert was austerely minimal in the manner of most galleries, but with a Santa Fe twist. The walls had rounded, adobe-style corners, and the paint was a shade of off-white most likely called Pueblo Pink or something along those lines. The floor was flagstone, the display stands were made of unfinished timbers, the display niches were rough-cut arches in the walls, and a couple of perfectly placed, dramatically spotlit Western accessories—an old saddle, a weathered Navajo blanket, and a ten-gallon hat with a bullet hole in the crown—instantly established the southwestern ambience, Ralph Lauren with a Native American twist. Counterpointing the southwestern mood, and elegantly stating the gallery's New York credentials, rows of high-tech tracklights sparkled in the ceiling, each focused precisely on a piece of art.

Also very New York in style was the gaunt, late-fiftyish woman coming toward Lucy from the back of the room. She wore a black silk shirt gold-belted over black leggings on a scarecrow frame. Her expensively punk-styled blue-black hair framed a narrow oval face made lovelier, or at least less time-worn, by what appeared to be a well-executed face-lift or two. Her diamonds—on ears, throat, hands—subtly sparkled and sang, "Oh, how I have money, and I like it." She said, "Hello. I'm Madeleine Rooney." Again, that deep, hoarse voice. The Madeleine Rooney package was five feet tall, chic, sleek, and trendy to a slightly alarming degree.

"Lucy Ripken," Lucy said, and held out a hand. "How are you? What a great-looking space!"

"Thanks. I just had it redone over the winter," Ms. Rooney said, and gave Lucy's hand a quick shake. Her fingers were cool and soft. "The courier dropped off the package a few minutes ago. I was just getting ready to unpack it. Where's your camera?"

"Outside in the car with my assistant. I thought we could talk fees first."

"Fine," she said, turning and walking away. "Is twelve hundred a day plus expenses suitable?" She tossed the words over her shoulder. "I'm assuming of course that you can do the whole job today. This is a rush."

"That's fine," Lucy said, pleased. Two hundred bucks more than she'd figured. "Expenses, including assistant, film, rush processing, the car, and miscellaneous stuff, will probably run another five hundred," she added, as Rooney dragged a small wooden shipping crate out from behind the slate-topped counter.

"I need film tomorrow. Can you get it done?" she said.

"No problem. And I've lined up a writer—two of them, actually. A husband-and-wife team. They'll be coming over at lunch. They work at the Aboriginal Museum and they know their stuff."

"Fine. You seem to have it under control. Darren said you were good."

"You talked to him today?"

"A few days ago. My regular photographer is in Vienna, and I simply must have this catalogue material at the printers the day after tomorrow."

"Well, you'll have film tomorrow, and I'm sure Quentin and Beth can turn around copy for you in no time."

"The Washingtons?" Rooney asked, and then, incongruously in the age of NO SMOKING, she placed a brown filterless European cigarette in her mouth and lit it with an elegant little solid gold lighter. She sucked in some smoke and coughed in a practiced manner.

"You know them?" Lucy asked.

"Of course. There aren't that many pre-Columbian experts in Manhattan, after all," she croaked. "I'm keeping the gallery closed today but I've invited a few special buyers in for a preview, so you'll have to work around them. Give me a hand with this, would you?" Rooney added, or rather demanded. Lucy whirled at the tone, ready to bite back. She bit her lip instead. Now that they'd agreed on money, Rooney had abandoned her efforts at politesse and assumed the role to which she was accustomed: boss.

"Sure." Lucy joined the woman in her cloud of imported toxins. "My driver's parked in front of a hydrant, but—"

"He can wait," Madame Rooney said, wielding a short crowbar. "You hold the crate steady, while I pry open the top." Lucy did as she was told. Madeleine Rooney quickly worked the top loose, then lifted it off to reveal a heap of styro peanuts. She plunged a hand in, pulled out an object buried in layers of plastic bubble wrap and tape, and began to unwrap it. A moment later, the first artifact was revealed. "Isn't it magnificent?" Rooney asked, holding up the object, a surprisingly naturalistic ceramic statue, about six inches high, of a young woman in an elaborate headdress and a robe embracing an older man, also robed. The faces were vaguely Asiatic. The door buzzed. They looked up. Simon Stevens's hulking silhouette loomed behind the glass. "Who's that?" Rooney snapped.

"My assistant," Lucy said. "Can you let him in?"

"Yes. But he does understand how delicate—and valuable—these pieces are, I assume," Rooney said, then went over and held down a button behind the counter. Simon stuck his head in the door.

"I'm all unloaded and the driver wants to split," he said. "I haven't got that much cash."

"Come on in," Lucy said. "Why don't you help Ms. Rooney for a minute? I'll take care of Ari. And close the door quickly. This stuff is very valuable." Simon strolled back, and Lucy could feel Madeleine loosening up, transforming herself into the coquette as she got a better look at the big, handsome boy. He was six-two, one-eighty, with jet-black hair and blue eyes. He could pass for a model, and still wasn't sure if he wanted to take pictures or be in them. "Simon, this is Mrs. Rooney," she said.

"Call me Madeleine," Rooney said, offering him a smile, the first Lucy had seen, and a hand. He shook it.

"Hi," he grinned, entirely at ease. "Simon Stevens. Nice to meet you. Great-looking gallery you've got here," he added, glancing around. "Wow, isn't that a Jaina Island ceramic?" he asked, noticing the object she was holding.

"Simon, I didn't know you knew pre-Columbian art," Lucy said.

"Surprise, surprise. I majored in art history, Lucy," he said. "Did two semesters on pre-Colombian. This is from the Yucatán—Late Classic period of the Maya. The moon goddess embracing an older deity, right, Madeleine?"

"My, you do know your stuff," said Madeleine, injecting a coy tone into her vocal rasp. "I wouldn't have known it if you hadn't told me, Simon."

"I'm going to take care of Ari," Lucy said. "Back in a minute. And you've got to help me bring the gear in, Si, so don't get too relaxed just yet." Simon preferred bullshitting around with clients to working. He was good at it—bullshitting around with clients—but that was only part of what she hired him to do.

Lucy paid Ari, adding a big tip for making him wait—got to keep guys like him on your side—and then she and Simon hauled the gear in the front door.

After some discussion and a look through a couple of art books and catalogues for comparison, Rooney decided she wanted 4 × 5-inch transparencies of the pieces. Lucy couldn't fault her for that, the large format film did look much better, but it meant she had a bit more work to do. They set up a display pedestal, and then Lucy broke out the bellows-style camera and began to assemble it while Simon rigged the lights. By the time they were ready to shoot the first one, Madeleine Rooney had the crate unpacked, and had lined up the pieces on the slate countertop in a neat row—several hundred thousand dollars' worth of ceramic and carved objects, all Late Classic Mayan in derivation.

There was a second two-figure statue, a variation on the first with slightly different versions of the same pair of deities embracing. Traces of yellow pigment added luster to this second piece. There were two shell objects, one of a man riding on the back of a sea monster of a sort, the other of a young woman whom Simon identified as Ixchell, the fertility goddess. The carved iconographic detail was intricate and extraordinary. There was a single carved obsidian object, a head in profile that probably had decorated the top of a scepter or sword, also highly detailed with iconography; and finally there was the most precious object of all, a complete, unblemished cylindrical vase, with polychromatic paint illustrations, in almost perfect condition, depicting a range of activities and beings—human, supernatural, and animal—in strikingly dramatic fashion. The imagery on the pot, at first confusing to look at, after a while sorted itself out, and the narrative action became evident. It was an amazing illustration of a worldview from a lost time and place, the Mayan civilization of the Yucatán. Lucy was awed by it, even as she contemplated photographing it. The pot would require several photographs to show all the sides. According to Madeleine Rooney, it was worth somewhere between two hundred thousand and five hundred thousand dollars, depending, Lucy supposed, on how the Dow did that week. Handle with care was an understatement.

They had shot several digital test shots, adjusted the lights, loaded a sheet of film, and were ready to make the first exposure when the buzzer sounded again at a little past noon. Rooney let Quentin and Beth Washington in the door.

"Luce," said Quentin, striding over to hug her. "How are you doing?" He was temperamental and somewhat delicate, tall, thin, high-waisted, high-strung, and long-legged, cranelike, with a large nose, curly hair, and a wide forehead over pale green eyes. He came from New England blueblood, complete with a DAR grandma. He had dressed, as usual, in slim-fitting jeans and a blue work shirt.

"Not bad," Lucy said. "Hey, Beth," she added, with a quick hug for Quentin's wife. Beth was five years younger than Lucy and Quentin. She was a solid, brilliant, handsome, brown-haired Jewish woman who came from Lower East Side radical stock like Rosa, except her parents had only made it as far north as Yonkers. Her father still practiced left-ist law, and was not rich. Beth and Quentin were an odd yet perfectly suited New York couple. "You guys know Mrs. Rooney," Lucy said, deferring to the money.

"Hi," said Beth. "How are you?" The gallery queen nodded recognition.

"Hello, Madeleine," Quentin said offhandedly, glancing at Rooney, his tone perfectly arch. "How are you? My God," he interrupted himself as he spotted the artifacts lined up on the counter. "Look at this! Beth, can you believe it! It's from Jaina! Fantastic! Where did you find these?" He approached the pieces, more fired up than Lucy had seen him since they all gave up recreational drugs. "Do you mind if I have a closer look at this?" He looked at Madeleine Rooney.

She nodded. "I don't have to tell you to be careful, do I, Quentin?" she said.

"No." He laughed. "I would hate to have to sell my daughter in order to pay for breaking one of these." He gently picked up the conch carving of the man on the sea monster and carried it over into the brighter light under a row of ceiling tracks. The doorbell sounded, and after taking a good look Madeleine Rooney buzzed in a client, then headed up to the door for personal greetings and an apology for the chaos in the gallery. Lucy heard her begin to crow at Mrs. Hopkins—or Agnes, as Rooney gushingly called the lady— about the new pieces. Agnes Hopkins carried a sleek black shopping bag in one hand and had tucked a small terrier under the other arm. Madeleine Rooney greeted the animal, named Duncan, with nearly as much enthusiasm as she had greeted its owner. The dog emitted high-pitched yaps and resentful little growls from its position under the lady's arm.

"Beth, have you met Simon Stevens, my photo assistant?" Lucy asked, tuning ladies and dog out. "Simon, Beth Washington."

"Hi," said Simon, "How ya doin'?"

"Beth, come here a minute," said Quentin impatiently.

"Hi." Beth shook Simon's hand quickly. "Excuse me, Quentin gets so excited about this stuff."

"Go on," said Lucy. "Have a better look." She watched with amusement, and perhaps a touch of envy, as Quentin and Beth huddled over the little shell figure, passing a magnifying glass back and forth. Lucy had thought the piece unquestionably lovely, but it didn't have the mysterious potency for her that it did for them. They knew where it came from, what it meant, who had created it and why, and knowing this made all the difference.

Ms. Rooney waltzed back with Agnes Hopkins to show her the goods. "Pardon the mess," Rooney said as she walked past, "I simply had to have this photography done today to get the catalogue printed on schedule, you see, dear?"

"Oh, don't worry, Maddy," said Agnes, rail-thin and elegant, just like Madeleine, as she eyeballed Simon. "I know how it is. I've been redecorating like mad, and there are workmen stomping around my house constantly." She passed Lucy without so much as a nod to indicate that she recognized her existence, although the terrier snapped fiercely in Lucy's direction. Lucy threw her black cloth over her head and gazed through the camera.

Quentin called softly, "Hey, Luce." She popped out from under the cloth and glanced at him. He waved her over, watching Rooney surreptitiously. Rooney and her client were too engrossed in admiring the goods on the counter to notice.

Lucy said, "Si, see if you can discover from Ms. Rooney where we can get some lunch." Then she joined Beth and Quentin in the corner. "What's up?" she asked.

"Lucy, where did she get this stuff?" Quentin asked, waving the small carving in the air.

"I don't know. I didn't ask."

"They're fakes," Quentin said quietly. "At least this one is, and I'd be willing to bet they all are."

"What?" Lucy snapped sharply. "But Simon said that—"

"Really well executed," Beth said, "but definitely forged."

"How can you tell? How do you know?"

"Look," Quentin said, holding up the piece. "See this?" he held the magnifying glass up to the figurine. "See these markings along the bottom of the fishy creature? These kinds of patterns aren't—they don't belong on a piece like this. This is what forgers do a lot of the time—take imagery off something they know, in this case, ceramic figurines—and re-create it somewhere else. But this pattern was never used in shell carvings. Least not that I've seen, and I think I've seen most everything around. No way this thing wasn't made in the last year or so."

"Jesus," said Lucy, her heart sinking. There went the job. She had a flash of inspiration, but it died even as the words came out. "Can you wait till I finish shooting them to—"

"Come on, Lucy," Quentin said. "We can't do that. She might be selling one to that dame right now," he said, glowering at the two women over by the counter.

"Yeah, you're right," she said. "Damn. Well, you want to do the talking, Quentin? I know I don't."

"Sure. Let's get it over with." He led the way to the counter, where Duncan greeted them with a renewed burst of yapping. "Um, excuse me, Madeleine."

"You want to talk fees, Quentin? Fine. Would you mind waiting a few moments? Can't you see I'm busy?"

"No, I don't want to talk fees, Ms. Rooney. I want to talk about the pieces. Privately, if it's all right."

His tone caught her attention. "Excuse me, Agnes," she said. "I'll just be a moment. Let's go into my office, Quentin. Don't let Dunkie peepee on the floor, now, Agnes."

"Now don't you worry," Agnes said. "Dunkie's a good little boy, isn't he?" she said, lapsing into baby talk and stroking her dog. Lucy followed the Washingtons and Madeleine

Rooney through a door behind the counter into her office. Prints, posters, and pieces of art were scattered about the glass-topped desk in the middle of the room. Lucy closed the door. The three of them faced Rooney.

"What is it, Quentin?" said Madeleine Rooney, anxiety surfacing in her voice. "Is there a problem?"

"Well, yes," said Quentin, placing the little carving on the desk. "This." He picked it up again. "See this?" he said, indicating the iconography on the sea monster. "This doesn't belong here, Madeleine."

"What do you mean, 'doesn't belong'?"

"This iconography is ripped off a ceramic piece. I don't know exactly which one, but—"

"What do you mean, 'ripped off'?"

"This is a fake, Madeleine," he said, not without some satisfaction. "I know Mayan work, and they never put these patterns on shell carvings."

"What are you talking about?" she said, snatching it away from him. "I have papers. These pieces were certified by a man in Santa Fe. I can't remember his name, but he was— Margaret Clements said—" She drew herself up. "I'm afraid you're mistaken. I have letters of authentication."

"I'll be happy to look at them," said Quentin. "But that doesn't change the fact that this piece is bogus. I think we'd be wise to check the others before you show them to anybody else, although I doubt that any of them are authentic. Why would a forger put anything real in with a bunch of fakes?"

"Wait here a moment," Rooney said, and bustled out of the office.

"Well, that could have been worse," Beth said.

"So much for my gig," Lucy said. "I can't imagine she's going to want this stuff photographed if it isn't what it's supposed to be."

They watched through the window as Rooney talked Agnes Hopkins and her dog toward the front door. "Sorry, Lucy," said Quentin. "Way it goes. Well, that bitch is out the door. Let's go check out the other pieces."

He led the way back into the gallery, where they joined Madeleine Rooney and Simon by the counter with its row of artifacts. Quentin picked another shell carving and examined it with his magnifying glass. "Yes, like I thought. Same deal. Another fake."

"I don't know what makes you so sure these are fake," said Simon. "I studied this stuff in school, and I'm not so certain."

"Forget it, Simon," said Lucy. "Quentin knows more about this stuff than you could ever comprehend."

"Now, wait a minute," said Rooney. "Maybe Simon has a point. Maybe you're making a mistake, Quentin."

Quentin looked exasperated. "Get serious, Madeleine. Do you think I would dare to screw up a call as important as this? No way. Simon, I'm sure you know your stuff, but you have no idea how good these forgers have gotten in the last couple of years. As the market for these pieces has grown, and the prices have climbed, a higher quality of hustler has jumped in. These dudes are experts. Believe me, if I hadn't seen it before, I wouldn't have known what to look for. Madeleine, you're wasting your time pretending otherwise."

"I'm not so sure. I want to talk to—I want Herman Forte to have a look."

"Forte?" said Quentin. "You're going to call Herman Forte? There's nothing he's going to tell you that I haven't already."

"There's too much at stake here. I simply must speak to someone with more authority," she said, and went back to her office. She closed the door.

"Who's Herman Forte?" Lucy asked.

"Dr. Herman Forte," said Beth. "He used to be our boss. A real classic New York academic shithead. But he's a Ph.D., and he loves ladies like Madeleine Rooney."

"Christ, I can't believe she's calling him," said Quentin. "Thanks for raising those doubts, Simon," he said. "Perhaps you'd like to come back to the museum with me and tell me how to do my job there as well?" He stopped abruptly, and turned his attention back to the objects, peering closely at the vase. "This one would have to be subjected to thermoluminescence to date it, but like I said before, I've never heard of anyone trying to pass off forgeries and real artifacts at the same time. I'd be willing to bet this is bogus, too."

"I'm sorry, Quentin," Simon said. "I was just trying to help."

"Don't make excuses. You fucked up, Si," said Lucy. "And where's lunch, anyway, you galoot?"

"There's a deli around the corner. What do you guys want?" he said sheepishly.

Rooney emerged from her office. "Herman's on his way over. Meanwhile, I'd like you to continue shooting, Lucy. I want these pieces in the catalogue."

"Really?" Lucy said, her spirits instantly lifted. Fake or no, what did she care if the lady still wanted pictures?

"Yes. Let's get on with it." Rooney picked up one of the shell carvings and placed it on the pedestal. "I'll just have to find someone else to write them up if you two aren't interested."

Quentin and Beth just looked at her. Quentin shook his head.

"I was just going to get some sandwiches," Simon said to Rooney. "Do you want anything?"

"I never eat lunch," she said. "But fetch me a bottle of Evian, Simon. Thanks."

"I'll have a Greek salad–type thing," said Lucy. "You know, feta, olives, yogurt, and cucumbers."

"Don't bother with us," said Quentin. "We've got to get back to work, right, Beth?" He glanced at his watch, an expression of contempt on his face.

"Right, Quentin."

"See ya, Luce," Quentin said. "Sorry," he added under his breath, "but this is total bullshit—and the last person I want to see right now is Herman Forte."

"That's cool, Quent, but she still wants her pics," she said.

"Go for it, Luce," he said. "A picture of a fake is just as pretty as a picture of an artifact."

"Let us know what Forte says, Lucy," Beth said. "Talk to you tonight. Ciao, Ms. Rooney," she added from the doorway, and waved as she sailed out.

Herman Forte showed up just as Lucy and Simon were finishing up their lunch. Forte was crew-cut and a boyish fifty, dressed snappily in a lightweight suit over a blue striped shirt and a bow tie. "Madeleine, how are you?" he gushed as they rushed to meet mid-room. They hugged and continental kissed and did their dance, then cut to the chase: the artifacts.

Madeleine Rooney took him by the arm and led him over to the counter, babbling all the while: "So Quentin Washington claims these are fakes but I don't know, this nice boy Simon says he doesn't think so, and I have papers, and I don't know; Herman, I can't believe Darren would let Maggie Clements send up a bunch of forgeries, do you?"

"Certainly seems unlikely to me," he said, picking up the obsidian head and looking it over. "Hmmmm. What did Quentin actually say, Madeleine?"

"Oh, something about the iconography along the bottom—who cares about the bottom, for God's sake?—belonging on ceramics and not on shell or stone pieces. Frankly, I don't see how anyone could know with such certainty that the Mayans didn't use the same patterns on different media," she said.

Forte looked at the iconography more carefully, then put it down and picked up one of the shell pieces and checked it out before setting it down. "Um, I don't know, Madeleine. I just don't know. Quentin may be right, I can't be sure. On the other hand," he added quickly, seeing her dismay, "He may be wrong. I'm not convinced either way, to tell the truth." He simply couldn't stand the idea of displeasing the lady.

"Herman," Madeleine whined, "Herman, what do you really think?"

"I think you should definitely go ahead with the photography and the catalogue. I'll have to think about it. Maybe I can get Louis Schultz to have a look."

"So they aren't fake? Washington was wrong?" she cried out.

"Now, now," he said, pleased to have pleased her, "I didn't say that. I said simply that there was some doubt. I'm not sure. I could go either way with this one. I think we need another opinion. I'll have to see what—"

"Fine. Lucy, we'll definitely finish up the shoot. Herman, do you have time to write these up for the catalogue?"

"I might be able to manage. It would have to be a rush, of course, with attendant fees. And I'd like to see the letters of authentication, if I could, Madeleine. I need to know who's seen the pieces."

"In my office. Come on back and have a look. Call your friend. Do whatever you have to." Madeleine could hardly contain her re-kindled excitement. And who could blame her, Lucy thought.

But on the other hand, how was this sycophantic snivelworm going to pull this off? Lucy wondered. If he was legit and the pieces weren't, he was putting his reputation on the line by authenticating them. Could Quentin have been wrong? No way. He was one of the smartest people she knew, and this was his work. He would never fuck up a call this important.

Well, for now, it was not her problem. "Well, Simon, I guess we oughta get to it, eh?" she said.

"Yeah. Hey, Luce," he added. "I'm sorry about what happened before, but—hey, maybe your friend was wrong, huh?"

"Not likely, Si, not likely. Let's just get the job done, eh? I don't want to hang around here any longer than necessary."